ACCLAIM FOR AARON PATTERSON

SWEET DREAMS

"*Sweet Dreams* was a book I read in two days. I truly enjoyed the read. It kept me wanting to know more. I'm looking forward to Part 2 of the WJA Trilogy!"

—*Sharon Adams, Novi, MI*

"Suspense thriller with a perfect ending, leaving me wanting more. An on the edge of your seat, all night read. I most certainly will be reading *Dream On*.

—*Sheri Wilkinson, Sandwich, IL*

"New authors come and go every day. Very few come on the scene with the ability to weave a tale that will make you sad to reach the end, longing for more. At a time when the world needs a real hero, Patterson delivers big with the WJA's Mark Appleton—an unlikely hero for the 21st century."

—*The Joe Show*

"Aaron Patterson spins a good tale and does it well."

—*W.P.*

"*SWEET DREAMS* is packed with action, suspense, romance, betrayal, death, and mystery."

—*Drew Maples, author of "28 Yards from Safety"*

DREAM ON

"Once again, Aaron Patterson has made a home run! *Dream On* is a wonderful read from cover to cover! I am now anxiously awaiting his next book *In Your Dreams*. I originally purchased his first book by mistake, and was pleasantly surprised at how much I enjoyed it... so now I'm hooked! Aaron has got to start writing faster!!! Although his books are definitely worth the wait! Bet'cha can't read just one! This guy has real talent for writing and keeping the suspense growing... the worst part about the book is the last page... I hated it to stop!"

—Ruth P., Charlotte, NC

"After reading Patterson's first novel, *Sweet Dreams*, I was really looking forward to reading *Dream On*. This book was amazing. I couldn't put it down. If you're looking for an exciting read, read this book."

—Paul Carson, Boise, ID

"I read the first book by Aaron Patterson (*Sweet Dreams*) and was very anxious for this sequel. I was not disappointed. This book kept me guessing with every page turn. It's very well written and I really enjoyed the technology employed, which makes it just a bit futuristic without being over done. This was a fantastic, suspenseful thriller that kept me guessing throughout the entire book. Mr. Patterson has become my favorite fiction writer."

—Donna H., Boise, ID

"This is the second book of Aaron's I have read and I have to say he is a very talented writer!!! I read this book in under twelve hours; it was so good I couldn't put it down. He managed to surprise me with a twist that I did not expect! It is filled with suspense and keeps you guessing throughout. I will be suggesting this book to everyone I know…"

—Amanda Garner, Oklahoma

Aaron Patterson

Sweet Dreams

Book One in the WJA Series

StoneHouse Ink 2011

StoneHouse Ink
Boise ID 83713
www.StoneHouseInk.net

First Paperback Edition 2009
First eBook Edition 2009
Second Paperback Edition 2011
Second eBook Edition 2011

The characters and events portrayed in this book are fictitious. Any similarity to a real person, living or dead is coincidental and not intended by the author.

Patterson, Aaron, 1979-
Sweet Dreams: a novel/ by Aaron Patterson. -1st ed. p.cm.

ISBN 978-0-9826078-1-7 (Paperback)
Library of Congress Control Number: 2010902250

Cover design by Paul Higdon

Published in the United States of America
www.StoneHouseInk.net

StoneHouse
ink

For my wife Karissa,
the love of my life and my best friend.

SWEET DREAMS
The Justice of Revenge

CHAPTER ONE

JULY. TEHRAN, IRAN. IT wasn't hot. It was hell. The heat would melt shoes to the pavement if a person stood in one place too long. The night air might bring some relief with its cool, musty smell of sand and sweat. However, it seemed this evening the cooling desert would not give up any of its pride and send a much-needed breeze into the city. No, this night was muggy, sticky, and just plain miserable.

Despite the heat, tonight was like any other night for Hokamend. Seated on a pillow in his private quarters, he was reading, like he did every night. This evening, the book was *The Fall of America*. He and his best friend, who'd been killed in a bus bombing six years earlier, had spent countless hours together going over, and over again, the plans and drawings of the Chicago metro system, trying to find the perfect place to set off the explosive.

Muttering a prayer for success to Allah, he looked through the open window at the sky and noticed it was devoid of stars. A storm was moving in to tease them with the possibility of sweet relief from the godforsaken heat. But he knew in the end the cloud would leave without so much as a drop of rain.

He envied his friend, who was in a place beyond this world, a place of which he could only dream. He turned back to his book, reminding himself of all the work yet to be done. Someone

had to complete the job, someone had to finish off those arrogant Americans.

His hatred for America and disdain for the people who infested the land made him want to spit. He pictured their smug faces and fancy cars. He would bring the infidels to their knees. He would wake the sleeping giant, then rip its head off.

A bodyguard walked past his door. He heard footsteps and it jolted him out of his daydream. His guards were the best money could buy. They walked in four shifts and in different patterns every hour to keep lurking enemies confused. Hokamend was a careful man, who never took chances with his own life. True, he demanded his followers give up their lives in service to Allah, but he was different. With a half-million-dollar American government bounty on his head, he was worth more, much more.

On the other hand, such a reward for betrayal could cause even friends to consider the offer. But he was no fool. Fingers, toes, even a tongue every now and then had a way of driving the truth home that under no circumstances should one cross Hokamend.

He slipped to his feet and walked to the double French doors leading out to a balcony to light up a cigar.

He touched the small scar above his right eye and smelled the cigar. "A battle wound," he would say. He was proud of his many scars. They proved his devotion to Allah.

A small flicker flashed against the night sky as he struck the lighter and drew on his hand-rolled Cuban. He scanned his property, searching for snipers or anything that might be out of place but found nothing amiss, which didn't surprise him. After all, this was the perfect location for his palace. Situated at the apex of a hill, the mansion was surrounded by a high wall with guard towers at each corner manned by armed snipers. Beyond the wall, two chain-link fences made a wide circle around the perimeter of the grounds. Razor wire coiled across the tops of both fences, and fifteen highly trained guard dogs roamed in between. If someone were to make it past the first fence and was lucky enough to avoid the dogs, then the snipers would ensure he didn't see another sunrise.

An open lawn devoid of obstructions surrounded the palace in a one-mile circle. Deliberately designed so an enemy could not hide behind anything, the grounds looked more like a park than a secure compound.

He watched the city lights in the distance twinkle and blink like little bat eyes staring back at him, trying to ascertain if he was friend or foe. He took a deep draw, let out a cloud of thick smoke and wondered when they would figure it out, if ever. *No, they don't have the stomach for it. They are weak.*

A mosquito landed on his arm and started sucking blood like a miniature vampire. He swatted at the pest but missed as it dodged just in time to save its worthless life. "Stupid bugs." he muttered. They were out in force tonight, and there was no cool breeze to fend them off.

The mosquito buzzed by him again. He swung his hand at it and cursed. This time, he made contact with the bloodsucker, spreading a red smear across his arm.

He swore again. The nasty pests were ruining his quiet time. With his busy life, he treasured this hour of the day when he could think and clear his head, not to mention enjoy a good cigar.

He felt another prick on the side of his neck. More like a bee sting than a mosquito bite, this one hurt. He rubbed his neck but didn't feel anything unusual. In fact, he didn't feel anything. Nothing at all. His fingers were numb, like hard rubber chafing against his neck. A cold shiver ran up his spine. It was as if someone else was touching him. He had sensation in the rest of his body, but his hands were dead.

The bite began to throb, and a terrible heat burned through his body. He stumbled back into his study. drenched in sweat.

Screaming, he fell to the floor, clutching his head with unfeeling fingers. He dug his nails into his skull, as if that would make the pain stop.

He yelled for a guard or someone—anyone—to help him, but no one came to his aid.

The pain sharpened, and his ears rang with a deafening sound like the air horns he'd heard as a boy just before a bomb exploded and more people died. Writhing on the floor, he shouted again for help. Then reality hit. No sound came out of his mouth. Just air.

Every nerve in his body flashed with impossible heat. Curled in a ball on the floor, he grasped his ears, trying to stop the noise that pounded against his skull.

Something was wrong with his ear. He pulled a hand away and blinked, not believing what he saw. Plastered in his lifeless palm, his right ear sizzled like a piece of hot bacon. He tried to focus, to make his brain work. But he couldn't think. The pain was beyond maddening. Mouthing a curse, he crushed the bloody ear in his hand as pain swept through his body like a wave of molten lava. The agony was so sharp and excruciating, all he could do was writhe on the floor, clawing at his head and face.

Outside his door, his bodyguards took wagers as to which one he would curse tonight for not getting him his drink on time.

* * *

MARK APPLETON QUIETLY MADE his way down from his rooftop perch, where he had just carried out another flawless hit. No one seemed to be aware of his presence, which was the way he liked it. Hokamend's guards wouldn't discover his body until the next morning. Most guards for hire these days were lazy drunks.

He'd hidden his blond hair under a dark baseball cap that matched the rest of his attire: black cargo pants, a long-sleeved, black shirt with patches on the elbows and a tiny pocket on the left arm for his throwing knife, plus black boots. His hands were covered in dark, lambskin gloves, which fit like a second skin. He silently slipped across the rooftop to a zip line, his access to this particular building.

Made of a small, woven cable used in airplane wings and developed by NASA, the eighth-inch line could support as much as three-thousand pounds. Using a high-powered air gun shaped like a small crossbow, he shot a tiny anchor at an adjacent building five-hundred yards away. Once the anchor penetrated the brick, it would spread to form a solid hold.

He slung his weapon over his shoulder, hooked to the line and started his soundless descent to the shorter building. A door on the rooftop led to a back stairway. He crept through the abandoned building, which was empty except for a homeless drunk here and there. He wrinkled his nose. The smell of urine and mold made even the musty air outside seem like a fresh ocean breeze. He made sure he didn't wake any of the drunks as he traversed the twelve flights of stairs.

Once he was on the main level, he made a right through a broken, wooden door into an empty room. Half of the wallpaper was torn off the walls, and the carpet was long gone, leaving warped plywood behind. This part of town reminded him of tornado country. Some buildings were beautiful and untouched by the bombs. Others were about to cave in on themselves. War had a way of leaving its mark on more than just the people.

He quickly disassembled his weapon, and as he did so, searched the room for anything he might have left or any sign that could tie him to the dilapidated building. He folded the gun in half where the black barrel and plastic stock met. The scope snapped off with a soft click. His weapon of choice was custom made and could fire a paper round up to three miles, if the wind was right. He shoved the gun pieces in a backpack and hefted it onto his shoulder. Once everything was secure, he pulled a small remote from his pocket and stepped outside, where he peered around the corner, made sure no one spotted him, and pushed the button.

He could hear a faint sizzling sound as the zip line above him melted, then turned to ash and floated down in small flakes. Good, no trace. He ran across the street and walked three blocks south.

Tehran, like most cities in the desert, came alive after nightfall. People smoked outside the bars and griped about the heat. He could hear laughter from inside one bar he passed. Outside another, he heard a thump, like someone falling off a chair, then the sound of glass shattering.

The streets were made of concrete and asphalt. Some intersections were lined with cobblestones. A multitude of blinking lights strived to draw traffic to look at what the stores had to sell. He made his way down a back alley, keeping his head down and avoiding eye contact. All he wanted was to get back to his place and get some sleep.

He stopped at a one-story shop with graffiti sprayed alongside the faded front door. A Persian sign above the door read *Sporting Goods*. The brick building wasn't much to look at with thick, black, steel bars imbedded in the wooden front door. The boarded up windows also had the local kids' handiwork spray-painted on them.

He inserted a key. The lock clicked. Using another key, he released the deadbolt. The heavy door creaked as he pushed it open and stepped inside. Pulling off his ball cap, he tossed it on the coat rack.

The shop was one open room with two rows of metal shelves in the middle stocked with a complete line of camping supplies: Coleman stoves and dehydrated foods ranging from stew to peach cobbler. If one was the old-school type, he could buy the original MREs and hope his taste buds were on vacation. The racks against the walls went all the way around the room and came to a stop at the front desk, which was topped by a cash register and a glass case containing pistols and knives. Behind the counter, guns of every shape and size, from shotguns to M16s, were racked from floor to ceiling. All of them had been previously owned but were in good working order.

The shop was not much, but it was clean, and it provided

a good place for him to hide as he researched his target. The owner was a native who worked for the same organization he did. As far as any one else was concerned, Mark was an out-of-town guest.

He stepped to the back of the little shop and stopped in front of a shelf full of books on how to fish and hunt and stay alive in the desert. He ran his fingers along the back of the books. When he located the fingertip-size button, he pushed it and a deep, groaning sound sliced the silence. The floor on his right split in the middle and opened up to reveal a concrete staircase. The hole was six-by-six and the concrete lid opened downward and hung like bomb bay doors on a plane. He started down and the floor closed above him with a solid thud. Wall lights flickered and came to life. At the bottom of the stairs, he stopped before a metal door with oversized rivets and bolts around the edges. A small, red light behind a glass bubble protruding from the wall glowed like an evil eye.

He placed his hand on the LCD screen mounted to the right of the door. The screen lit up and proceeded to run a scan of his handprint. He leaned down and spoke into a box, making sure to pronounce each syllable perfectly. "Appleton, Mark."

The red sensor above the door hummed as a red laser shot out and fanned at the end. Beginning at the top of his head, it scanned down his body, taking readings of his frame and measurements of each bone like an X-ray, though much more advanced. The light turned green when the scan was finished, and the door unlocked and slid down into the floor.

What lay beyond was not a concrete bunker or a dingy underground hideout. Instead, it was a house. Not a real house, but it was as much of a house as one could get this far away from home. The first room looked like a typical American living room, minus the picture window. To the right was a kitchen with a black refrigerator and stove plus a microwave oven. To the left was a sitting area with a fireplace and a fifty-inch, surround-sound plasma screen television and a Blu-ray player. A couch with big, fluffy cushions faced the TV, and a camelhair rug graced the floor.

He punched a code on a keypad mounted on the wall on the far side of the living room, and a hidden door opened. The whooshing sound it made always reminded him of a Star Trek movie. Lights inside the room flashed on to reveal case after case of weapons and ammunition. He unpacked his backpack on a metal table that stood against a wall near the front of the weapons room. After he cleaned and oiled his gun, he placed it in an eight-foot glass case next to a Glock. Every wall supported similar cases containing guns, C4 explosives, landmines and rocket launchers. Most of the weapons and ammo boasted his personal touches, from bullets made of paper to guns powered by air and sound waves.

At his touch, the door whooshed back into place and blended into the wall as if it never existed. He stretched, pulled off his shirt, and ran his fingers through his hair. He craved a cool shower and a shave. The stakeout and events leading up to the kill had taken a year of stalking and many long, boring nights waiting for a clear shot.

The cool water felt good as it cascaded over his lean body and washed away the stress of the day.

He thought about the terrorist he'd just killed. He knew he should be sad or feel a little guilty about killing another man, but he couldn't bring himself to even feel bad. All the things Hokamend had done—the bombings of schools and playgrounds that had killed and maimed dozens of children, the snipers who shot twenty-plus people at a time in major American cities before anyone realized a massacre was in progress.

He turned off the water, muttering, "It's time for the terrorists of the world to live in *fear* instead of us fearing them." After he shaved, he grabbed a pair of shorts from the dresser in his bedroom and slipped them on. "Much better," he sighed. "Nothing like a comfortable pair of shorts."

In the kitchen, he pulled a microwave dinner from the freezer and threw it in the microwave for three minutes on high. He turned the package over and saw that this dinner offered a tasty slab of chicken with mashed potatoes and a brownie to boot.

He chuckled. "K certainly wouldn't approve. A microwave dinner and a soda?" He could hear her exclaim, "Not healthy!" and see his wife's playful frown.

The smell of fake chicken filled the kitchen. He was too tired to cook tonight. Plus, he hadn't had a chance to restock his refrigerator. Lifting a fork from the first drawer to the left of the sink, he sat down on the leather couch and began to eat.

"Not bad, for a TV dinner," he announced to himself in-between bites. Not like K's cooking, though. Not much like anybody's cooking.

Now that he was on the subject, he couldn't help but think about K and his daughter, Samantha. It had been three years since... He shook his head, trying to shove the thought from his brain. *Wow. Three years. Time flies.*

Finished, he got up and threw the empty container in the trash, feeling a little celebratory. He was done with the mission and that meant only one thing.

Vacation—after a good night's sleep.

He turned off the lights and his alarm clock and crawled into his king-sized bed. He was going to sleep in, which would be a nice change from the multiple all-nighters he'd pulled in the last year. He closed his eyes and drew the covers up around his chin. No matter how hot it was outside, he had to be under the covers.

Once he had breathed in deep and let it all out in a long sigh, he relaxed his legs and arms. His eyes were getting heavy and now, he knew, no matter what that they were going to come. Thoughts of his family would consume his mind until he fell asleep, which usually took a couple hours, but tonight he had a feeling he would fall asleep right away. He wished he could see K and her sparkling hazel eyes and the smile she reserved for him and him alone.

Then there was little Samantha, with her cute pigtails

bobbing as she ran down the steps to meet him. The workday tensions melted when he felt her tiny arms hugging his neck. She always smelled like soap and lavender, no matter how dirty she was or how long she'd gone between baths. It seemed like just yesterday he was home holding K and Samantha in his arms. He hated to go to bed alone, again. So alone.

Three years earlier...

CHAPTER TWO

THE CLOCK ON HIS office wall read one o'clock. But it seemed like the hands weren't moving. Mark stared at his computer, trying not to look at the clock. The incessant *tick-tock* seemed to mock him.

His boss, Hank leaned in the doorway. "Mark, I need that file on the Hoffman project. I've got a meeting in an hour with Hoffman to go over any changes he might want to make before we move on. Oh, and could you run me another set of blueprints, just in case?"

"No problem. The blueprints are printing as we speak. I'll finish up Hoffman's file and get it to you in five."

"Thanks, man," Hank said over his shoulder as he swiveled to dash back to his office.

Hank Douglas was a man of speed. Not only was he quick-witted, but it seemed like he even talked on the run. If he was speaking to an employee, he was walking past the person or rushing to a meeting, or the elevator door was closing between them as he added a few final remarks.

Hank was also the CEO of Synergy Engineering and Design (SED), one of the top five engineering firms in the country. The company designed multi-million-dollar homes for celebrities, including quaint vacation homes in Sun Valley,

Idaho, commissioned by major movie stars. For some, twenty-eight million was a small price to pay for a good room when on vacation.

In addition, the company had a commercial division responsible for buildings like Trump Towers Asia and the beautiful, yet urban, Parchment casino in Las Vegas, Nevada. Everything operated out of the Douglas Building in downtown Manhattan, which was located on Broadway across the street from the Marine Midland building. It was twenty-five stories of glass and stone jutting from the earth in what one would say was an impossible construction. Twisting metal mixed with stone made the building look like something from a science-fiction movie.

The top of the skyscraper was crowned by thirty-foot pine trees, which cast long shadows over the pond that sat in the west corner. The garden-like park was open to the public, and the employees enjoyed walking during their lunch and coffee breaks on the winding path that looped throughout the park. In the summer months, a family of mallards returned each year to grow fat from all the free food tossed to them.

Mark, who rarely had a chance to enjoy the rooftop park, was in charge of the residential department. His staff designed houses from basic design-build to landscaping and interior design. He was the chief engineer with twenty-one other designers under him. Altogether, SED employed almost a thousand people and was on its way to becoming one of the most sought-after firms in the nation.

Mark had grown up in the small town of Cañon City, Colorado, an old mining town that had morphed into a tourist town after the gold ran out. Tourists enjoyed a railroad ride that offered scenic tours of impressive gorges, long bridges and views of people whitewater rafting. The population of the town was only fifteen thousand. Moving to New York after growing up in a small town had been a bit of a shock to his system. Nevertheless, he managed and now loved the city and had learned to overlook its ugly spots.

When he finished high school, he went to Harvard's School of Engineering and Applied Science to study civil engineering. After getting his degree, he worked as an intern with SED, thanks to Professor Greenheart, who not only took a liking to Mark, but also knew Hank Douglas' family. Ten years later, Mark found himself in upper management.

After a year with SED, Mark met his wife, K. She was an art teacher in a local high school and loved kids more than anything in the world. Until she met Mark, that is. They met at City Baptist, where Mark faithfully attended every Sunday to get his mind and heart right. The Sunday she walked in and stood surveying the room, the light from the morning sun illuminating her in the doorway, his mouth had hung open like a schoolboy's. Suddenly, he believed in love at first sight. She was everything he had ever dreamed and more.

K was beautiful. She had long, blonde hair that was naturally curly and hazel eyes that changed to a fire green when she was angry. He liked to get her good and mad every now and again just so he could see the fire in her eyes. Her skin was fair and smooth as fresh milk. She'd glanced at him as she took a seat in the pew in front of him. Needless to say, he didn't hear a thing that was said that morning. Afterward, in the parking lot, he had stumbled over himself and asked her out. She had agreed, because sometimes miracles do happen.

After dating for a year, with a few maddening fights that ended with those fiery green eyes flashing warning signs at him, they were married beneath the shadow of the Rocky Mountains back in his hometown. They'd had a beautiful wedding surrounded by aspens blazing with color. Red and orange leaves covered the ground where they stood, gazing into each other's eyes. The lake behind his parent's house looked like glass and seemed to smile with approval as he and his bride kissed for the first time as husband and wife. After a ten-day honeymoon, they'd settled in a little house he'd purchased in upstate New York. It was the all-American house with a small yard, a big old oak tree in the back, and a porch swing painted white on the front porch.

"It's perfect," she'd exclaimed when he pulled his hands from her eyes. He loved to surprise her, and this one took some doing. He had signed the papers before leaving for Colorado, hoping and praying it would be what she wanted. It was not exactly a purchase that could be returned to the store for a refund. He had breathed in a silent sigh of relief when he saw her favorable reaction.

Their daughter, Samantha, was born a year and a half later. She was everything they had hoped for in a daughter, with her mom's smile and her daddy's dark blue eyes. By the time she was two, she thought she was sixteen and capable of doing things for herself. "I do it," was a common phrase in the Appleton household.

Mark clasped his hands above his head and stretched. It seemed like just yesterday he first saw K sitting in that little church pew, and now tonight was their five-year anniversary. He looked out the window of his office and noticed a throng of people filling the sidewalk down below.

He turned back to his computer. He had made reservations a month ago at an exclusive restaurant called The Leaf. It was going to be a great night. Samantha would be at her grandparents' house overnight, and he would be showing K around the honeymoon suite at the Hilton Garden Inn in less than five hours.

He was glad for a project to keep his mind busy, so he wouldn't be thinking about tonight. But the clock still mocked him. There was something about Fridays, how time seemed to go by slower than any other day of the week. He sighed. No matter how hard he tried, his mind was not on work today. All he could think about was the evening to follow, and K.

He clicked the mouse a few times, hit Print, and hurried to the print room, grabbing the blueprints as they slowly rolled off the plotter. He drummed his fingers against the metal top, anxious for the printer to finish its job. Finally. He folded the last one, and after a few minutes of arranging the completed file, started down the hall to Hank's big corner office at the far end of the building.

"Hi, Mark. Big night tonight, right?" the receptionist asked as she poked a pencil into her hair.

"Yeah. I'm going to get out of here after I get this file to Hank. Oh, did you—"

"Yes, I called the flower shop after lunch and made sure K got them. The delivery guy said she cried and cried because she wanted *chocolate*, not flowers." He threw a paper clip at her.

She giggled and ducked out of the way just as the phone rang. Grinning, she picked it up. "Synergy Engineering. How may I help you?"

After he dropped off the file and prints in Hank's office, he took a shortcut through the break room to his office. He quickly cleaned up his desk, making sure everything was in place— pencil holder on the left, picture of Sam and K next to his PC. Everything else had to be in its particular drawer or folder. Was he a little OCD? Maybe, but everything in his office, and in his life for that matter, had a place. Why not put it there?

On his way to the elevator, he passed Bert, one of his designers. He threw his keys into the air then caught them, and with a smirk, said, "I'm out of here."

Bert looked up from the plans he was working on. "You be good tonight." He winked. "Big brother is watching you."

"I'll try. You have a good weekend, Bert. I know I will." He stepped into the cherry-wood-lined elevator and pushed the button to the parking garage.

The elevator door closed just as Bert started to respond. Mark laughed out loud. "I just pulled a Hank!"

He drove from the parking garage onto Broadway, just missing a bright yellow cab, whose driver acted as if his path was a racetrack, not a clogged city street. He flipped on the radio, even though he already knew the traffic report: bumper to bumper all the way home, tangled metal pileups, distracted cell phones users, and, in general, everyone paying attention to everything but their driving.

The radio crackled. A firm, commanding voice said, "Cindy Winters is reporting live from David's Island Correctional Facility, where we have a breaking story unfolding. We go live now to reporter Cindy Winters. Cindy, can you tell us a little bit about what's going on out there?"

"Well, Tom, the prison alarms are sounding, and I'm looking at about fifteen fire trucks. I've been told that every paramedic within the surrounding areas has been called to the prison."

Mark was jammed up on the expressway, trying to decide if he wanted to change lanes or just wait it out. He turned up the radio and waved at an angry woman with a little white dog sitting on her lap. She waved back but with only one finger. New Yorkers were so good-natured. K liked to call them Yorkers but Mark had his own pet names for them.

The news story went on. He half listened. Was there a prison break, or maybe a riot? That sort of thing happened more than anyone wanted to think, but from the sounds of it, it didn't sound like a riot. David's Island used to be an internment facility for prisoners of war, and most recently was used as a Bible camp for kids. Planners even had hopes of putting a nuclear power plant on the island, but it never happened, for one reason or another.

Now it was a maximum-security prison for some of New York's finest, and not the boys in blue. One long, two-lane road found its way from New Rochelle to the seventy-eight-acre island. The buildings were only one-story tall, and outside of the guard towers, old red maple trees hid most of the prison from view, so the people of New Rochelle couldn't complain that an ugly prison was blocking their view of Long Island Sound.

"Cindy…" Tom's voice broke into Mark's thoughts. "Can you tell us what's going on out there?" After a brief pause and the thump of a microphone, Cindy's sweet, professional voice came back on.

"Tom, I just spoke to a guard, who said it seems that there

has been a mass food poisoning. He said the inmates were
in the cafeteria eating their lunch, when everyone suddenly
became ill and passed out. They think it was the food, or
maybe it was an outbreak of some kind. We don't know all the
details yet, but we do know experts from the Center for Disease
Control are on their way."

"Is this something confined to people who ate the tainted
lunch, or have others gotten sick as well?" Tom asked.

"From what I've been told, it is only affecting the people
who ate the food served here today."

"Thank you, Cindy," Tom droned. "That was Cindy Walters
reporting live from David's Island. We'll keep you informed of
this breaking story as..."

Mark turned down the radio and gazed out over the sea
of metal as it slowly crawled away from the city. He had
never heard of food poisoning happening so quickly. He had
experienced food poisoning a few times, and at least for him, it
always took an hour or so to kick in.

His mind turned to his date with his beautiful girl. He
would be home soon. He could almost see K and her special
smile. He knew he would see it tonight and might even get her
to flash it at him more than once.

He reached to the passenger seat of his modest Honda
Accord and felt the velvet box with the bright-red bow tied
around it. He had bought it two week ago and now traced its
delicate corners. Would she like it? The moment he thought
he'd figured out what she might like or hate, the rules changed,
and he had to try again. But, he didn't mind. It added to the
mystery that was woman.

After getting off the expressway, he turned down a side
street, cut across to Carwall Avenue and turned right. Mt.
Vernon was only thirty or so miles from the office, but it took
over an hour to navigate the distance. Tall, old oak trees hung
their branches over the road like great monsters of a day gone
by. He smiled at a little redheaded boy shooting hoops into a
makeshift basketball hoop he'd nailed to a tree. The boy looked

his way with a half smile on his freckled face and went back to shooting.

At the third house from the end, he saw Sam's tricycle in the front yard, lying on its side with one pedal up in the air as if surrendering. He pulled the silver Honda into the driveway and heard a crunch. When he got out, he saw the cracked body of what used to be little Suzy. He picked the doll up and tossed it in the back of the car to dispose of later. Sam had never been too fond of Suzy. She wouldn't miss the doll.

He was about to reach for the front door knob when the front door of his home flew open and Samantha ran out to meet him. "Daddy, Daddy, Look—*Look!* I drawed a horsey!" She shoved a tattered piece of paper at him. It looked like she must have used an entire red crayon on her work of art. He smiled at his daughter and noticed how her blonde hair had started to curl up at the ends. He hoped it would be curly just like K's one day.

"Wow, and what a beautiful horsey it is, Samantha!" Picking her up, he hugged her and kissed her cheek.

Sam's three-year-old arms wrapped around his neck. She hugged him as tight as she could. "I want to fly."

He laughed, threw her in the air and caught her as she giggled uncontrollably. He settled her on his shoulders. "Okay. Let's go find Mommy." He knew if he got his daughter going, she would want him to make her *fly* all night.

"Mommy!"

K came down the stairs wearing a knee-length black dress with a scooped neckline. She was five-foot eleven with blonde hair that looked like ripe summer wheat ready for harvest. Her long legs made the dress look even more stunning.

Mark's heart jumped in his chest. It was going to be a good night, a very good night. He lifted Sam from his shoulders.

"Oooh, pretty, Mommy!" She wiggled out of Mark's arms and ran to K's side to stroke the dress.

Mark kissed K softly on the lips, fully aware of their watching daughter. "You look fantastic, honey." Her perfume

SWEET DREAMS | 29

whisked through his senses. He vowed to make up for the
abbreviated kiss later.

K's eyes sparkled and her smile said she knew she looked
good. And that she was going to use her charm for everything
it was worth tonight. "Come tell me about your day while I get
ready." She turned and started back up the stairs.

Mark followed her and sat on the edge of the bed, watching
her as she continued her preparations for the evening. Sam
milled about his feet, trying to take his shoes off and giggling
when he pushed her over. Each time, she popped up and tried
again. He told K about the slow day and how he didn't get
much of anything done except think about their date tonight.
He left out the part about the snarling traffic and the news
report. It all seemed like a distant memory now.

K looked at their daughter. "Sam, where's my other
earring? The silver and black one?"

Samantha looked up at K, her eyes wide and innocent, her
hand behind her back.

Mark could see the earring she clutched like a pirate who'd
just found the key to a hidden treasure. He chuckled.

"Pretty earring," Samantha said, not willing to give up her
precious loot.

"Sam, Mommy needs it." K leaned over and tried to reason
with Sam, her bright, hazel eyes opened wide.

Sam slowly put out her hand and opened it, revealing the
missing earring.

"Thank you, Sam, for helping Mommy."

Sam's lip pooched out, but she forgot about the loss when
she found a piece of string on the floor, and walked around the
room announcing that it was a necklace like Mommy's.

When the doorbell rang, Sam jumped up and ran down
the stairs yelling, "Gramma, Grandpa!" K's parents loved to
babysit Samantha, which was especially nice when they needed
someone to look after Sam overnight.

Scooping up the bag with Sam's teddy bear and other
overnight necessities, Mark made his way downstairs to say

hello to his in-laws and to hug his daughter goodnight.

Sam was jumping up and down, giggling. She loved to go to her grandparent's house. Her blue eyes were wide as she grabbed her sippy cup with one hand and Grandpa's hand with the other and pulled him toward the car.

"Samantha, come give me a hug and a kiss," Mark said. He laughed as she ran back, gave him and K quick hugs and kisses, then skipped back to the car, snagging her grandpa's hand on the way.

He watched as his in-laws' dark-blue, Chrysler Minivan backed out of the driveway and turned onto Carwell Avenue toward their home in the West Hamptons. Bill and Holly Bardwell had lived in the Hamptons since before people had to be wealthy to own a home there. K had grown up in the same house as her father had.

Now, the Bardwells ran an exclusive bed and breakfast in their home during the summer months. Bill was in real estate and had done very well for himself over the years. Holly was in love with art, and that is where K got her love for the arts, as well as her talent. She and her mother used to spend hours looking out at the sunsets from the back porch of their home, painting what they saw, and sometimes not only what they saw but what they felt.

When the minivan disappeared and they'd waved their last wave to Samantha, K returned to their bedroom to finish putting on her make-up, while Mark changed into a black pinstriped suit with a white shirt and a blood-red tie. He ran some water through his short, blond hair and made it spike up a little.

K laughed at him when he announced he was ready to go. "Hey, some people don't just fall out of bed looking good. I have to try a little harder than you do." She tied part of her hair back with a thin silk ribbon and let the rest fall on her shoulders, then glanced at him and smiled.

It was *that* smile, a smile worth waiting all day to see.

* * *

KIRK WESTON SAT IN the third row of the briefing room. He looked at the other occupants. There were twenty or so people in the room, and everyone was wearing a suit but him. The FBI had called the Detroit Police Department and requested he fly to New York to help them with an urgent case. Which didn't make sense.

He was on the bottom of the food chain back home in Detroit and had a hard time believing anyone would request his presence on an out-of-state case, especially the feds. He also wondered why his captain hadn't balked.

He rubbed his hand across the dome of his shaved head. He knew he was a good cop. A guy doesn't make detective by hanging out at the donut shops and showing up late for work. But he also knew his outright disregard for authority cost him a lot of brownie points with the stripes.

And he was more than annoyed they'd pulled him off the case he was working. But it seemed, from the dark looks on the faces of the others in the room, that everyone else was in the same boat. Not that his other case was all that important. Just a rapist who had a bad habit of picking targets under the age of sixteen. No biggie. Let some other slob go after the guy. "Stupid feds," he muttered just loud enough for the two gentlemen in front of him to hear.

They nodded their agreement.

He could see badges from New York, Boston, even Washington. He was the only one not in uniform. No matter. He felt more comfortable in jeans and a white T-shirt, and no one was going to tell him what to wear, anyway.

A well-built man with thick, black hair that spiked on top of his head like a tiny army of soldiers made his way to the front of the room. He adjusted his green tie that had no business next to his salmon shirt, unless he was appearing in a sad Christmas play. He looked up through thick glasses and cleared his throat.

"Ladies and Gentlemen, my name is Mathews, special agent in charge." He pulled up a PowerPoint on a computer as he glanced around the room, a somber look on his face.

"As most of you know, yesterday there was an incident at the David's Island Correctional Facility. If you'll look on the screen behind me, you can see that the inmates in this photo appear unconscious."

The picture showed hundreds of men in orange jumpsuits lying face down on the floor and others still sitting in their seats with their faces buried in their food. Fifty or so paramedics and firefighters appeared to be working on the victims. The photo was of the main mess hall or cafeteria, taken from a high angle, maybe from a balcony

Kirk shifted in his seat. *So they ate bad shrimp.*

Metal tables that looked like elongated picnic tables sat in neat rows, and in the top part of the picture, a long counter with glass behind it was probably where the cooks prepared the food.

"As reported on the news stations, the poisoning affected every inmate in the building. Only the inmates showed signs of poisoning. The guards are fine." He paused. "Now for the real story." Mathews took off his glasses and switched to the next photo.

A slow muttering rippled through the room.

"These people are not unconscious." He waited until the crowd quieted. "Every inmate you see here is dead."

Whispers and gasps, especially from the women, sounded as the officers began to comprehend what had happened.

Kirk smirked. That particular prison housed some of the most vile criminals in the country, and now they were all dead. Justice had been served.

Mathews raised his hand. "People, please cut the chatter. I'll turn it over to Captain Jacobson, who has been with the FBI for over twenty-five years and has been at the scene of the crime from almost the moment the attack was reported."

A tall, lanky-looking man with bottle-cap glasses stood up. Kirk decided his strong, commanding voice didn't match his appearance.

"Here's what we know. First, every inmate died within

seconds of exposure to the food. Not all of them actually ate the food. Next, not one guard has died or even become ill, even though some of them ate the same food. And last, but not least, so far, we've found no trace of poison or anything abnormal in the food or in any of the victims." The captain showed several more slides, then asked for questions.

Kirk studied the slides with new interest, not because a bunch of slime bags died, but because he loved a good mystery. He wanted to know how it was done, to see if he could crack the case and look into the eyes of the mastermind. The prison yard had body bags littered from one side of the picture to the other. Individuals in hazmat suits with the letters CDC stamped on their backs like a bold black warning looked like they were testing something. Kirk guessed it would be the air and food. More photographs showed agents going through the cells looking for any clue that would lead to an answer to the cause of death.

A thin, redheaded agent wearing a pale-gray suit, who was sitting in the front row, raised her hand.

"Yes, Sally, go ahead," Jacobson said.

"So you're saying you've found no poison in the food, no toxic substance in the air, and nothing out of the ordinary?"

The captain arched an eyebrow as he pulled up the next picture. "That's not completely true. We found this tag inside of every inmate's pillow. They were sewn inside as if it they had been placed there by the factory." The picture showed a cut-open pillow with a small piece of cloth containing the initials WJA. "We're looking into every possibility. I need you all to be on top of this case, and unless we get anything that proves the contrary, we will be classifying this case as a mass homicide."

Captain Jacobson looked around the room one last time, then turned the meeting back over to Special Agent Mathews and took a seat next to Sally in the front row.

Mathews split the room and gave each of them assignments. Each person was handed a cream-colored file folder stuffed with photos and case records. The file contained everything one did and did not want to know about the inmates housed at David's Island.

They were to follow up with the families of the deceased individuals to see what, if anything, they could learn from them. It was a shot in the dark, and Kirk thought they were barking up the wrong tree. They should be looking into the WJA note, the pillow factory, and the food delivery service. Someone had to have seen or remembered something that could help.

Mathews dismissed everyone with the old "go out there and make us proud" speech, or something like that. Kirk was only half listening as he hurried out of the room and headed for the exit. He pushed open the door to the parking garage.

Lights lit on a rented, dark-blue Ford Crown Victoria as he beeped off the alarm. The car was a hard habit to break. He had driven a Crown Vic for as long as he could remember. He liked knowing what he had under the hood. Inside, he tossed the files in the back, where they scattered all over the seat, photos fluttering to the floor.

He turned the key and peeled out of the garage, driving in the direction of his hotel. He had to think, to really think. Did he want to do this? Did he even have a choice? His career was almost over, anyway. One more cluster mug, and his boss would have him patrolling a mall parking lot for the rest of his life. He hunched over as he drove, his back was aching again. The stress and the flight hadn't helped.

"Ah, screw it!"

He flipped the car around and headed for the expressway in the direction of David's Island, ignoring the honking horns and the angry gestures of the drivers he'd just cut off. He had to see the crime scene for himself.

CHAPTER THREE

THOUGH THE VIEW OF the New York skyline was breathtaking, Mark stared into K's eyes. He couldn't remember when she looked more beautiful. He reached into his pocket and pulled out her gift, then placed it on the table and slid it toward her with a smile.

"Oh, Mark, Honey, you shouldn't have. All I need tonight is you." Her eyes sparkled as she untied the red bow. The lid of the narrow, black box made a faint popping sound as she opened it.

K gasped and put her hand to her lips. "It's beautiful." She lifted an intricate, silver chain from the silk lining. The diamond pendant suspended from the necklace caught the moonlight that swathed the balcony in white and twinkled a response.

He moved to her side of the table to kneel behind her chair and hook the necklace for her. Nuzzling her ear, he whispered, "This has been the most wonderful five years of my life, sweetheart. Never in all my wildest dreams did I think marriage would be this good."

She nodded, tears glistening like stars on her eyelashes. "Me too."

He kissed her shoulder, then pulled her to her feet. They

embraced for a long, tender moment. His cheek against hers, he murmured, "Dance with me, my love?"

A string quartet played softly in the background as they danced, holding each other close. The balcony of The Leaf sat fifteen floors above the city and overlooked Brooklyn Bridge. All around the terrace, orange flames flickered from tall torches. His wife's soft skin glowed in the firelight. Despite the cool breeze, he felt warm and content holding her in his arms. He was the luckiest man in the world.

After Beethoven's *Moonlight Sonata* ended, they joined hands and walked to the edge of the balcony. The city was alive with the lights that filled the sky around them, making the stars pale in comparison.

"Thank you, honey, for five wonderful years," whispered K. "And for tonight. This has been an incredible evening." She leaned her head on his shoulder.

He felt a shiver vibrate through her body. "Are you cold?"

"Just a little." The weather was warm, but a gentle wind off the East River cooled their skin.

"I'll get the check and be right back. I have another surprise for you." He hurried off to find the waiter.

After taking care of the bill, Mark wrapped his arm around his wife and hurried her down the elevator to the lobby. Their car was waiting for them at the entrance to the restaurant. When they walked out the door, a short man wearing a white shirt and a red vest with the restaurant's signature cursive *L* stepped from behind the wheel. Mark gave him a fifty and opened the door for K.

As soon as he got behind the wheel, she tugged on his arm. "Where are we going?"

He grinned. "You'll see when we get there."

She pretended to pout, a look he always loved. Before he pulled into traffic, he kissed her long and hard, silencing her protests.

The streets were busy, but then again, it was Friday night in New York City. He'd booked the Hilton Garden Inn, the hotel where they'd spent their wedding night before heading to California for their honeymoon. He couldn't wait to see K's reaction when she realized he'd booked the same room they'd shared their first night of marriage.

As they drove up in front of the fourteen-story, stucco-and-glass building, the valet, a thin-faced, grade-school-looking kid, took the keys and delivered the car to the parking garage. K giggled as she clutched Mark's hand and pulled him up the stairs and into the front lobby. "Mark, you *sneak*. How did you get us a room? They're always booked."

"Not just *a* room. I got *our* room!"

She smacked his arm with her purse.

He grinned and deflected the blow. Sam got her energy— and her orneriness.

Inside the lobby, smooth, cream-colored, marble floors were topped by red-leather couches and fluffy chairs in the same, soft shade of red. A fireplace glowed in the sitting room. Mark checked in and they took the elevator up to their room.

The room was everything they remembered. It was as if they had stepped into a time machine and it was their very first time together as husband and wife. A fire burned in the living-room fireplace, sending soft orange-and-white light throughout the room. Candles flickered on the nightstand.

K's eyes reflected the light from the fire, dancing like fireflies in the spring. Her soft hands took his, and she led him to the bedroom through a set of French doors. Her long, blonde hair was that of an angel. Mark touched a strand, which curled around her shoulder. He tried to say something but she put a finger to his lips, reached behind her, and closed the door.

Mark knew from the way he felt tonight, how his heart pounded in his throat, that what they had was something special, something not found by accident. This was love, true love. It couldn't be faked or manufactured. Every day, he fell more and more in love with his wife, and he *so* looked forward to growing old with her.

"I love you, K."

* * *

REPORTERS SWARMED THE YARD like ants scurrying around an anthill. The prison had an odd presence about it. It was like Death had moved in, and even after he'd done his work, the stench of his soul lingered.

Kirk was used to seeing guards high up in towers or roaming the grounds, and inmates in orange jumpsuits working out or playing courtyard ball. However, this facility looked like a movie set without the cameras rolling.

Most of the bodies were already at the CSI crime lab for their final examination. He got out of his car and flashed his badge at a potbellied officer wearing dark sunglasses and holding a radio in his hand, who was trying to restrain the media mob without much success. The cop glanced at his ID and let him pass. The poor guy had probably been fighting off FBI tweaks and NYPD all day, so what was one more goon tromping around the crime scene? He squinted over his shoulder at the reporters and muttered, "Stinkin' vultures. They all want a piece." He looked around. Finding the poor sap who was supposed to be in charge was easy. He would be the guy in the cowboy hat barking out orders, a blueprint of the prison in one hand and a cup of coffee in the other.

Kirk sauntered over to him. "Hey, Cap. You the man around here?" He didn't bother to take off his mirrored-finish sunglasses, though he knew it was a sign of disrespect. He'd never been good at the whole butt-kissing thing.

"Yeah. Who wants to know?" The captain's thick mustache curled as he spoke, and he talked out only one side of his mouth.

"Name's Kirk Weston, DPD. I'm here with the FBI to look around." He held up his badge.

The captain glared at Kirk from under his wide-brimmed hat. "Fine. Just don't touch anything. There isn't much to see, but knock yourself out anyway." It was obvious he didn't appreciate an outsider stomping around in his crime scene.

Kirk didn't blame him. Heck, he didn't want to be there.

"Thanks." He turned toward the front door, ducked under the police tape and headed in the direction of where he thought the cafeteria might be.

The correctional facility—or as he called it, *prison*—stinking liberals liked to gussy up the place to make it seem like a four-star resort—had the usual amenities. To the west, for the inmates' viewing pleasure, stood a concrete wall with razor wire affixed to the top. He stared at the building in front of him. Not many windows or bushes. To his surprise, there were no petunia gardens to brighten the drab surroundings. The felon lovers must have fallen down on the job.

The front doors stood open and unguarded, which was highly unusual for a maximum-security prison. A paramedic wheeled by him pushing a gurney with a black body bag strapped to it, another paramedic right behind him pushing a similar load. Kirk wandered into the building and down the hall. Following the smell of stale milk and instant mashed potatoes, he turned left and walked through two sets of double doors by using a borrowed card key into the cafeteria.

Trays of food still sat on the tables. Others had fallen to the floor and spilled gravy and corn in a splash of yellow and brown across the concrete floor. It was like time had frozen, and everyone had disappeared. Metal tables were lined up in neat rows, just like in the pictures he'd seen earlier, but with one distinct difference—no one sat at the tables, stunned looks on their faces, fear in their eyes. A few rows over from where he stood, crime scene investigators were collecting samples and placing them in labeled plastic bags.

"I thought you guys would be done by now." The sound of his own voice intruding into the silence of the huge room surprised him.

One of the agents, a short man with thick, blond hair that kept falling in his face, looked at Kirk. "We *were* done, but after we didn't find anything abnormal in the samples we gathered the first time, we decided to come back to retrieve samples from the food bins in the kitchen, as well as something from every tray."

"It doesn't make any sense," said the other agent, a slim brunette in her mid-twenties dressed in a white, button-up top and black slacks. "If it was in the food, it would have killed the guards who, according to them, ate the same thing as the rest of the inmates."

"What about something airborne?" Kirk asked. "A gas or something."

"No. That would have done the same thing. It would have killed anyone within range." The short agent, looking to be in his thirties, scratched his head and pushed a loose strand from his face.

"Do either of you have a card?" Kirk asked. The pretty brunette reached in her pocket and pulled out a white business card.

"I'm Cassy—"

"Good to meet you. I might call you in a few days to see if you have anything new. I'm working with the FBI on this one... Never thought I would work with the feds..." His voice trailed off.

"No problem. This one's a mystery to us all," she said.

He looked around a little more, then stepped into the kitchen where he spied a file cabinet in a back corner. He pulled out the top drawer and sifted through the files, one by one. Finally, he found a paper that looked like a purchase order.

One hundred pounds of flour, twenty-five cases of mac and cheese... All the items on the P.O. looked like they came from the same place: Simco Foods.

He shoved the paper into his pocket. *Finally, I've got a lead.* He looked through the rest of the files but didn't find anything about where they had acquired their bedding. He wrote a note to himself on a beat-up old notebook he kept in his back pocket and closed the file drawer.

In the main hallway, he found a hall that led to the cellblocks. He peeked inside several cells, but nothing seemed out of order, except the lack of prisoners. Once he was back in his Crown Vic and driving again, he glanced up at the sky, which was cloudless except for one out-of-place, determined-looking rain cloud. He turned on the radio and had just tuned in to an 80s rock station when the downpour hit.

He slowed and steered with both hands through the deluge. It was almost impossible to see more than ten yards in front of him.

He glanced at the dark scar on his left forearm. It had been raining like this back in Detroit when he earned the scar. He'd caught up with a suspected drug trafficker, but as soon as he showed him his badge, the idiot ran. He had pounded the pavement after the dealer and cornered him in a dingy alley behind a laundromat on Sixth Street. The chase ended in a slippery, bloody shootout. He'd been grazed by a bullet, but the criminal—idiot, as Kirk liked to call him—was dead, thanks to two well-placed bullet holes in his heart. He patted his Glock .45 in his side holster and remembered what his shooting instructor had said repeatedly—*never leave home without it.*

The sun would be setting in a few hours. He wanted to scope out the food warehouse before it closed and had to work fast before his boss got wind that he'd gone AWOL.

Whatever. He'd just tell him one of the dead convicts' mommas told him her little boy had a friend who works there. He smirked as he turned off the expressway and headed toward Manhattan.

CHAPTER FOUR

MARK ROLLED OVER, TRYING to ignore the sun rays that streamed into the suite and convince himself he had more time to sleep.

Warm October air drifted through the open window, filling the suite with the scent of maple trees and roasted coffee beans as it mixed with the diner a block up the street.

He looked over at K, touched her soft skin and traced the outline of her face. She was everything to him. He thought of how happy he was, and for a brief moment, wished he could freeze time. He wanted to be like this forever, to lie next to his true love, his soul mate, and drink in her beauty.

But finally he said, "Good morning, honey," and watched her open her beautiful eyes and smile at him. "It's ten o'clock, sweetheart. We should get going. I think checkout is at eleven."

She mumbled something, then snuggled deeper into the pile of pillows and blankets.

He kissed the top of her head and stumbled to the bathroom, where he turned on the shower and stepped in. The hot water hit his back. He sighed as he began to wake up from his morning fog. Steam filled his nostrils, and the water massaged his muscles.

"Baby?" he yelled from the bathroom.

"I'm up—I'm up," she moaned. "That is one comfortable bed."

Leaving the water on, he tiptoed out of the shower, wrapped a towel around his waist, and snuck up behind his wife, who was bent over the suitcase. He grabbed her from behind, making her jump and scream.

"Mark! You scared me." She pushed him on the bed, ran into the bathroom and locked the door.

He was still laughing as he dried himself. He pulled a pair of jeans from the suitcase and slipped them on. It was a perfect day for a broken-in pair of jeans and a T-shirt.

After they checked out of the hotel, they drove to K's parents' house to pick up Sam.

Kate looked up from the grocery list she was making. "After we get Sam, I need to go to the store to buy a few things for dinner tonight. I think the Super Mart on Third Street has an Office Depot right across from it," he said. "I need to get a few things there, so I'll drop you off and pick you and Sam up after I'm done."

K nodded but asked him to try to keep it under twenty minutes. He smirked. She knew he would wander around forever, ogling the latest gadgets, if she didn't give him a time limit.

When they pulled into the driveway leading to her parents' three-story house, he could see Sam waving at them from the front bay window, a huge smile lighting her face. He smiled and waved in return. The apple of his eye, his pride and joy, the sweetest, most beautiful little girl on earth.

He parked the Honda and they both got out to meet K's parents at the front door. Sam jumped into his arms. He squeezed her tight before turning to his in-laws. "Mom, Dad. Thank you for watching Sam for us."

K hugged her parents. "Yes, thank you so much. We had a wonderful evening together."

"Our pleasure, as always." Her father smiled, revealing his perfect, white teeth, and patted Sam's arm. "Booboo was happy, too, wasn't she, Sam?" K and her older sister, Lily, owned a white horse they affectionately named Booboo.

Sam nodded enthusiastically.

"That old horse needed a little girl to ride her. She misses the little ones." He handed Sam's backpack to Mark and shook his hand.

K thanked her parents again for babysitting.

"Anytime," her mom said. "We love having her around." Holly was a slim, fit woman, who walked a mile every day, rain or shine. "Nothing makes you feel young again like a child running around the house."

Mark set Sam down. She hugged her grandparents, then ran to the car and jumped in the back seat. He watched her climb into her booster seat and buckle herself in. After more goodbyes and thanks, he opened the car door for K before settling into the driver's seat.

On the way to the store, Sam told them all about her adventures. "Grandpa tickled me, and Gramma gave me candy and… and…" was all they heard from the back seat. He shook his head, smiling at her nonstop chatter, and squeezed K's hand. "Like mother, like daughter," he whispered.

She snatched her hand away and slugged him in the arm. "Huh-uh. She gets that from *you*."

He stopped the car in front of the Super Mart entrance.

K opened her door, grabbed her purse, and walked around to get Sam out of her booster seat.

Sam giggled as K unbuckled her. "Can I ride the horsey?"

In the rearview mirror, Mark saw her point toward the mechanical horse next to the front of the door.

"After we're done with our shopping," K said as she set her on the pavement. "Then you can ride it two times."

"I can?" Sam ran to Mark's window. "Will you watch me, Daddy?"

"Sure thing, sweetie."

K leaned in to kiss Mark through his open window. "I'll only be about twenty minutes or so, so don't get mesmerized in

Office Depot and forget us. Sam will never forgive you, if you miss her rodeo show."

He nodded. "You're right. I'd hear about it for weeks."

She pointed to his lap. "Better buckle your seatbelt, bud." Then she smiled. "Love ya."

He couldn't help but smile back. His sweet wife looked radiant without even trying. But he didn't see any reason to buckle up for a ride across a parking lot.

"Sure. See you in twenty." He waved one more time at Sam, then turned into the middle lane and pointed the car toward the Office Depot on the far end of the asphalt. Glancing in his rearview mirror, he could see K holding Sam's hand as they stepped through the open sliding doors.

Before the doors closed, a man bolted from the store at a full run, his shirt flapping, and terror etched across his face. A high-pitched whine filled the air. Mark stomped on the brake as the hair on the back of his neck stood on end. "Wha—"

He gripped the steering wheel and stared at the lone, frightened figure sprinting toward him in the mirror. Something was horribly wrong.

Sam! Kay! He had to get to them, but every limb felt like it weighed a thousand pounds. He wanted to cover his ears to muffle the screeching noise, but his fingers were clamped to the steering wheel. Sam had to be screaming in terror.

Then the sound overtook him, shooting through his body like a bolt of lightning just before a blast of hot air burst the rear window and an incredibly bright light blinded him. His chest slammed into the steering wheel. His head hit the windshield.

The metallic taste of blood filled his mouth. *K! Sam! Were they all going to die?* He heard the sound again. This time it was a word in his mind. "*KABOOM!*" He ducked, his head smashing into the leather seat as the side windows exploded into a million daggers of death.

The car lifted off the ground like a rocket and flipped end over end. He covered his head with his arms and jammed his legs into the floorboard, wedging himself against the seat and the door, trying not to be thrown from the car.

The force was like a carnival ride, pulling everything away from the center of the car as it tumbled through the air. He pushed with all his strength at the dash and seat, desperate to stay in the vehicle. The car landed on its top, slamming him into the roof.

The car stopped moving, but the heat was overwhelming. He had to get out. He pulled his upper body through a broken window, then dragged his legs out and rolled onto his back. He gulped in a deep breath, but the acrid air burned his lungs. He sat up and blinked, trying to focus. His family. He had to find his family.

He scrambled to his feet and turned to face the supermarket, but it was gone. Where was the store? He took a step toward where he thought the store should be, but his legs gave away, and he fell onto crushed glass and concrete and split his forearm open, sending a flash of hot pain all the way up his arm.

Furious flames and thick, black smoke filled the air. Metal fragments and glowing embers rained down around him. Cars were on fire. One of them suddenly exploded. Nearby, a man missing one leg lay draped over an overturned, mangled shopping cart, a pool of ruby-red blood forming below the cart.

He choked back the urge to vomit and turned away. Through the ever-darkening haze, he could see the supermarket walls had been sheared off at about four-feet high, debris piled like garbage on the outer rim. The blast must have been in the center of the store.

No! He pushed himself to his feet and bolted toward the building, screaming. "K!" He reached the spot where the front doors had been and dug into the mass of hot bricks and rubble with his bare hands. "Sam!" They were alive somewhere in the rubble. They had to be! This was a mistake, a nightmare— "No," he sobbed, "it can't be."

His hands were soaked with blood as he clawed through

the dirt and concrete. He found a strap. It looked like the straps on Sam's backpack. A fresh flood of hope filled his heart. He pulled, and the strip of fabric popped up. It was only three inches long and burnt at the end, but he knew it was hers. He threw his head back and screamed for God to save his little girl, but his only answer was the ever-increasing wail of sirens.

Tears coursed down his face, and the inferno around him began to spin. He fell to his knees, feeling something sharp cut through his jeans just before he heard the thump of his head hitting the ground.

* * *

KIRK SAT IN THE parking lot of Simco Foods, a huge, metal warehouse with a little office stuck to the front like a tumor. The building was stained with rust, and the weedy parking lot looked equally neglected.

Taking out his gun, he dropped the clip, made sure it was full and popped it into place. Pulling the slide back, he checked to see if a bullet was in the chamber. He'd never been a boy scout, but he was always prepared. One thing detective work had taught him was that one never knew what a person would do when his back was against the wall.

After locking the car, he went through the front office door. The receptionist was an older woman with gray speckled hair and more wrinkles than a bulldog. She looked up at him through her gold framed glasses. "Can I help you, young man?" Her voice quivered just as he remembered his grandmother's did when he was a boy. He had loved going over to his granny's house. She always had a dish of M&Ms on the coffee table.

He pointed to the Detroit Police Department badge on his hip belt, flashing her half a grin. The FBI had issued them all identification, but he didn't want to use it, if he didn't have to. No one ever looked at the city stamp on the badge, anyway. "I'm Detective Weston, and I'm investigating a homicide. I would like to ask you a few questions."

"Well, I don't know if I can help you with that. We don't

get much excitement around here." She fumbled with the tiny chain around her neck that was hooked to her glasses.

"Your company delivers to David's Island, doesn't it?" He looked at the faded pictures on the wall. One was of a mountain lake and the other an ocean scene. They looked to be at least thirty years old, like the rest of the office. He smiled and tried to act half-interested in the answer, so as not to give the old woman a heart attack.

"We deliver to the prison every Friday. Now, let me see…" She shuffled through several folders stacked neatly in an upright file rack on her desk. The phone was clean, and a small photo of a little boy, probably her grandson, sat next to a pencil holder. "Here it is. Yes, Gus Martinez was the driver last Friday." She handed him a paper with a photocopy of the man's driver's license.

He stared at the picture, memorizing the features. "Is he here? I need to ask him some questions."

"Hold on. Let me check." Pulling out what looked like a time sheet, she glanced at it and nodded. "Yes, he should be out back cleaning his truck. You can go talk to him, if you like." She pointed to a door behind her.

He thanked her and headed toward the door, then looked over his shoulder and asked, "Besides food, what else do you deliver to David's Island?"

"Just that. We are a food-service plant. We provide anything edible, but that's all."

He nodded and pushed through a set of double doors, ignoring the mandatory safety glasses warning pasted to the wall.

He looked up. Metal beams stretched between metal columns. The ceiling had to be forty-feet tall and the length well over the size of two football fields. At least that's what he'd ascertained from the outside. He could not see all of it from where he stood. Loading docks ran along the east wall, and to the west, he saw what must be huge, walk-in freezers. Forklifts drove in and out through hanging, thick, plastic strips that groaned and popped each time.

He shook his head. The forklift operators drove like lunatics, honking and zipping back and forth, barely missing each other as they stocked shelves and loaded and unloaded trucks. He saw a stocky thirty-something Hispanic man with thick, black hair and a thin mustache sweeping an eighteen-wheeler at the fourth loading dock from the end. He double-checked the picture in his mind. It was Gus Martinez, all right. He walked toward the truck, careful to stay out of the way of the forklifts.

Martinez looked up from his broom.

Kirk knew exactly what he was thinking, that he could tell he was a cop from the badge on his belt and the way he walked.

The driver shifted his feet as Kirk approached.

"Are you Gus Martinez?"

He nodded but didn't say anything.

"I'm Detective Weston. I have some questions for you, if you don't mind." He was pulling out all of his nice-guy charm. Even added the sappy bull, *"If you don't mind."* He was on a roll now.

"Sure. Am I in some kind of trouble?" Martinez blinked, then blinked again.

"No, no trouble. I just have a few questions about your deliveries to David's Island."

Martinez shuffled his feet again and looked at the floor."Um… What you need to know?" His English was broken but understandable. His dark, unkempt hair had streaks of gray running through it. He shoved his hands into his pockets and jangled his keys.

"Well, as I'm sure you know from the news, there was an incident out there on Friday, the same day you delivered food to the place."

"Some people got sick. I saw on news." He looked toward the big rollup door then back at Kirk, his eyes darting.

"No. They all died, Gus. The media was just trying to keep everyone from panicking, just in case it was an outbreak of some kind." He tensed. The guy was gonna run.

Martinez's eyes widened. "Died? But they said—" He suddenly swiveled and bolted for the door.

Kirk swore and pulled his gun, diving after him, but missing the fleeing man's shirt collar by a hair.

Martinez jumped off the dock ledge.

Kirk dropped to the pavement and sprinted after the fleeing man. His temper rose, and he could feel his heart kick in as adrenaline surged through his body.

Martinez rounded the corner.

Kirk hit the corner and dropped his shoulder into the cinder block wall to slow his momentum then, with his gun drawn, whipped around the side of the building.

Nothing...

He heard a car engine start and saw a green, paint-chipped Caddy squeal out of the parking lot, just missing a light pole and throwing gravel as it hit the street.

He yanked his keys from his pocket as he ran. Hitting the auto-lock button, he jumped into his rental car, fired it up, and took off out of the parking lot. He could see the taillights of the runaway Caddie in the distance, weaving in and out of traffic as though driven by a drunken psychopath.

Kirk Grabbed his cell phone from his belt and dialed 911.

"911. What is your emerg—"

He cut the operator off. "This is Detective Weston, DPD. I'm in pursuit of a green 1990's Cadillac heading west on..." The street sign whipped past him as the driver of an oncoming car slammed the brakes, swerving out of the way. "...Fourth Street. Just past Beacon Ave. Send backup. Suspect is Hispanic, hundred-and-eighty pounds, wearing a dark jacket and gray pants." He dropped the phone on the seat and grabbed the wheel with both hands to make a hard left, sending the phone onto the passenger-side floorboard.

He caught up to the old Caddy, thanking his lucky stars he drove a Crown Vic. Cars flew by like blurs of light, horns honking. Then it hit him. They were on the wrong side of the street.

"Gus, old buddy, you just messed with the *wrong cop!*" Gritting his teeth and swerving into the right lane, he pushed the gas pedal to the floor, and the car surged forward. He saw a sharp, right-hand curve in the road ahead and knew it was his chance to gain the advantage.

The two cars screamed down the industrial road, his front bumper within nudge range of the rear bumper of the Cadillac. As they started into the curve, Kirk jammed his foot to the floor, waited for the gear to drop and smashed into his target. He crammed the steering wheel hard to the left, propelling Gus Martinez into a spin.

Bumpers locked and the two cars spun in an ever-widening circle. Kirk fought for control, hoping he looked like some sort of super cop in complete control of the spin and the impending outcome. But that was wishful thinking, and he knew it. A white minivan slid through the intersection, t-boning the Cadillac and knocking the cars apart. Gus's car slid away, then flipped over in a shower of sparks and grinding metal.

The minivan bounced onto the curb, smoke erupting from its crumpled hood. Kirk stomped his brakes, cranked the wheel away from the minivan, and skidded to a stop. He jerked his door open and crouched behind it, aiming his .45 at the overturned Caddy. He heard brakes squeal and an airhorn blast, then saw a woman burst from the minivan and a semi-truck jackknifed onto its side behind her car. The truck slid toward them, scraping the road like a huge snowplow, metal grating and twisting in a tortuous grind.

The semi ground to a halt beside the Cadillac. Martinez crawled out a broken window and slipped behind the rear fender of his car. An instant later, he popped around the side, a gun in his hand, and opened fire. Kirk fired two shots that pinged off the rear fender. He scanned the area for movement and saw the flash a microsecond before he felt the sting in his leg. He swore. Martinez had aimed below the door. Last thing he needed was a bullet in his leg.

Furious, he jumped around the door and ran toward the Cadillac, ignoring the sharp pain crawling up his leg. Martinez peeked over the chassis of his car, saw Kirk and ducked, but not before Kirk shot him in the shoulder.

Twisting with the impact, he fell backward onto the debris-strewn pavement.

Kirk dove to the ground, skidding on his belly across glass shards and spilled fluids.

Gus rolled over, gun raised.

Kirk fired two shots in rapid succession that hit the dark-haired man squarely in the forehead.

For a moment, Kirk lay in the middle of the street hearing only the thumping in his ears. He grunted as he pulled himself to his feet and brushed glass and dirt from his arms. He made his way to the back of the car, where Martinez lay in a widening pool of blood.

He pounded his fist against the car. *You had to kill the guy, didn't you, Weston? He pushed your buttons, and you just had to make him pay!* His only lead, and he'd killed the man. He could hear the sound of emergency vehicles closing in on them.

CHAPTER FIVE

MARK TRIED TO OPEN his eyes. They felt heavy, like they had weights on them. Finally, he forced one eyelid open, but instantly closed it against the painful, blinding light.

Head throbbing, he waited a moment before squinting through both eyes. He was lying on a bed in a medium-sized room with a television mounted on the opposite wall. A man on the screen wearing a suit, apparently a weatherman, pointed at clouds rushing over a satellite picture of the United States, talking rapidly. But all he could hear was a monotonous beeping sound.

Mark turned his head. The sound seemed to come from the machine beside the bed. He heard rustling and saw someone in scrubs pass his door. *So I'm in a hospital,* was his first thought. His second was, *Why?*

He tried to sit up, but a sharp pain shot through his side and knocked him back to his pillow. But it wasn't just his side. His whole body ached. Eyes wide, he stared at his torso, which was swathed in bandages, and at the tubes that protruded between the strips. Had he been in a car accident? Had he fallen? Had he—?

Then he remembered. And his heart shattered. He shuddered, recalling the horror of watching his family walk into the grocery store just as a frantic man dashed out. He relived the explosion. Saw the ball of fire flashing toward him.

"Nurse! Nurse!" he called. "I need help! Someone help me!" Despite the bandages on his hands, he frantically felt the bed for the call button but couldn't find it.

A nurse rushed into the room. "Mr. Appleton, are you in pain?" She glanced at his chart then reached for his wrist. "I'm glad to see you awake."

"Please," he croaked as she took his pulse. His mouth was so dry, he could barely speak. "My wife. My daughter. Where are they? They were in the grocery store. Have you seen them? Please…" He gripped her hand and stared into her face.

She took his hand in both of hers. "Mr. Appleton, I am so sorry…" She swallowed. "Everyone inside the supermarket died in the explosion. Only four survivors were found outside the building, including you. I am so sorry about your family." Tears filled her eyes. "I wish I could give you hope, but I can't."

"No, it can't be!" He pushed himself upright. "Tell me it isn't true!"

She shook her head, tears now pouring down her cheeks.

His heart exploded into a million pieces, like the windows of his car. He covered his face with his hands and began to rock as he wept. He had to think, but he couldn't marshal his thoughts. He could barely breathe. How could he live without his family? K and Samantha were his life, his everything. The nurse patted his back and asked him if he wanted anything.

He shook his head.

She offered him water.

Again, he shook his head. Though his throat was parched, he couldn't drink, not with Sam and K dead.

She told him she was going to find the doctor and hurried out of the room.

Still rocking, he wrapped his arms around his sore ribs. He should have gone into the store with them, should have protected them from... from whatever it was. Or died with his family.

Finally, he dropped onto his pillow and stared at the ceiling, wishing he could sleep, then feeling guilty for wanting to escape the pain.

The doctor came in, looked him over and checked his charts. He offered his condolences, asked how he felt, but Mark didn't respond. Instead, he asked what caused the explosion. The doctor told him no one knew, but the authorities were already investigating.

Later that evening, Bill and Holly visited. His mother-in-law's eyes were red and puffy. Bill looked like he was about to pass out. Without even a *hello,* Mark turned his back to them. It was selfish, he knew. They had lost their daughter and granddaughter, but he could not feel anything beyond his own deep, dark grief. He couldn't shoulder their grief, too.

He refused to eat, so the nurse added something to his IV. He really didn't care what she did. The only reason to get well was to find out what happened, find out what had incinerated his family. Even if it was an accident, he would find the negligent person responsible for killing his family and... He wasn't sure what he would do. But if the explosion was intentional, the bomber would pay—and pay dearly.

* * *

"YOU, MR. WESTON, ARE off the case!" Captain Jacobson jabbed a long, bony finger at Kirk's nose. "The last thing I need is a rogue cop running around *my* city. All you had to do was interview the families in your file. Was that so hard? Now we've got a dead witness and miles of rubble I've got to explain to the media. Who do you think is going to pay for all the damage?"

Kirk shrugged his shoulders. "I was just doing my job— following a lead."

Jacobson's face darkened. "I want you on the next plane back to Detroit," he hissed. "Your superiors are expecting you." He plopped into the chair behind his desk and motioned for Kirk to leave.

Kirk stood, pulled the purchase order from his jacket and tossed it onto the desk. "You might want to look into this." He cursed and left the room, slamming the door behind him.

Interviewing the inmates' families was a joke. This was a well-planned job, and he had a feeling the FBI had a good idea who did it. Maybe they could have stopped it. But then again, who gave a crap about a bunch of dead cons? Their massacre would save the taxpayers' money.

He flagged a cab outside the FBI building. "Hill View Hotel." He slumped into the backseat and closed the door, his bandaged leg aching from the short walk. Rubbing his chin, he thought about what his next move should be and decided to check into a different hotel. If that bottled-capped captain thought he was going to send him packing, he had another thing coming.

His cell phone rang. He pulled it from his belt and looked at the number. It was his boss, who was sure to have a few choice words of his own for him. He silenced the ringer. "This one, I'm doing on my own."

The cab stopped in front of the hotel. Kirk dug in his wallet and tossed the driver a fifty. "Keep the change."

Hill View was a simple hotel in the midst of other cheap hotels. The lobby stank of cigar smoke and stale coffee. He didn't bother to look at the scabby rail of a man behind the short counter they called a front desk.

He packed his clothes, which were thrown all over the floor, making sure to grab one of the fluffy, white robes as a gift to himself. "Thanks. I needed one of these."

He stuffed the robe into his Under Armor athletic bag and zipped it shut, thinking how strange it was that a dump like the Hill View had robes. *Let them charge me.*

Outside the hotel, he slung the bag over his shoulder, put on his sunglasses and headed for the Avis car rental agency several blocks away, though walking was painful. He gritted his teeth each time he added weight to his sore leg. The only comfort was the knowledge he'd sent the goon that shot him to the morgue.

He had to flash his badge to get the woman behind the counter moving. Noting in the computer that he'd smashed his previous rental car didn't help her uncooperative mood, but he promised her the FBI would take care of it.

Once he was behind the wheel again, he felt much better. He'd requested a Dodge Charger, and they happened to have one left. He was especially pleased that it was black.

He sat for a moment in the agency's parking lot, contemplating his next move. He couldn't get Martinez's words out of his mind. *They said.* Who was *they*? He needed more info. What he needed was a hacker. He needed Mooch.

He'd picked up Mooch a few years back for hacking into the eBay website and changing every auction to "Buy it Now for One Dollar". EBay officers had ended up in a lawsuit for the billions lost in that one day.

But Kirk didn't arrest Mooch. Instead, a working relationship was forged between the two. It was always good to have a computer whiz owe one a favor. In this case, it was a big one.

"It's time to pay up, kid." He dialed his cell as he drove, weaving in and out of traffic, only to be stuck behind three Yellow Cabs.

"Pick up," Kirk muttered.

The other end of the line crackled and a young voice came on the line.

"Hey, Mooch, I need that favor you owe me. I'll be online in ten minutes. Stay close to your phone." He pushed the End button before Mooch could say anything more than hello.

Slipping his phone into his pocket, he turned down Fourth Street, looking for a coffee shop. He needed some caffeine. If he was cut off in traffic one more time, he would no doubt lose it.

He spotted a small coffee shop at the next corner with a *Mean Bean* sign above the window, pulled down the alley behind the brick building and parked in back. Grabbing his laptop from the front seat, he locked the doors and strode in the back door as if he owned the place.

The walls of the *Mean Bean* were painted mocha brown and black and decorated with burlap sacks, along with pictures of coffee beans and newspaper clippings of the shop's ribbon-cutting ceremony, which made at least one local paper.

He ordered a plain, black coffee from the pretty, brown-eyed brunette at the counter. On a different day, he might have flirted with her, but "thanks" was all he offered today. He headed toward a booth at the back and slid across the vinyl seat.

As his laptop booted up, he glanced around the nearly empty place. One guy with a woven cap on his head was hunched in an easy chair reading a book, and a couple of ladies were laughing and talking in hushed tones over what looked like scones and tea.

When he heard twenty-year-old Mooch's voice answer his call, he jumped right in. "Mooch, bring up the Transportation Department."

* * *

MARK WAS RELEASED FROM the hospital the next day, though he was a long way from healed. The doctor told him he had to take it easy for a month, so his ribs could heal properly. He had three broken ribs, lacerations over his arms, legs and back, and his hands were swollen and bruised.

However, considering what he had been through, the doctor said he was lucky to be alive. He didn't feel lucky. Lucky people don't watch their families die and lose all that matters to them in an instant.

He took a cab home, even though Bill and Holly had offered to drive him. He wanted to walk through the front door alone. He didn't know how he would react when he returned to an empty house.

He stopped in the foyer, where K's scent lingered, and closed his eyes. He had to get through this. There was no one to hold his hand and do it with him or for him. He walked upstairs, looking at all the family photos that hung on the wall. How could this have happened? Just yesterday, he'd awakened in the hotel after an incredible night with K. Just yesterday, he'd hugged little Sam and felt her squirm with energy and excitement as she showed him her new toy puppy dog she'd named W*oofie*.

K smiled at him from the bathroom. He could see her putting on makeup, brushing her hair. He smelled her perfume, ran his fingers over her clothes in the closet.

He stumbled back to the bedroom. He *couldn't* do it. Couldn't go on without K and Sam. This house, this home they'd made together wasn't a home anymore. It was just another house on a street where other families lived, played, and loved each other.

A wave of emotion racked his body. He fell onto the carpet, weeping bitterly. What would he do without them? He could not live in this house filled with memories, memories that would increase the pain of his overwhelming loss. He wanted to remember K and Sam, but knew he could not live surrounded with the life he'd had with them. He had to leave.

The phone on the nightstand beside the bed rang. Startled from his grief, he crawled to his feet and checked the caller ID. It was Hank, calling from his cell phone.

He hesitated. He didn't feel like talking to anyone, but Hank was his boss, a boss who'd been close to his family. He dried his eyes on his shirtsleeve and picked up the receiver. "Hello."

Hank's voice was soft. "I'm so sorry, Mark." He paused. "I, I don't know what to say. The explosion was a horrendous thing, but knowing K and Sam were in that store…" It sounded like he choked back a sob. "Everyone here is in shock. They're all thinking of you and praying for you."

He swallowed, the sound audible on the phone. "The next few weeks and months are going to be rough. Take as much time as you need to get through this. We'll cover for you. I'll help however I can—line up meals, funeral arrangements, legal matters. A shoulder to cry on. Whatever. Just let me know."

Mark sniffed and wiped at his nose with the back of his hand. "Thanks, Hank. K's parents are taking care of most of the funeral arrangements. They scheduled it for Wednesday morning." Just the thought of attending K's and Sam's funerals made him want to throw up.

He took a breath. "I think after that, I'm just going to get out of town for a bit…" His voice drifted off. "I'll keep you posted."

"Okay, buddy. Call me if you need anything. I mean it."

Mark hung up the phone and sat on the side of the bed. He looked around their bedroom, memories threatening to overwhelm him. Endless nights of lovemaking. K in the morning, her hair spread across her pillow. Sam cuddled between them, kissing first one parent, then the other. He couldn't spend one more night in his house, a house that was once a home.

But he couldn't think of anywhere else to go. Maybe he should get something closer to work. The only reason they'd lived outside the city was for Sam's sake, but now… He shook his head and lifted a picture from the nightstand of him and K standing in front of their house. K's beautiful smile radiated as she beamed at her newborn daughter sleeping in her arms. He took the photo out of the frame and held it to his chest.

Finally, he forced his feet to go to the garage, where he gathered empty boxes and took them into the house to pack the few things he couldn't live without. Family photo albums. Samantha's teddy bear. K's Bible.

He packed two suitcases worth of clothing, looked around the house one last time, then loaded the boxes and suitcases into the silver BMW Hank had had delivered to replace his destroyed Honda.

He stopped by K's parents place to ask them to watch the house until he decided what to do with it. Handing them the key, he said, "I've got everything I want out of it. Take anything you want."

"We can't do that!" Holly exclaimed.

"I left K's jewelry and clothing. Maybe you'd like a memento or two. Or one of Sam's stuffed toys. The rest—furniture, kitchen stuff, all if it—can go to the Salvation Army or the Rescue Mission. However you want to dispose of it. I'm not going back."

His mother-in-law pulled him close, holding him for a long moment. "I'm so sorry this has happened, Mark, but please don't leave us. You're like a son to us."

He sniffed, fighting for control. "I'll keep in touch." He turned and walked away, knowing he was leaving his old life behind, forever.

Finding an apartment turned out to be easier then he'd expected. After a few calls to apartment buildings his company had designed, he located an upscale, fully furnished apartment he could move into immediately.

When the leasing agent left with the signed lease and his deposit in hand, Mark dropped onto the overstuffed sofa, his hand over his eyes, his mind in a fog. What day was it? Sunday? "Yeah, it's Sunday."

He grabbed the remote on the coffee table and clicked on the news channel.

"Yesterday was a busy day here in New York." The anchorwoman looked grim. "A car chase in the Northeastern Industrial Park area resulted in a shootout that left one man dead and a Detroit detective wounded."

He only half-listened as he bit into a ripe apple from the gift basket on the coffee table. Had she already talked about the supermarket explosion? Did he tune in too late?

"The shootout left over three hundred thousand dollars in collateral damage. At this time, we have no comment from NYPD, other than that the situation is under investigation. In other news, we still have no information as to the cause of the explosion at the Super Mart yesterday. Sources say a ruptured underground gas line may have been the culprit. The blast killed more than two hundred people and destroyed the entire building. We now go live to Andrea Kilpatrick, who is at the scene, where investigators are still trying to pinpoint exactly what happened. Andrea?"

"Yes, Susan. I'm standing in front of where Super Mart once was. As you can see, there isn't much left here." The camera panned the rubble.

Mark's stomach lurched.

"The police say they are not ruling out foul play, but so far they have not found anything to lead them to believe this was more than a very tragic accident."

"Andrea, is this something that might have been caused by faulty wiring or a gas line that needed to be repaired? Could the store have prevented this?"

"The investigators have not released a statement. In fact, they say it could take months to get to the bottom of this. We will let you know as soon as we hear something from the local authorities."

"Thank you, Andrea. A relief fund has been set up for—"

He shut off the TV and walked over to the kitchen counter, where he'd left his cell phone. He dialed the police station. He needed answers, and his gut told him the explosion was not an accident. The image of the terrified man rushing from the building right before it exploded burned in his mind.

"Yes. Hello. This is Mark Appleton. I need to speak to whoever is in charge of the Super Mart investigation."

The dispatcher connected him to a Detective Bruce Owens, who answered in a deep voice, "What can I do you for?"

"Hello, Detective. My name is Mark Appleton. My wife and daughter were killed at the Super Mart yesterday." His voice broke. Just saying it aloud made him want to weep, but he choked his grief back and went on. "I was told you're the one overseeing the investigation." He tried to sound firm, in control of his emotions, but his voice cracked anyway.

"Yes, Mr. Appleton. I'm the one in charge of the investigation. I've been meanin' to call you, but I didn't want to push too hard, with what you've been through—"

Mark interrupted. "Can we meet tomorrow? I just got out of the hospital." He wanted to get it over with, find out if they had anything besides the crap the media was reporting.

"If you can be here around ten o'clock, I'll make sure I'm in the office. The officers at the front desk will show you to my office."

Mark thanked him and hung up the phone. Bruce sounded like a good-enough guy. He hoped he wasn't a hardened detective whose main concern in life was finding out what time the donut shop opened.

* * *

AS THE LAPTOP DOWNLOADED the patch Mooch was sending over, Kirk thought about how little he knew about the internet, which usually caused him more problems than solutions.

His laptop hummed quietly.

"Mooch, what's taking so long?" He hated to wait for anything or anyone, especially a low-life hacker or fast food.

"Well, *excuse me*. I'm only trying to hack into a government website and still keep us out of jail. If they see us, we're screwed!"

Kirk could hear him tapping keys.

"This is hard enough over the phone, getting you a link and—"

"Fine, Mooch, fine. Just get me to last Friday. The address is Five Sixty-Four West Fuller Avenue. Simco Foods. Do you have cameras around that area?"

Mooch's voice cracked like a teenager. "Yeah. I can see almost anywhere in the world. I hack into the street cameras, into the Crimson Satellite that isn't running, so they say."

"Not running?" Leaning on his elbows, Kirk peered at the coffee beans beneath the glass that topped the small wooden table where he sat and took a sip of his coffee.

"Been broken for years, too expensive to fix, but I can still use it for looking around. Me and my buddy Chucko—do you know Chucko? Anyway, we rigged it to take snapshots, just not live action stuff."

Kirk shook his head. "You get off on this stuff, don't you?" He saw something come up on his computer screen, an aerial view of the Simco warehouse. "What day was this taken?"

"It's the day you wanted, Friday. Hold on. Here's the video from the loading dock cameras."

"Run it from about eight a.m. in fast forward."

The video showed semi-trucks pulling up, loading, and driving off. He looked for Martinez's face among the drivers but didn't see him. He watched the clock at the bottom of the screen spin by.

"Wait! Back up a sec. I think that's it. Stop it there." Kirk cursed as he looked at what was plain to see—Martinez loading his truck with boxes.

"What are we trying to find here?"

"I'm not sure. Can you follow that truck? Can you go in real time?" Putting his coffee down, Kirk scooted his chair closer to the table.

"We better make this quick. We'll be spotted if we stay on too long. I'm running a Radian Jammer, but it'll only work for about five minutes."

"Just do it. We won't get caught." And if they did, he'd have no problem throwing Mooch to the wolves.

The truck left the warehouse, headed toward the interstate, then disappeared. "Where'd he go?" Kirk frantically punched buttons on his laptop and almost spilled his coffee all over it.

"Man, you're jumpy. Hold on. He's out of range. I'll have to switch back to *Crimson*. But it will be in stills, so don't blow a gasket."

The screen showed snapshots of the loaded truck, but Martinez headed the wrong way. That road didn't lead to David's Island, and Kirk was positive he had delivered a load there on Friday morning.

He watched as the truck pulled onto a dirt road that led to an old abandoned sawmill. The parking lot was overgrown with weeds, and one side of the building looked like it had collapsed.

"Can we get a shot behind that mill? I can't see the truck." He tried to sound nicer, even though his body heat was rising. He'd never liked computers, and now he was at the mercy of a hacker devoid of scruples.

"I can get a partial, but the mill is blocking the line of sight."

He could hear Mooch typing and munching on what sounded like potato chips. This only added to his stress level. The truck was now out of sight, with the exception of the rear bumper, but remaining in the same spot with each time-stamped photo. Then he saw a shadow beside the vehicle.

"There. Go back one. Yes, that one. Can you zoom in on the shadow of the truck?"

The picture zoomed in closer. It was clear now. There were *two trucks*. Somehow, he didn't think this was an accident.

"What's that? Another person?"

"On it. I see her."

"Her?" Kirk strained his eyes. The picture zoomed in on the second shadow. He could see long, dark hair blowing in the wind. It was a *her*. "Okay, Mooch. Let's see if we can get a look at this chick."

Sitting back in his chair, he took another sip of his coffee and watched the screen. His hunch was right. Martinez had been up to something, and now he had proof.

But picture after picture revealed nothing new.

The woman stayed in the shadows. It was as if she knew exactly where to stand in order to prevent a clear camera view of her. As the stills flashed by, he saw someone who looked like Martinez unloading the boxes from his truck and loading new ones from the mystery woman's truck onto his.

"Mooch, where is this spot? Give me an address." He needed to check out this drop-off site firsthand.

"Uh, oh! Pull the plug, man! They got us!" Mooch screamed like a girl in Kirk's ear. He jerked and dropped his coffee on the floor. A red warning sign flashed on his screen.

He dropped his phone, grabbed the laptop, flipped it over and yanked the battery out. He didn't know if it would do any good, but it was the only thing he could think of at the time.

He picked up the phone. "Okay, Mooch. I'm out." He took a breath, as winded as if he'd been chasing a perp. "Did they see us?"

"Nope, but holy cow, that was close. Good thing I have a breaker switch on my desk, for just such an occasion." His voice sounded like he'd just won a Super Bowl game, and his breathing came in short bursts.

Kirk wondered if the poor kid ever got out in the real world for some real time, real life exercise. "I need you to make copies of those photos of the mystery woman and those trucks. E-mail them to me as soon as you can, and find out anything you can on where that other truck went. Oh, and by the way, if you do this for me, I won't tell the FBI it was you they almost caught a minute ago."

"Awww, thanks man. You're a saint."

"Just do it, Mooch. I'll even get you an FBI T-shirt."

Mooch cursed.

Kirk laughed. There was nothing in the world Mooch hated more than the feds. He packed up his laptop, stepped over the spilled coffee, and slipped out the back door of the coffee shop.

He looked at the address Mooch had given him, then shook his head. He would have to wait until morning. He needed to get some sleep. Plus, he was getting hungry and irritable.

He crawled into the car, his leg throbbing. It felt better than yesterday, but was still plenty sore. For a moment, he sat in the driver's seat staring out the window. The woman bothered him. Who was she? What did she have to do with the prison massacre?

Finally, he checked his phone and saw he'd missed two calls, both from his boss. He started the engine. The case might cost him his job, but it was too late now. He knew how it would work. Return home with a win and save his job. But go home with nothing, and it would be *hello early retirement*.

CHAPTER SIX

THE THREE-STORY RED BRICK police station was fronted
with a wide parking lot littered with police cruisers. Near the
front door, Mark saw what looked like a SWAT team truck,
a van painted white with a blue stripe down the side lettered
NYPD.

He took a deep lungful of the morning breeze, which
warmed his face and tossed the flag that fluttered high atop a
pole in front of the building, trying to prepare himself for the
upcoming ordeal. The last thing he wanted to do was relive the
day his family was stolen from him, but there was not much
luck he'd avoid it this morning.

Double doors led to a front desk area, where everyone
seemed to be in a hurry. He dodged an officer taking a reluctant
prisoner, then approached the front desk to get clearance and
directions to Detective Owens' office. "Hello. I'm here to meet
with Detective Owens. He's expecting me."

A petite, pretty, blonde receptionist looked up at him with
bright, sunny blue eyes and a big smile which lit up her face.
She checked her computer. "What's your name?"

"Mark Appleton."

"Yes. He's in the big conference room down the hall and
to the left. It will be—oh, never mind. I'll show you. I give

terrible directions."

She giggled and jumped out of her chair. Walking around her desk, she almost skipped down the hall. She was bubbly, which made him wonder where she was from. New Yorkers had never been known for being particularly friendly, and members of the NYPD were rarely accommodating, or even helpful. Maybe she was new or had had one too many gun shot wounds to the head, making her a little loopy. She chatted as they walked past a big, open room filled with dozens of officers behind rows of desks. The place was busy. But then, it was a big city.

"Here you go, Mr. Appleton." She shook his hand with vigor, then bounced off back to her desk.

He was annoyed when he opened the door to the room she'd led him to. The place was so packed he had to squeeze in the back to the final, remaining chair. The mood was somber. People talked in hushed tones, whispering and looking around. He guessed there were about three hundred in the room.

A slender man with a stack of papers in his hand strode in a side door. He reminded Mark of Shaggy from *Scooby Doo*. He had wavy blond hair and a polo shirt that looked like it was blue at one time but had faded so much it looked almost white. He stopped at a small table with a laptop on it.

"Good mornin', everyone. For those of you I haven't met, I'm Detective Bruce Owens. Because many of you contacted me about this tragic event, I decided to call a meeting. It's better y'all hear it at one time and not from the media. I've never been good at this stuff, but here it is."

"Before I start, I want to say I'm very sorry for y'all's loss. There is nothin' to prepare yourself for this kind of tragedy. I want to help y'all get through this, and I'll tell you everythin' I know up to this point. Afterwards, if any of you folks have questions, I'll try to answer them the best I can."

The screen behind him came to life as he worked the laptop's remote. The first slide showed an aerial view of what was left of the store. A gasp rippled through the room. It looked

like a war zone picture instead of what used to be a popular
New York shopping center.

Detective Owens glanced around the room. "I'm sorry. I
know this is hard to see. It's okay to leave the room if this is
more than you're able to take in right now."

One couple got up to leave, the man's arm around a
sobbing woman.

Owens said, "Thanks for coming," and turned back to
the screen. "As you've already figured out, what you folks
are lookin' at is what used to be the Super Mart. We've had a
group of experts workin' at the scene night and day since the
explosion Saturday mornin'. We still don't know how many
people were killed, but so far we've recovered two hundred
and thirteen bodies."

The sound of soft sobs floated through the room. Mark
clenched his fists and choked back one himself. He had to keep
it together and be strong for K and Sam.

The detective's slow drawl continued. "Here's what we
know so far. This incident has been ruled out as a terrorist
attack. We haven't found any traces of a bomb, or anythin'
that would suggest foul play. The nearest we can tell is that an
underground gas line ruptured, then exploded."

Whispers rustled through the room. Mark frowned. The
picture looked like a bomb had gone off. A big one. Not that he
was an expert, but come on. There had to be more to it than a
ruptured gas line.

The tall detective went on. "The gas line was part of a main
feed that ran from a nearby apartment complex, then tied in
with the Super Mart before connectin' with the city gas line in
the street. The line was old, and the city was in the process of
replacin' it, but they hadn't got that far down the line yet. Are
there any questions so far?"

An older man in the front row raised his hand. "How do
you know it wasn't a terrorist who did this? It sure looks like
a bomb from that picture." He pointed at the screen behind
Owens.

"Well, sir, we would have found traces of C-4 or other high explosives, and parts of the bomb. There would be traces of it everywhere. Everythin' in this darn accident that we've found is consistent with a gas-based substance." He picked through his stack of papers, pulled out a single sheet, and started to read.

"Traces of natural gas and fossil fuel were found. Based on the saturation level in the boiler room, we have reason to believe the gas leak started there, and the boiler ignited. The explosion then caused a chain reaction, setting off the entire underground gas line. If it weren't for the automatic shut-off valves, the explosion could have extended farther down the line."

A few more questions were posed and answered, though a feeling of despair and grief seemed to fill the room. Mark thought about how pointless and unfair it was. If it had been an act of terror, he and the others could at least direct their anger and emotions at the killers. They could have some closure when the instigators were brought to justice. But this? Who could they blame? *The city was trying to fix the problem. They just didn't make it in time.*

When Owens finished with the last slide and the last question, Mark followed the crowd as the families of the missing and deceased quietly filed out of the room. He wanted to talk with Detective Owens, but his mind was blank, like he'd fallen into a trance. Though he remembered the day it all happened, it seemed so long ago, almost as if it was in another lifetime.

"Mr. Appleton?"

Mark blinked and glanced up.

Owens motioned for him to join him at the front of the room.

Mark made his way to where the detective was standing.

"Thanks for comin' in. I apologize for not tellin' you about this meetin'. After we talked on the phone, I decided to get all the people who had a family member killed in the explosion together, so I could fill everyone in on the investigation at the same time." Shutting down his laptop, he put it under his arm and walked toward his office, motioning for Mark to follow.

"I wanted to get a statement from ya and go over what you saw that day. You were one of only four people who survived the explosion." Setting his computer and papers on top of other stacks of paper, he pointed to a chair.

Mark took a seat. When he sat, his ribs came alive with a pain so intense he could barely breathe. He took a shallow breath and sat back, even though that position hurt as well. "Well, there isn't much to tell," He grunted through the cutting pain. "I had just dropped off... um—well, my wife and daughter..." He dropped his head into his bandaged hands and stopped talking as a vision of K and Sam walking into the store filled his mind.

"Take your time," Owens said.

Mark looked up. The detective was leaning on his elbows, looking intently at him with what appeared to be real concern. First, there was the happy person calling herself a New York cop at the front desk and now a Texan who actually seemed to care.

He regained his composure and continued. "I was headed to Office Depot, but just as I turned away from the Super Mart, the building exploded and flipped my car upside down. After I got my bearings, I ran toward the building, trying to find them. That's about it."

He paused to let the detective, who was taking notes, catch up. "There was one thing unusual, though. Right before the explosion, I saw a man running from the building, looking scared, as if he knew the explosion was going to happen."

"Hmmm..." Owens' eyebrows lifted. "Can you remember what he looked like?"

Only because the memory of the fleeing man had been burned onto his brain cells did he have any idea of what the man looked like. "He had on a red ball cap, a blue jacket, and blue jeans. I think he had dark hair. It was sticking out from his ball cap on the sides. He looked to be in his early twenties. Just a kid."

Owens scratched his head, making his blond hair flop as if it was made of yarn. "I'll have my folks look into it. His body would have been outside... We might be able to ID him."

"So you really think it was just an accident? I mean, it is sure hard to accept that your whole world can be taken from you because of an old gas line." This time, he didn't blink back the tears, and something about letting them fall made him feel better.

Detective Owens leaned back in his chair, which squealed in protest. "I'll do everything in my power to find out for sure, but I'm afraid it looks that way." He played with his fingernails. "I'm so very sorry, Mark. If there is anythin' I can do..."

Mark shook his head and stood up. It was too much to process right now.

The detective stood and stuck out his hand.

Mark shook it.

"Thanks a bunch for comin' in," said Owens. "I'll be keepin' in touch with you about that guy you saw. If we find him, I may need you to come in to ID his body."

Mark nodded.

"And if you remember anythin' else, I mean anythin' you think might help, give me a call." Reaching into his pocket, he pulled out a business card. "This has my cell number on it as well as the office number."

"Thank you. I will," Mark said. "Please let me know if anything turns up."

"I guarantee it."

He made his way out past the front desk, where the receptionist smiled and waved at him as he passed. The meeting had turned out a lot different than he had thought it would. Now he had to try to figure out what he was going to do. He didn't feel like living anymore, not without K. A part of him wished he had died in the explosion with her and Sam.

Poor little Samantha. She must have been so frightened...

The sun hit him in the face as he left the police station, but he couldn't enjoy it. He looked at the people walking, living, yelling, and cursing around him and thought of K, who couldn't get mad or cry anymore. She and his innocent little girl, who had never done anything to deserve a violent death, were both gone.

He walked past his car in the parking lot and crossed the street, dodging an SUV. The driver of the white Escalade honked, but Mark ignored him

A couple blocks uptown, he found a small park with a slide and a swing set, where kids played and parents watched and looked at their watches. Sam would have loved the park. It had a big swing with green rubber seats. He could see her laughing and calling out to him to push her higher and higher. Seated on a faded wooden bench, he broke down and cried. And cried, not caring who saw him or what they thought.

"Sam, my sweet, beautiful Sam."

* * *

A KNOCK SOUNDED ON Kirk's door. He stirred but didn't respond. All he wanted to do was sleep in for a change. No one knew where he was, and he hadn't asked for wake-up service, so what crazy, suicidal person would have the audacity to knock on his door so early in the morning?

The knock came again. He blinked. The sun splitting through the curtains glared into his eyes like a nagging wife. Groaning, he pushed himself to an upright position. His feet hit the floor with a thud. "Bah!" He wasn't a morning person. For that matter, he wasn't a night person. And, for sure, he wasn't a people person.

Finally, he got to his feet and dragged himself to the door, where he found a newspaper and a list for the different breakfast options on the floor. This hotel was a few steps up from the last one. It even had a little fridge filled with bottled water and liquor. If you touched it, you bought it.

"Eggs and toast, or a breakfast sandwich, served until eight

a.m." He looked at the alarm clock on the nightstand. Eight
thirty. Oh, well. He didn't want their dry, lukewarm breakfast
anyway.

He decided a shower would wake him up. On his way to
the bathroom, he clicked on the television, turning it up loud,
so he could hear the news through the sound of the water. After
he undressed, he took the bandage off his leg and looked at the
gunshot wound. It was scabbing over and would heal quickly.
Just another scar to add to his collection.

The water felt good and even made him smile for a brief
moment. Until it hit his wound, that is. He could hear the
anchorwoman jabbering on about some high-pressure system
that was coming in.

"And in other news, the NYPD is investigating
cooperatively with the FBI on the food poisoning incident out
at David's Island last week. They have no new leads as to how
the food was contaminated, but they assure the citizens of New
York that our food is safe."

"Safe. Ha. I bet they've still got their agents chasing
around family members, asking about what kind of childhood
they had." Grumbling, he finished shampooing his mostly
bald head, then dripped water on the bathroom floor when he
reached from the shower to the counter for a razor to shave. He
pulled the curtain back and thought about what he knew about
the case so far.

He had a bunch of dead inmates but no dead guards, tags
with the letters WJA on them, and a mystery woman involved
in a food drop. The woman *had* to be connected with the WJA
thing. WJA. Was it a code or the name of a terrorist group?

He turned off the water. What would Deb have to say
about this one? He pushed the curtain open. Why was he
suddenly thinking about his ex-wife? Granted, she was nice to
think about, but their marriage had been one raging fight after
another.

Stepping out of the shower, he shook his head. Maybe it
was because she was great at helping him crack cases. She was

a great sounding board.

He'd stayed married to the fiery redhead longer then he should have, but then again, he should never have gotten married in the first place. She always spoke her mind, a little too much, which was not a good combo with him.

Finally, the fighting got to be too much for her, and they'd split two years ago, no kids. *A clean break,* he told himself, like he'd told himself dozens of times, but he still loved her. He just couldn't bring himself to change the way she wanted. It was better this way, he reminded himself. But then again, he had told himself countless lies.

As he dressed, he reminisced about how he'd met Deb in front of a stand of tomatoes during one of his rare visits to the local supermarket. She was only five-feet-tall and not even a hundred pounds. For a second, he'd thought she was just a kid. But then she'd turned and smiled at him, and it was all over. Four months later, he asked her to marry him.

His cell phone vibrated on the nightstand like a rattlesnake ready to strike. The sound jolted him back to the present. He didn't recognize the number, but decided to take the call anyway, after he turned down the blaring TV.

"Detective Weston."

"Hello, Detective. This is the crime lab. I mean, this is the lady from the prison. I gave you my card."

Kirk tried to remember her name. "Ah, yeah, hi, uh…"

"Cassy Meyers."

"Right. Cassy! How ya doing?"

"The FBI gave me your phone number yesterday morning. I've been so busy with everything going on, but I remembered you wanted to know when we found anything new."

Kirk grinned. She must have asked the FBI for his number before he ticked off the big dogs.

"So, what did you find?"

"After testing all the food samples and coming up empty, I decided to look into the guards' blood work and found something very interesting." Her voice became animated.

"The guards?"

"Yes. I thought since we didn't find anything in the inmates' bodies or in their food, that maybe we would find something in the guards' blood that the inmates lacked—and we did! Are you ready for this?"

"Yeah, hit me with it."

"Okay. The guards all had traces of Dypethline in their systems, a drug used specifically to protect the immune system."

"Okay... So the question is—why would they need a protected immune system? And protected from what?"

"Wait. It gets more interesting. This drug is—well, it's pretty experimental, and still in test form. As far as we know, it's never been tested on humans. We don't even know who else would have access to it besides the government."

Kirk fought to process the information. *Stick with the facts.* "So, how did they get this drug into their system?"

"I'm not sure. However, this opens up more options. If they were protected, then, like you said, they were being protected from something—something that would have the exact opposite effect of Dypethline." The phone was silent as she waited for the information to sink in.

The picture started to clear up. "What you're saying, Cassy, is that this drug, Dypethline, has a partner drug that is its polar opposite. If a good drug helps the immune system, the partner drug kills the immune system. And from the looks of it, it seems they also can cancel each other out." He paused for a moment. "So, basically, whoever did this poisoned all the food, but it didn't affect the guards or whomever had Dypethline in their blood."

She laughed like a child who'd just learned to ride a bike for the first time. "Very good, Detective. You catch on quick. All I have to do is find out what its partner drug is, and we have our killer. I've been searching but haven't found it yet."

"This Dypethline—who manufactures and supplies it, and who has access to it?"

"I'm not sure of the source, or if they're still testing it, but I read an article about it a year or so ago in a medical journal."

A thought ran through Kirk's mind, almost too much to believe. Did the government or the FBI have something to do with the killings? Was that why they had all the misfits running the investigation?

"Could you do me a favor, Cassy? Keep this conversation under your hat for the time being? I need to check into a few more leads, and the FBI isn't too happy with me at the moment."

"Sure. Until I find out definitely what we're dealing with, I'll tell them the truth—that we still don't have answers."

He folded his phone and put it into his pocket. This was getting more twisted by the second. He had a feeling his friends at the FBI were swimming in waters much too deep for them.

CHAPTER SEVEN

MARK HIT THE BUTTON on the BMW's key fob and opened the car door. He started to get inside but stopped when he saw a white envelope lying on the leather seat. He glanced around the parking lot. Someone had been inside his car. How did they get in? Who? Why?

He checked the lock and the window, looked at the outside of the door. No evidence of tampering. He walked around to the passenger door. No dents or scratches on that lock or doorframe.

After another scan of the cars in the police lot, he picked up the envelope and settled into the seat. The paper looked and felt expensive, probably linen. Frowning, he ran his fingers across the letters embossed in large print on the front. WJA. *What does WJA stand for?* Finally, he opened the envelope and pulled out a single sheet of paper. He unfolded it.

NO ACCIDENT!

No accident? What was that supposed to mean? A sickening feeling washed over him. Was someone telling him the explosion was not an accident? That it was planned, an attack of some kind?

He crumpled the note and shoved it into his pocket. He wondered if he should show it to the detective, but didn't have the energy to go back in and talk. Whatever it meant, he didn't have the energy to think about it now. All he wanted to do was crawl back in bed and dream about his family.

* * *

KIRK BIT INTO THE juicy cheeseburger, then cursed out of the side of his mouth when sauce dripped down the front of his blue T-shirt. "Aw, man… This is my favorite shirt!" Holding the burger in one hand and steering with his wrist, he swiped at the drip with a napkin. The car swerved. He grabbed the wheel with the napkin and returned the car to the correct lane.

He looked down. His cleaning job was only making the stain worse. It was hard to get a shirt to fit these days, with his abs turning into a one-pack. He had once been a gym rat, but then life, marriage, divorce… Now he couldn't see his belt for the belly that hung over it.

The road turned to the right, just like in the pictures he'd printed from the e-mail Mooch sent him. He wanted to see the old mill for himself. He probably wouldn't find anything more than dusty tire tracks, but it was all part of being thorough.

He could see the dilapidated building standing out against the horizon, a sleeping giant. It looked like the entire building had been constructed of plywood and old, tired planks. He slowed the car, popped the last fry into his mouth, and burped in satisfaction. Nothing like a burger to chase away hunger pains.

Parking his Charger in the front of the mill, he turned off the ignition and pulled out his .45 from its shoulder holster. Pulling the action back, he checked the chamber. It made a clicking sound as it snapped back into place. He holstered the weapon, checked the perimeter one last time, and got out of the car. He checked his watch. One o'clock. He had some time to check the place out.

He walked to the front of the rotted building. Chains and twisted boards crisscrossed the front doors. Most of the windows on the two upper floors were broken. A washed-out sign across the side of the building read: LAKELAND MILL.

He pushed through the weeds to the back of the property and found what he was searching for. Multiple, wide tire marks, which wound around to the back of the building. He followed the tracks to the corner, where he stopped, leaned against the wall, and drew his weapon.

He listened for a moment, then slipped around the corner, stopped, and scanned the area—the doorways, the windows, the adjacent out-buildings, the trees behind the buildings. He'd been in too many situations to assume he was alone. He lowered his gun. The area was clear, with only a few tumbleweeds stacked against the side of the structure like bums in an alley.

Footprints were everywhere. Most of them, it appeared, belonged to Martinez, or a man with very wide feet. Then he saw what he was looking for—a second set of prints, smaller ones. The mystery woman.

He checked his surroundings, then re-holstered his gun and pulled a digital camera from his pocket. He snapped several shots of the footprints and of the tire tracks.

He saw where the second truck had parked behind the structure, just out of sight from the road. Squatting on one knee, he peered at the tracks, which looked weird, not like tread marks from a normal delivery truck. The rear tracks were about twice the size of the front ones. Probably some kind of armored truck… Like those banks use to transport money.

He straightened and started toward the silo tower ten yards behind the main building. The tower was about fifty feet tall with a cone-shaped top and a rusty ladder strapped to the side that ran all the way from the bottom to the top. Though it was probably empty, the silo still emanated sawdust and dirt, a smell strong enough to make his eyes water.

Then he saw the newly painted letters blazing in the sun high atop the tower: WJA. "What in the—?"

He pulled out his camera and took a picture, thinking someone had spent some time painting the giant lettering. It was not a hack job, like what he was used to seeing from the local taggers back in Detroit. This was very professional.

He dropped the camera back into his pocket and turned just in time to see a billy club crash down on his forehead. A flash of light filled his vision as he crumpled to the ground. He heard the thud of his head hitting the dirt as he grabbed for his gun. Before he could find the holster, another blow smashed the back of his skull.

* * *

MARK OPENED THE DOOR to his apartment feeling like he'd been cheated. His life had been turned upside-down—for what? The thoughts of K and Sam tortured him every moment of every day.

When he closed his eyes, he saw them. When he walked down the street, they were with him. When he drove his car, he heard Sam's chatter in the back seat. Felt K's hand in his. He could barely eat. Could barely think.

He ran his hand through his hair. He had to return to work. He'd call Hank tonight and tell him he was going to work tomorrow. That was the only way he would get his mind off his own personal hell.

On the kitchen counter, he saw the bottle of wine that had been in one of the gift baskets sent to his hospital room. He didn't remember who sent it, but it was just what he needed at the moment.

He rummaged through the silverware drawer. After he found a corkscrew, he managed to pop the cork, despite his bandaged fingers, and pour himself a glass. He'd always thought people who drank to smother their pain were cowards. Now he wasn't so sure. At least for today, he needed a break from the agony.

He held his glass to his nose and breathed in deep, inhaling the rich scent of the red wine and the promise of relief. He sat on the couch, the bottle in one hand and the wine glass in the other.

But his back, still sore from the rollover, seized as he sat, sending daggers of pain up and down his body. He dropped the glass. It hit the floor, and a red stain instantly spread across the area rug. He groaned, set the bottle down, and painfully maneuvered off the couch.

After he cleaned the rug and hung it outside on the balcony to dry, he returned to the couch. This time, he lowered himself slowly, careful not to send his back into orbit again.

He reached for the now empty wine glass he'd placed beside the sofa, looked at it, then back at the bottle on the coffee table. With a sigh, he set the glass on the end table. He could not numb the pain and the grief. He wanted to live, to feel. Bad feelings were just as much a part of life as good ones. This was how he would remember how much he loved K and Sam. The pain was his love for them, which would never die.

* * *

A THROB OF PAIN rushed through Kirk's head, waking him from his forced slumber, his skull pulsing with each heartbeat. He opened his eyes but couldn't see anything. He waved his hand madly in front his eyes.

Nothing.

Gingerly, painfully, he probed the back of his skull with his fingers.. His hair felt wet and tacky. Blood. He grunted, surprised he was happy to be alive. He rolled onto his back and felt for his gun. As he suspected, it was gone.

He sat up and pushed himself to his knees, his head throbbing. The smooth, cold floor felt like it was made of metal.. Taking baby steps, he shuffled his way around his new home trying to imagine what it looked like, but he didn't have much of an imagination. Hands in front of his face, he waved them back and forth, searching for a wall or---. He wouldn't go there. Whatever he found, he didn't want to find it with his forehead. He started to take another step, then stopped, his heart in his throat. His right hand felt something... Not something. *Nothing.* Nothing but air up above him, in front of him, behind him, to the left or to the right.

Not good.

He lowered himself to his belly. Hugging the floor, he

rubbed the floor with his fingertips in ever-expanding swaths. Finally, he was able to trace the edge.

The floor was two-inches thick and rounded, as if he was lying on a large Frisbee. He crawled in a circle to define his prison, determined to find the wall the cliff was attached to. That would be the safest place to be, he reasoned, so he wouldn't roll off in his sleep and fall into nothingness.

"No wall?" he muttered. "Something has to be holding this thing." He felt sweat drenching his armpits and could smell fear seeping from his pores.

He felt along the edge once again, hoping against hope he was wrong. But he found no wall, no supports, no cables to suspend it. Nothing but this crazy, floating, metal Frisbee and, as far as he knew, a deep, dark hole above and below him. He moved to the center of the disc to contemplate this new information.

Click, click, pop, pop.

Blinding, white light made him twitch and snap his eyes shut. He tried to open them, but after total darkness, he blinked uncontrollably.. He squinted and shaded his eyes with his hand, trying to make out what was in front of him.

The room was about fifty feet in diameter, with a dome ceiling and warehouse lights hanging high above him, like huge, monstrous eyes staring at him. He was lying on a round chunk of metal fifteen feet in diameter. He wasn't in the middle, like he'd thought. He pulled himself to the center, and as he did so, the disc swayed.

He flattened himself to the floor, breathing hard and hugging it for all he was worth. At any moment, the disc could tip and pitch him over the side.

Way below him—the room had to be at least a hundred feet to the bottom—he could see a single door. He searched the perimeter. As far as he could tell, that door was the only way in and out of the huge, round room. The walls were smooth, their silver sheen rippling as they bounced the light back and forth. He felt like he was inside a gigantic oven.

Straight ahead, at eye level, a mirrored window broke the monotony of the glossy walls. He recognized it for what it was. A two-way. Just like the ones at the station back home. It was better to be on the other side of the glass.

"Hello, Mr. Weston." A deep voice thundered and circled the round room.

Kirk flinched. His heart pounded in his ears. "Who are you? How do you know my name?"

His voice echoed off the walls, making his headache even worse. "Please do not talk, Mr. Weston. All you need to know is that you are a prisoner here. As you can see, if you try to escape, you will die in the attempt.

"Look around, Mr. Weston. You are in what we call the MAG Chamber, a room built with magnets and specially engineered metals. The walls, the floor you are sitting on, even the lights, are set to an exact range and magnetic strength. A magnetic field supports you, a field we can control with ease."

He rose to his knees. "What kind of people are you? Do you—"

The floor dropped from beneath him so quickly that he left the disc and was airborne. As suddenly as it started, the floor stopped. He crashed into the disc with a thump, the breath knocked out of him.

The floor began to rise. "Mr. Weston, we asked you not to talk. If we want your comment on something, we will ask."

He rolled onto his back and made a thumbs-up motion.

"The rules are as follows. No talking unless asked a direct question. Do not try to escape. You will be killed on-sight if you try. Last but not least, welcome to the WJA."

The sound system squealed and clicked off. The room was as silent as before. Then, just as fast, the lights shut off with the same sound of breakers popping.

Kirk breathed in a sigh of relief. His pounding head couldn't take any more loud noises or bright lights. He rolled onto his side. *Now what?*

* * *

"HELLO HANK." MARK TURNED up the volume on his cell phone. "I just wanted to let you know I'm coming into work tomorrow." He knew he would get resistance from his boss, but he wasn't going to take no for an answer.

"Mark, come on. You've only been off for like, what, a day?"

"I really need this right now, Hank. I have to get my mind off everything. Just give me some small project to work on, and you won't even know I'm there. I need to keep busy."

Hank sighed. "Fine, but you're going to take some time off later in the year…when you can enjoy it. Are you sure you're ready to come back this soon?"

"I can't just sit around here…" The silence was sharp. He knew it made Hank feel uncomfortable.

Hank heaved a sigh. "All right, all right. See you tomorrow."

"Thanks. I'll see you first thing in the morning." He hung up the phone, then stared out the window. He had to get back into a routine. Memories of K and Sam were consuming him. He wanted to remember them, and he felt somewhat like a selfish pig not wanting to think about them. But he couldn't do it right now. Not now.

He sat in front of the TV and flipped through the channels, going from the extreme to the ridiculous. He could find a hobby, something new to learn to keep himself busy. Golf? Fishing? Maybe he would join a gym and try for the six-pack he always wanted but had never found the drive within himself to go all the way.

He stopped flipping when he saw the program on the Discovery Channel. They were running a series called *The History of Weapons.* He watched for a few minutes and was surprised how interesting it was and how many different guns there were: semi-auto, full auto, pistols, machine guns. They even showed one that could shoot around corners. He remembered that Bert down at the office had invited him to go shoot with him at the firing range a few times. He'd always had other things in the way. Now, it sounded like fun. This might be the thing to take the edge off. He might even like it.

He'd used a thirty-thirty hunting rifle when he hunted with his dad back home. It was one of his few memories from his childhood. For some reason, he only remembered bits and pieces. Deep down, it bothered him. He *should* be able to remember. He'd ask Bert if he could go with him. It would be good to have proper instruction on how to shoot a handgun, maybe even get good enough to enter a competition someday.

"Whoa there, bud. Let's just take this one step at a time." He was the type who threw himself into projects with all of his soul and energy. It might be too early to dive in headfirst.

* * *

THE NEXT MORNING, MARK walked into his office avoiding as many coworkers as possible. He didn't want people to feel sorry for him or look at him like he was made of glass. He set his briefcase on his neatly organized desk and sat carefully in his chair. The wrap around his ribcage helped to ease the pain, but he was still sore. Sitting was the hardest thing to do with broken ribs. Then there were his hands. He hoped he could move his fingers enough to use his computer.

Hank walked in. "Hey, Mark!"

"Hi, Hank." He raised his hands. "I'll take it slow, I promise. No need to baby me." Hank had a heart the size of Texas, but he didn't want to take advantage of it.

Hank frowned. "You sure you're up to this? You broke a few ribs, you know." He emphasized the work *broke*. He glanced at Mark's bandaged hands.

Mark rolled his eyes. "I'll be okay; I just move slower than usual, so no making Bert run back and forth to the copier for me."

"Fair enough. I asked Maria to give you a hand for a few weeks, just to get you coffee and run errands for you." Maria was the receptionist with shimmering brown-gold eyes who made sure Mark never forgot meetings or birthdays.

Hank wasn't asking. That meant he couldn't argue the

point. Not that he would have anyway. Maria was a good friend. It would be nice to have her around.

"Thanks, I'll appreciate her help."

Hank looked at his watch, mumbled something about being late for a meeting and hurried out of the office.

Mark clicked on his computer and was shuffling through papers in his briefcase when he saw Maria coming toward his office, a skip in her step. She was a slender woman with brown hair that was always up in weird-looking buns or clips. If he had to guess, he would say she was in her mid-twenties. She was always on the verge of laughing or giggling. That was one of the reasons he got along with her so well. She always enjoyed a good joke or prank.

When she walked in, he said, "Congrats, Maria, on moving to an admin position. Sorry it had to be me you got stuck with."

"I wouldn't have it any other way." She walked around his desk to give him a hug, then stepped back. "How are you doing?"

He closed his eyes for a moment then looked at her.

"As good as can be expected, I s'pose. I just wish everyone would be themselves. No need to be so glum on account of me."

She sat in one of the low-backed chairs across from his desk. "We all care about you. It's hard to know what to say or how to act. You know what I mean? We want to help you through this hard time, and well… We're worried about you. We hurt for you."

He smiled. It was a weak smile, but it was the best he could do.

"Just know if you need anything, anything at all, you know where to find me." She stood to leave.

"Yeah, I guess it'll take some time… for everyone. Thanks, Maria." He was relieved when she started for the door. Talking about what happened to his family was about to overwhelm him. He needed to change the subject.

"Hey, do you want a coffee, or something to eat?" she

asked. "I'm heading up to the cafeteria."

He nodded. "I could use an Almond Joy mocha and a bagel with cream cheese. Didn't have any breakfast. Thanks." He grinned as she left his office. This assistant thing was going to be nice. Maybe he could find a way to keep her on permanently.

CHAPTER EIGHT

One Year Later

CHRISTMAS EVE. THE OFFICE was all but deserted. Christmas fell on a Friday this year, and that made Mark, as well as the rest of the office, happy for a long weekend. The year had gone by without a second thought to his scarred body and broken heart.

He dreaded going home to an empty apartment. Christmas had been the highlight of the year for his family. Despite his grumblings, the minute they'd eaten their last bite of pumpkin pie on Thanksgiving Day, K would shove him and her dad out the door to hang the Christmas lights. Didn't matter what team was playing who on television.

He shook away the memory, dropped a couple projects into his briefcase to keep himself busy over the weekend, and snapped it shut. He knew he should move on with his life, but he kept falling back into the memories. *Wallowing in his grief*, as he'd heard a therapist on television say. His friends and coworkers told him time would heal his heart, but he had his doubts.

He turned off the lights, shut the office door and locked it. As he turned around to head for the elevator, he almost ran over Maria. "Maria! What are you still doing here? It's Christmas Eve."

"Oh, I had a few things to finish before I took off." She hesitated. "Um, Mark, I was wondering if you might…" She shifted her feet, looking down at the floor. "I…um. I don't have anything going tonight. If you want—"

He decided to rescue her from the awkward moment. "Sure. I would love to, but this time at my place. I haven't decorated, but my neighbor gave me a potted tree, so maybe I could stop and get some lights and tinsel or whatever, and you could help me decorate. I'll even make some of my famous eggnog."

Maria's steady, faithful friendship had seen him through the last year. They'd shared dozens of long walks between the trees of the rooftop park. He talked about K and Sam. She listened. Not once had she made him feel weird or out of line.

Her brown eyes lit up. "Oh, cool; I was hoping you wouldn't have anything going on. I mean, not that I hoped you would be alone, but—"

He laughed and took her arm, steering her toward her desk. "You're a dork, Maria. Get your stuff. I need to hit the stores before they close." As they rode the elevator to the parking garage, he listened to Maria's happy chatter and watched her eyes sparkle and switch from gold to brown to gold again. Her knee-high boots, striped red-and-green dress and the pencil that secured her brown hair seemed to enhance her effervescent personality. She laughed, and he smiled. They were becoming great friends, but that was all. He was not ready for another relationship. It was just too soon.

* * *

KIRK HAD NEVER BEEN a fan of beards, or any facial hair for that matter. That was for the bums too lazy to work or shave. In this case, however, he didn't have much of a choice. He ran his hand through his full beard and long hair that now intertwined, a year's growth, as far as he could tell. He tried to keep track, but without the sun or anything to mark the passing time, he was lost.

The lack of seeing the sun, clouds, moon and stars, or even a nasty rainstorm, depressed him almost as much as being marooned on a sterile, metal island. He still didn't know why they kidnapped him or whom he was dealing with, outside of the initials WJA.

They were a high tech bunch, though. The room looked like something right out of a movie. Metal walls, wires interlaced in them, and the floating floor made him feel like Frankenstein's experiment gone wrong. They fed him twice a day, whether he was awake or asleep. As his stomach was fully aware, the times were varied, probably so he couldn't tell if it was day or night.

The guards, or as Kirk liked to call them, *Creepers*, were always masked and never spoke to him. The handful of times he'd tried to engage in conversation, they had punished him with extended darkness or extended time between meals. But when they wanted to feed him or allow him to use the bathroom, the lights would flash on and the disc begin to lower.

By the time his eyes had adjusted, he'd see the door at the bottom of the room open and two masked men walk into the tall, round room. About once a week, or so he figured, they would let him shower for five minutes, the timing and temperature controlled by a force outside the shower stall.

The hallway leading to the bathroom had two doors, one on each side. The door to the left led to the bathroom, a simple affair, with metal walls and floor, a steel toilet, and a roll of toilet paper. No sink, not even a light.

The door to the right opened to a small shower room with a showerhead in the metal ceiling and nothing else, except the floor drain. The Creepers controlled the water, which was always ice cold.

First, soapy water rained down on him for a couple minutes in the pitch black room, then equally cold rinse water. Finally, the spray would stop and warm air would shoot out of the same nozzle to dry his goose-bumped flesh. The moment the air stopped, the door opened and the Creepers would hand him clean clothing and watch him dress.

Each time he showered, he felt like he was in a human car wash and, each time, he imagined the flashing signs. *Wash. Rinse. Dry. Exit carefully, 'cause you don't know what the dudes on the other side of the door are going to do.*

He still wondered how the men got into the hallway. There wasn't any other door. No other way in or out of the shower or bathroom. The hallway ended with a metal wall just like all the others. Nevertheless, there they were, covered with black, skintight outfits and masks pulled over their heads like creepy gang-bangers.

He'd given up on the mystery of the door a long time ago. He had bigger things to think about, like how not to go crazy just sitting all day, every day, on a fifteen-foot disc. To keep himself sharp and strong, he made use of his free time—which was pretty much all the time—to exercise, just in case the opportunity to escape presented itself.

First, he did push-ups and sit-ups for approximately half an hour. This was easy enough, but the pull-ups proved a little more challenging. He would make his way to the edge of his round home, look over the edge at the hundred-foot drop, bend and grab the edge, which was only about two inches thick, just enough to hold onto.

Then the fun part. He'd lower himself over the side and hang from his fingertips. The first time he tried it, he fell and broke both legs. He woke up on his disc with a cast on each leg and an ache in his back.

After a few weeks, and after the casts came off, he could stand up and move around without much pain, so he resumed exercising. Once a day, at least that's how it felt to him, someone would lower the disc about twenty feet above the floor for approximately an hour. That's when he'd do his pull-ups.

He had tried to escape half a dozen times, but this always ended badly. The Creepers seemed easy enough to take out, so the first time he tried, he threw a left hook at the taller of the two. A cracking sound shattered the silence, then a mist shot from his gray jumpsuit, filling the small room in seconds. He was instantly paralyzed and awakened on the floor of his circular home with a splitting headache.

The agony that shot through his body when he regained use of his limbs was nearly unbearable, like a million fire ants crawling and biting the ends of every nerve with sadistic pleasure.

This day was no different from any other. He started with push-ups and sit-ups. After a lot of practice, he was now able to do handstands on the edge of his metal disc and hold them for the length of a song. Today, he could hear the words of *Ride the Lightning* from Metallica's lead singer fill his mind as he held his legs straight up in the air. His one-pack was all but gone, and he could tell he was about thirty pounds lighter. Every muscle felt like a rock.

The sound of the lights popping on brought him to his feet as he waited for the weekly announcement.

"Good day, Mr. Weston. We have a special treat for you today."

The voice was the only one he'd heard for over a year, and it was the only thing that brought him any comfort. He felt like he knew the person behind the voice. Though the man was his captor and his enemy, he was his only friend.

"You may not be aware of it, but today is a special day. Christmas Eve. You have been in our care for over a year now."

The pit of Kirk's stomach turned as he realized how long he'd been there. He'd known deep down, but hearing it confirmed, made him nauseous. "As a token of the Christmas spirit, we are releasing you."

Kirk stood motionless as he heard the news, then began to rock with dizziness, the disc wobbling beneath his feet. His mind warred with possible outcomes—none of them were good. They were going to kill him. Or, maybe they would leave and let him die of starvation. Or kill him when he stepped outside under the long-forgotten sun and breathed fresh air for the first time in months. This was some kind of sick joke.

"Do you have anything to say?"

He was silent.

"You may speak, if you like."

He opened his mouth, but his voice cracked due to lack of use. He swallowed, but all he could do was squeak out a noise that sounded like a cross between a grunt and a squeal.

"Not to worry, Mr. Weston. You will have plenty of time to recover." The disc started to lower, then came to a rest on the main floor. The door to the small hallway opened, and, for the first time, no Creepers stood guard.

The lights hanging high above the floor flickered and pulsed like a movie screen. The silver walls shimmered like a desert mirage. He blinked his eyes. What was happening?

Then, in one swift motion, the walls that had comprised his prison disappeared. Behind them, large magnets twisted in a circle, humming like the smooth, greased motors of a mad-scientist's machine. Those were what held him in the air?

He started to shake, and his knees gave out. He fell onto the disc but felt dirt beneath his hands. He looked up and could see past the wires and cables running all around his magnet prison to the warehouse beyond. The second-floor window, where he assumed the voice had come, from was a suspended office that looked like a cargo container sitting atop thick, steel beams.

The place looked vacant, but he knew they were watching him. He pulled himself to his feet as two Creepers stepped out from nowhere. They motioned for him to follow them as they made their way through the door and down the hall to the back wall, where they stopped, turned from him, and walked through the wall.

He walked toward the wall, a sinking feeling rushing over him. He could have at any moment walked through the same wall and out to freedom. His mind had kept him there, imprisoned for months upon months. Just like an addict, the only thing standing in his way was himself. Suppressing the urge to vomit, he followed the men.

When he walked through the hallway wall, he found

himself standing inside of what looked like a giant warehouse that stood over one hundred feet tall. Bright, blessed sunlight streamed into the building through a huge, open door at the opposite end.

He squinted as he walked toward the door, shading his eyes from the burning, yellow light. When he reached the door, he turned and looked back at the place where he'd spent over a year of his life. It was a scary but beautiful sight. The engineering and the work put into the building was incredible. He looked one last time, then headed out into the sunshine.

As he stepped into the morning air, he was overwhelmed with emotion. Too afraid of what his captors might do next to celebrate, and too happy not to celebrate. Either way, he was free, even if for a moment.

His eyes slowly adjusted to the new light, but as he looked around, his heart sank. Sand. Nothing but sand every direction he looked. The desert was the last place he thought he might be. Maybe the city, or in some outbuilding in the woods, but not the middle of the desert.

He walked a few hundred feet, then turned one last time to look back at the building that had housed him for the last year of his life. It stood monolithic in the sunlight. How did they do it? Why? Squinting, he studied the building. Would he be able to describe it? To find it again? Would anyone ever believe him? No, they'd just assume he'd lost his mind.

As he scrutinized his prison, it suddenly vanished. He blinked. Like a wisp of hot air rising off the desert floor, it was there, and then it wasn't. He shook his head in amazement.

No wonder they let him go without blindfolding and transporting him somewhere else. He'd never find a nonexistent barn. On the other hand, they'd left him to die in the desert, so maybe they figured he wouldn't live long enough to go looking for them.

Off to the west, if he still remembered directions, something glinted in the sunlight, burning his eyes. The more he stared, the more it looked like a city of some kind. He'd heard that desert travelers saw mirages. Was this one of them. Should he stay put or—? There was no *or*. Stay, he'd die. Walk, he might die. "Well, why not?" He croaked.

Though he was hot for the first time in months, he resisted the urge to tear off his clothes. He knew he could die of sunburn and dehydration before he made it two miles. The morning sun was already heating up the earth, and the sand was warming under his bare feet. This was going to be hard to explain to his boss back home. If he ever made it home.

* * *

MARK DROPPED MARIA OFF one level up, then took the elevator down to the second floor, where he normally parked. He looked around the mostly empty lot as he walked toward his car. Most of his coworkers were home sipping cider with their families.

Family. No, he wouldn't go there. Not tonight. Maria was coming over, and they would have a good time together. For her sake, he wouldn't ruin it doing the wallowing thing.

He eyed the few other cars parked here and there. An old Ford coupe with the license plates hanging crookedly took up two spaces, like the driver was worried someone might dent its already rumpled exterior. Then he noticed the black Lexus. He had seen it several times before and figured it belonged to someone in the building. But something made him feel extra wary this time, like someone was watching him.

The lights flashed with a beeping sound as he unlocked the door to his BMW. He started to toss his briefcase to the passenger side but saw a packet on the driver's seat and stopped. Strange. No one else had a key to his car. Well, maybe Hank. But, he would have said something, unless it was a Christmas present.

Then he saw the symbol and sucked in a quick breath. Now his sixth sense was at full attention. He glanced around the darkened parking lot, then back at the parcel. *WJA*. The package had been left by the same person or persons who left the note in his car right after the accident.

He scanned the garage, searching for the letter-carrying messenger, but saw nothing suspicious. He walked around the car. Like last time, the doors and locks looked fine. Again, he surveyed the all-but-empty garage and peered at the Lexus with renewed interest. Somehow, it seemed out of place. He knew the cars of the workaholics who stayed late, holiday or no holiday, but he didn't know the owner of this car. His heart pounded as he walked over to the black car.

He cupped his hands, trying to see through the dark tint on the car's windows. Nothing moved on the other side. He stepped back, worried someone might see him and think he was up to something.

He walked back to his car, tossed the mystery package onto the dash, started the ignition and pulled out of the parking space.

His tires squealed on the ramp to the first level. He considered tossing the package out the window for the first curious skateboarder who came along. He was always finding junk beneath his windshield wipers advertising free weight-loss pills or other products of equal importance. However, the *WJA* symbol spiked his curiosity, and the fact that it was inside his locked car made him nervous. Might not be something a kid should pick up.

He exited the building wondering what the package contained. It looked too bulky to be a mere note like the last time. Picking it up, he squeezed it and shook it, reminded of the techniques he'd used as a young boy to figure out what was inside his Christmas gifts.

It was lightweight but solid. Maybe a CD or DVD. He tapped the package against the dash in time to the music on the stereo and admitted to himself he was burning with curiosity. Was this connected with the note? The note that read *No Accident*?

He couldn't stand it any longer. He steered the car onto a side road and parked in front of a diner under an old street light. The moment he stopped the car, he tore open the parcel

and turned it upside down. A disc inside a clear, plastic case fell
into his lap, along with a small note that read:

Surveillance Footage / Super Mart. The date printed on the
DVD was the same day of the explosion.

His vision blurred and his heart began to pound so hard he
could barely breathe. For months, he had fought to not think
about that horrible day every moment of every day, but now it
all came crashing back.

He grabbed the gear shift and threw the car into drive. The
BMW lurched into the street.

*Who did this to me? Who do think they are messing with my
mind like this?*

No matter who they were, he had to get home, had to see
what was on the DVD.

Chapter Nine

KIRK TORE STRIPS OF cloth from the legs of his jumpsuit and tied them around his feet, but the makeshift shoes didn't do much to protect his feet from the scorching sand. The backs of his white hands began to blister. Too many days living in the dark like a sewer rat. And, though he squinted, the bright sunlight stung his eyes. And he could tell his forehead was burning.

On the bright side, he was finally free and, though his long hair was hotter than blazes, it protected his cheeks and his throat from the merciless sun. He trudged forward, telling himself being lost in an endless desert was a whole lot better than being trapped for months on end on a chunk of suspended metal. He shielded his eyes with his hands, trying to see how much further it was to the city.

The buildings of the city looked to be about a mile off— unless he was seeing a mirage, so he kept walking, dragging each step through the hot, heavy sand. Soon he would be back to civilization and water. The thought gave him new strength. That was another positive. If he hadn't used his imprisonment to get in shape, he wouldn't have made it this far.

Finally, he stumbled into a small town. From the looks of the stucco-and-stone buildings and the dark-skinned people who stared at him from beneath white headdresses as well as black burkas, he was in a Middle Eastern country.

Water. He had to find water. Several yards further, he found himself in the center of the food market. The colorful fruit and vegetables displayed on the bright rugs looked incredibly delicious and juicy. His dry mouth watered.

He looked around. Everyone was staring at him. He raised his bent fingers above his mouth as if drinking, then held out his palm. Surely someone would feel sorry for him and offer a pale, burnt, ragged gringo a drink. The vendors looked at each other. Finally, a grizzled man stepped toward him, stopped in front of him and reached into his robe.

Kirk stiffened and moved back as the townspeople circled him. The man was going to shoot him. He couldn't run, he couldn't hide. And, maybe after all he'd been through, it didn't matter. At least he'd die free.

His gaze never leaving Kirk's, the man slowly pulled his arm from the folds of cloth.

Kirk couldn't help but drop his gaze to watch the man's arm motion.

Before he could blink, the man thrust a plastic water bottle at him, his dark eyes bright and wary.

Kirk nodded and took the bottle. Was he seeing things? Water bottles with Arabic lettering on the side in an impossibly small desert town? But the thin plastic felt real. He removed the cap, tilted his head back, and drank the entire liter. Hot water had never tasted so good.

He twisted the cap back onto the bottle and handed it to the man. Who knows, maybe the town had a recycling program.

The crowd dispersed, evidently satisfied he was human, despite his appearance. He looked around. Phone... He needed to find a phone. He glanced up and down the dirt street that ran between the run-down buildings but saw nothing promising. No phone booths. No cell towers or satellite dishes.

He spotted an uncovered, curly-haired head above the noisy market crowd and realized he was looking at a tall white man with a camera strap around his neck.

Maybe the guy spoke English. Knowing he could be a reporter or one of the Creepers, he hesitated only a moment before hurrying toward him. At this point in the game, it didn't matter.

Up close, the Caucasian's hair looked like a wild bush. His beard was patchy and clumpy, growing in some spots and bare in others. Kirk touched his arm.

The man stared at him, one eyebrow raised as if he was trying to determine what he was seeing.

"Do you speak English?" Kirk croaked.

"Yes. Are you okay, sir? You look like someone drug you across the desert." The man had an accent Kirk couldn't place.

"Something like that. I need to get to a phone right away. Any chance you know where there's one I can use?"

"I have one back at my Jeep. It's a satellite phone, the only type of phone that works out here in the middle of nowhere." He jetted out his hand. "My name is Geoff Martin, *National World Magazine.*" A big smile crossed his face.

"Kirk Weston, Detroit PD." He shook Geoff's hand, glad to meet someone with whom he could finally communicate. Talking felt good after so many months of silence, despite his painfully parched throat.

"Oh, a police officer. What brings you to the United Arab Emirates?"

"The UAE?" So that's where he was. "How the… uh… well," he stuttered. "I'm working on an investigation. Can't talk about it." The last thing he needed was to end up as lead story in a magazine or newspaper because of some dumb reporter—if that's what this guy was.

"I understand. I have not seen much of anyone from the States, but no worries. Follow me, and I'll get you that phone." They walked down a side street in between two apartment buildings. The clothes on balcony railings hung limp and lifeless.

They came to an open lot with a handful of cars. He saw a

Jeep off to the left. He could tell it didn't belong to one of the locals due to the oversized tires and Warn winch on the front.

Geoff opened the door, reached into the glove compartment, and pulled out a large phone with a thick, foldout antenna. After dialing a few numbers, he handed the phone to Kirk. "Just dial the area code, then the number of the party you're trying to reach, and push this button." He pointed to a green button near the top of the phone.

Kirk thanked him and walked out of earshot of his new friend. For a long moment, he stared at the keypad. Finally, the number came to him and he dialed. Wow. It had been a *long* time since he'd made a phone call.

The phone rang twice before his boss answered. Jacob C. Michelson was a veteran in the DPD pushing thirty years of service. His crabby attitude showed every year of his miserable life.

Kirk swallowed to wet his throat. "Hi, Chief."

"Who is this? Speak up." The chief's voice was as firm and commanding as ever.

"It's me, Chief... Kirk, Kirk Weston." He could hear Michelson gasp.

"Kirk? Holy cow, man. We thought you were dead. Where did you disappear to? What are you doing? Why did—"

Kirk butted in, knowing his boss would drown him in questions if he let him continue. "I'm okay, but I need some help. I was kidnapped—but I escaped. Now, I'm stuck in a little town somewhere in the Middle East." He braced himself for the barrage.

"What!? Who took you? You'd better tell me what's going on. Weston, I mean it!"

"Yes, sir, I'll tell you everything. Just get me home."

"All right. I'll make arrangements, but you need to get to an airport. And fast. There's some kind of wacky crap going down over there. Call me when you get to an airport, and I'll get you home." Kirk thanked him and hung up the phone.

Geoff was sitting on the hood of the Jeep munching on a

Power Bar. He pulled another one from his pocket and handed it to Kirk.

"Hey, thanks. Been awhile since I ate something besides MREs." At least that's what he'd imagined was the source of his tasteless food while imprisoned. "And thanks for letting me use your phone." He handed it back to Geoff.

"No worries. The magazine pays for it. So–you got a hold of your friend?"

"Yeah. Now, I've got to get to an airport. You know where the closest one is?"

"Sure. About a hundred miles that way." He pointed off to the east with his Power Bar still in his hand.

"One hundred miles!" Kirk cursed and kicked the nearest tire on the Jeep.

"Tell you what. I'm just about finished with the photos I need from this region. I'll drive you, on one condition."

Kirk cocked his head. "What's that?"

A wide grin spread across Geoff's face. "You let me buy you some clothes and shoes, and maybe a shave and a drink."

Kirk managed a smile and took the generous man's outstretched hand, shaking it with all the strength he could muster. "Thanks a bunch, man. You have no idea." He hadn't met a decent person in so long, he didn't know how to respond other than to say *thanks*.

* * *

MARK RUSHED INTO HIS apartment without even closing the front door behind him. Throwing his car keys on the coffee table, he pushed the DVD into the player. The television screen flashed to life.

He held his breath. He didn't know what he expected to see on the video, but he had to see it. As the DVD started to play, the screen morphed from blue to black, fuzzed a little, then cleared up.

Suddenly, the screen split up into four boxes, each showing a different part of a store. It was the Super Mart, all right. He could see the sign on the wall behind the meat racks on the screen in the upper, left-hand corner. His heart, which was already racing, pounded faster. He looked at the date and time on the bottom of the screen. Nine a.m.

Three hours before the explosion. He watched with feverish anticipation, though fearing what he might see.

One of the views was of the front door of the store. Another showed an aisle, another, a stockroom filled with shrink-wrapped pallets stacked on floor-to-ceiling racks. The views rotated as the camera turned a hundred and eighty degrees and back again.

He sat on the edge of the coffee table. What was he supposed to see? He leaned closer to stare at the screen. He saw people walking around, doing their shopping. As far as he could tell, everything looked normal.

"Wait. What's this?" He paused the DVD and all four screens froze. Up in the right-hand display, he saw someone who looked familiar. Where had he seen that kid before? Then he remembered. It was the man he saw running out of the store just before the building exploded.

He hit the play button and watched the guy wander around the store. He looked left and right as if he was nervous or distracted. The kid looked to be in his late teens, or maybe twenty, with dark brown hair and thick eyebrows. Mark fixated on the kid, who seemed to be looking for something. One by one, he picked up boxes of cereal, jugs of laundry soap and cans of chili as if he expected to find hidden treasure.

The time stamp at the bottom of the screen read eleven a.m. Forty-five minutes before the bombing. Eventually, the dark-haired youth picked several items, paid, then walked out the front door.

"That can't be right. I saw him run from the building." Mark scanned the screen, looking for any sign of the suspicious man who'd apparently left the building.

Nothing.

He paused the video, closed his eyes, and tried to clear his head. He needed to calm down, so he could think. This was the right day, judging from the date and the times on the display. The police had closed the investigation. This was the proof he needed to have the case reopened. He breathed in deep as he scooted off the coffee table and sat on the floor. Ignoring a shiver, he wrapped his arms around his chest.

He started the video again. Thirty minutes went by in real time as he scanned each screen for anything out of the ordinary. So far, there was nothing, except the young man who had left the store and had not returned.

Then, as if he was following a cue, playing a part in a sick movie, the youth re-entered the store with a determined look on his face. Mark jumped to his knees. This time, the guy acted like he had a purpose. He walked through the aisles toward the middle of the store in smooth strides, as if he knew exactly where he was going.

Mark slowed the video to see where the guy was going— then lost him. He crawled closer to the screen, frantically scanning each camera view, trying to find the mystery man. *There!* He came into view in the soup aisle when the camera rotated, then was lost again as the camera panned back the other direction.

When the camera picked him up again, Mark noticed his dark coat looked bulkier than the previous time the kid was in the store. Or maybe he hadn't noticed the bulge. Either way, he could tell he had something hidden in his coat.

He watched him grab a phone affixed to one of the pillars in the center of the building near a Gatorade display. He glanced both directions, then spoke briefly into the receiver. Then he pulled out a phone from his jacket and switched it out with the store phone.

Mark frowned and backed up the video. A sick feeling came over him as realization dawned. The kid was not talking on the phone. He was undoing the clips that held it in place. Like any magic trick, he used the skill of diversion, but this one beat them all. After he switched the phones, he slipped the old one on a rack behind him and covered it with bags of brown sugar.

Someone pushing a cart walked by and gave him a sideways glance but moved on without a second look. The kid began to dial the phone, but he dialed way too many numbers to be calling someone. The camera rotated again. Mark held his breath, waiting to see what was going to happen next, though he knew exactly what happened. But he couldn't help but watch.

The camera panned back. The kid hung up the phone and pushed a button on the top of the phone and bolted. Through the lens focused on the front door, Mark saw him run into an old woman, who tumbled to her knees. The kid almost lost his balance but managed to stay on his feet and charge toward the exit, right past K and Sam, holding hands as they walked to their death.

A bright flash of light obliterated the screens just before everything went black.

He dropped his head in his hands and began to weep uncontrollably. He'd watched his family die again, right in front of his eyes. His entire body shook with grief.

The sound of a man's voice brought his head up with a snap. Through eyes swimming with tears, he could see a man on the television screen. He was sitting in a big, black executive chair behind a huge desk. Oak bookshelves filled with books in every shape and size lined the wall behind him. There had to be thousands of them.

Mark wiped his eyes and peered at the man. He had kind eyes and a gray beard trimmed to perfection. Everything about him spoke of refinement and wealth.

"Mark, please forgive this intrusion in your life, especially on Christmas Eve. I know the preceding has been painful and confusing for you, but I'm here to help you. My name is not important at this time. All you need to know is that I'm a friend."

Mark tried to pause the machine, but the pause button on the remote would no longer work. He tried the buttons on the

DVD player, but they didn't respond to his touch, either.

"I'm truly sorry for your loss, but we felt you needed to know the truth. This was not an accident, as you just saw. I need you to listen to what I'm going to tell you, because you'll only get one chance to hear what I'm about to say." The man leaned forward in his chair, and took off his glasses.

"I can't help you in what you must do next. All I can do is point you in the right direction. The rest is up to you. This crime is more than what it looks like on the surface. If you want the truth, you need to find Pat Rotter.

"You need to do this alone. Do not go to the police. We don't know how deep this goes in our governmental agencies. For your safety and ours, you'll need to keep the police out of this.

"Now I must go. Find Pat Rotter. He can tell you everything you need to know." He paused, then pointed at the camera. "Never forget, Mark—justice will prevail."

Mark stared at the screen as it darkened, his mind racing. Did the police know it was a bomb? They told everyone it was a gas line. Why would they lie to the public, to the families who'd lost loved ones?

He had so many feelings rushing through him, he didn't know if he should be sad or angry, or if he should just kick the wall. *What is going on?*

"Mark? Are you okay?" Maria stepped in the door. "It's freezing in here." She stared at him sitting in front of a black, fuzz-filled screen.

He turned.

"Oh, I'm sorry. You must be watching old Christmas videos of your family." She started to back out the doorway. "I can come another time. I should have realized the holidays would be hard for—"

"Maria... uh... I'm okay. I just..." He couldn't hold on any longer. He desperately needed someone to talk to. He crawled to the couch, collapsed onto a cushion, and began to sob.

He heard Maria close the door, then felt her settle in beside him. She pulled him close and wrapped her arms around him. "It's okay to cry, Mark. Just let it out."

As he cried into her shoulder, he thought how stupid she must have thought he was, but he didn't care. He had just relived the deaths of his wife and child. To top it off, the explosion wasn't some random act of terror. Plus, the man on the video had hinted the police might have been in on it.

* * *

KIRK TURNED TO LOOK behind the Jeep, to make sure no one followed them. But all he could see was the cloud of dust the tires churned up as the vehicle sped through the desert like a cheetah on the run. He settled into his seat and fell asleep. When he was bounced awake, he asked Geoff where they were going.

"Dubai, or rather, the airport in Dubai." The Jeep jerked through a pothole as they bumped onto a paved road. Kirk was happy to see other cars on the road. At least they were headed back to civilization.

"You made a go at the sleeping thing," Geoff said. "You must have been exhausted to sleep through a ride like the one we just had." He smiled in his goofy way, which looked all the goofier with the wind blowing his crazy hair all over his head.

Kirk rubbed his sore eyes. His long beard and hair flapped in his face, as well. He made a mental note to avoid children. He'd scare them, for sure. "Yeah, I could sleep for about a year, just to catch up. This Jeep isn't bad, compared to what I've been sleeping on."

The journalist's eyebrows rose. "So, uh… What were you doing out in the desert wandering around?"

Kirk grunted. He should give him something. He'd been more than generous. "Well, most of it would be pointless to tell you. But to sum it up, I woke up in the desert with a lump on the head, dragged from an important case in New York. I've been gone for over a year now."

Geoff's eyes widened. "Whoa. What did they want?"

"That's the weird part. They never asked for anything

or even said why they took me. It about drove me crazy not knowing why I was kidnapped." Kirk had a good idea of whom he was dealing with, but he needed more proof. He needed to find out what this WJA group was—then take them down.

"Hmm, you're a cop. Maybe it had something to do with one of the cases you were working on."

Kirk eyed Geoff, who probably didn't know how close he was to the truth. He yawned. "I just want to get home and sleep in my own bed."

The road got busier as they neared Dubai. He wondered what kind of city it was. He had never been outside of the States. The sun was on its way down as they approached Dubai. He was surprised how much it looked like Florida, with palm trees, restaurants, and casinos lining the streets and skyscrapers dotting the skyline. Cars bustled about the thoroughfares. Some had only one tire in the front and resembled small, covered motorbikes. Most of the cars were tiny compared to the huge trucks and SUVs many Americans drove.

"Well, here we are! Welcome to Dubai, the city of surprises." Geoff waved a hand at a beautiful skyscraper that seemed to jut out of the earth. Covered with glass, the structure circled up into the sky like a sail on a ship that had just caught the wind.

"Impressive."

Geoff steered the Jeep onto what appeared to be a freeway. After they passed a sign with an airplane symbol on it, Kirk breathed a sigh of relief. They were getting close.

"I called my office while you were passed out. They gave me permission to use the company jet. I need to get back to the States. If you like, you can join me. The passports and all the mumbo jumbo of getting a flight out of here on a commercial airline would take you weeks, if not longer." He grinned, showing all of his white teeth.

"If you're going to fly out of here anyway, I'll be glad to join you." He could see that his new friend was a giving person. Shaking his head in amazement, he wondered if Geoff was his polar opposite and some higher power had thrown them together as a cosmic joke.

After Geoff parked the Jeep in the rental-parking garage, the two tired, dusty, windblown travelers made their way to a hangar at the back of the main airport. Kirk smiled when he saw the twin engines of a G5 Learjet through the open hangar door. It was a beautiful plane with white paint that glinted in the evening light and the magazine's logo on the tail.

Before the plane even took off, he fell into one of the beds in the back of the plane. Finally, a real bed, one with a mattress and a blanket. He'd soon be back home in Detroit, but how was he going to explain to his boss why he was over a year late for work.

CHAPTER TEN

CHRISTMAS DAY MARK AWOKE from the nightmare he'd been dreaming to find he was living it. He rubbed his eyes and looked around his bedroom, trying to remember the previous evening. Was the video real or a twisted part of his brain wanting to make sense of the explosion? But, in reality, things made even less sense than before.

"Oh, shoot… Maria!" Jumping to his feet, he grabbed the robe draped across the back of a chair and threw it on. He opened the door and sniffed. The apartment smelled like pine trees solution.

"Morning, sunshine!" Maria smiled from the kitchen. "You're just in time for breakfast." She cracked an egg and dropped the contents into a skillet. "I hope it's okay I borrowed your couch last night. You were so upset, I hated to leave you alone. Are you feeling better this morning?"

"Uh… yeah. Guess I let too much tension build up from everything… and… Wait! The video!" He scrambled to the DVD player, then sighed with relief when he saw that the disc was still in the tray, which meant it was real. Now he had the proof he needed.

He looked over at Maria, who was watching him with wide eyes.

"You sure you're okay?" she asked.

"Yeah, I just... Well, you wouldn't believe me, anyway." He stared at the disc in his hand. He'd told her everything he was feeling but left out the parts of the story that made him look crazy.

"Mark, I'm your friend. Remember? I have no reason to distrust or disbelieve you." She turned off the flame and moved around the kitchen counter to sit on the edge of the couch. "What's on that DVD?"

He sat next to her and started at the beginning. He told her about the mysterious appearance of the first note in his locked car, then about the package that had also appeared in his car, again locked, containing the second note and the disc that had turned his world upside-down again.

She touched his arm and watched his face as he told his story, a soft smile on her lips.

When he finished, he looked away, hoping she wouldn't laugh and insist they drive straight to the asylum.

She ran her finger over the raised lettering of the WJA logo on the package. "Wow! So, the whole thing was a planned attack, not an accidental explosion. You should tell the police or the FBI or somebody."

"I would, but we don't know what or who this WJA is. They could have made up the whole thing, created this video— although it looks real enough. I need more proof. And the only lead I have is this Pat Rotter person."

Maria's big, brown eyes lit up. "I'm great at finding stuff on the web, Google and all. I was a bit of a techie nerd in college." She laughed. "I got into trouble my sophomore year for hacking into the Center for Disease Control website."

He grinned. "Of all the places to hack into. You must be a nerd." He cocked his head. "I thought you were a good girl, but all this time, you were hiding a priceless, useful talent."

He laughed and pushed her off the arm of the couch. He was amazed how much better he felt after letting his emotions out last night. Maria had a way of making him feel not so broken, almost whole again.

"You better be nice to me, or I'll burn your eggs." she teased.

Mark waved his hand in the air, signaling that he was not listening. He walked over to the DVD player and shoved the disc into the player. Maybe he'd learn more about the mystery kid. The screen flashed white, then all at once went black with the words *Top Secret* scrolling across the screen.

"What!?" He tried to take it out and reinsert it into the player. But this time, he saw a timer in the lower left-hand corner of the screen. Nine... eight... He hit the eject button.

Nothing.

"Come on! Eject!"

Six... five...

Grabbing the DVD player, he yanked it from the entertainment center, ripping the cords from the back. He ran to the bathroom, tossed the player into the tub, and ran out, slamming the door behind him.

He glanced at Maria, who watched him with wide eyes. He knew what she must be thinking. *Time to get in the car, Mark. I'll drive you someplace where nice men in white coats will take good care of you.*

"What?" He tried to look sane, although it probably wasn't every day she saw a grown man rush his DV D player to the bathroom and slam the door shut. He sniffed. Smoke was seeping under the bathroom door into the hallway. He started toward the bathroom but jumped when the smoke detector above his head screeched to life.

He yanked the bathroom door open. "Aw, man." His DVD player had melted into a plastic puddle in the middle of the tub and had already filled the small room with smoke.

Maria followed him in, hands over her ears.

He motioned toward the bathtub. "Now I don't have any proof that I'm not imagining all this." She coughed and waved her hands at the smoke. "This is proof enough for me," she yelled over the sound of the alarms.

Someone in the next apartment began to pound on the wall.

Mark switched on the bathroom fan and ran out of the room to disconnect the alarms.

Maria opened the windows and the door of the apartment, then returned to the kitchen where she turned on the fan over the stove and went back to her cooking.

When all was quiet again, she lifted the spatula."I believe you, Mark, but I still think you should contact the police. Just tell them the truth."

"Maybe you're right." He reached for the phone. "I'll call Detective Owens right now. But I doubt he wants to see me after giving me the cold shoulder about the first note."

"Well, this is note number two, and you have the video—er—had it. But you'll have to wait 'til Monday. Today is Saturday. Plus, it's Christmas, you know."

"Oh, it is, isn't it? So what would you like to do today? That is, if you don't have any other plans."

She flipped the eggs. "I was actually hoping that this... uh... Well, not this, but that... You know what I mean. I wanted to spend Christmas with you." She lowered her eyes, looking like a chastised puppy that could not bear another rejection.

He pretended to think about it. "Well, I guess, since you're here, and I'm not doing anything, we could spend the day together." But she didn't laugh. Just looked at him with those puppy-dog eyes.

He raised a hand. "Hey, I'm just teasing. I've love to spend Christmas with you."

She threw a potholder at him, then lifted two plates from the cupboard. "Tell you what. Let's eat breakfast. Afterward, if you help me with the dishes, I'll help you hunt down this Pat guy."

He put out his hand.

"Deal."

* * *

THE TOUCH ON HIS arm awakened Kirk from a deep sleep.

He jumped to his feet, grabbed the neck of the man who stood over him and shoved him against the wall of the plane. But when he saw it was Geoff, the guy who was giving him a ride back to America, he released him and backed away.

"Sorry. I thought you were... Never mind." He sat on the bed and rubbed his eyes, remnants of his dream about the cylindrical, metal prison and the Creepers crouching at the edges of his memory.

Geoff sat down across from him, breathing hard and holding his neck. "No worries. I'm just glad you let me go before you killed me. Remind me never to mess with you!"

Kirk eyed the reporter. *Does anything ever get this guy down?* "I had a rough year. Didn't think I'd ever get out of that place. You wouldn't believe it if I told you." He stretched and looked out the window at the snow-covered ground below them. "Where are we?"

"About an hour from Detroit. You've been passed out for over seventeen hours. By the way, Merry Christmas!"

"You're kiddin', right?" Kirk shook his head, trying to clear his jumbled thoughts. "Well, Merry Christmas to you, too. Sorry you have to spend it with me, I never was much into the holidays."

"I thought as much. I love celebrations—so festive and fun. People get in the giving mood. And then, you've got to love Santa!"

Kirk grunted in disbelief. He hated Santa and the dumb elves. Most of all, he hated the arrogant red-nosed, whatever-his-name-was reindeer. "Well, you can have it all to yourself. It's just a way for the stores to get more money out of people, and make the rest of us feel guilty when we don't participate."

Geoff laughed. "Hey, you hungry? I can get us some dinner, if you like."

"Great. I'm starved."

* * *

GEOFF WENT BACK TO where the food was stored, opened up the mini fridge, and pulled out two sandwiches. Looking around for some napkins, he felt his phone vibrate and rumble in his pocket.

Looking at the number, he answered in a hushed tone.

"Yes, I'm on my way back now… Sure, I'll keep you posted." Hanging up, he gathered the sandwiches, grabbed two Cokes, and headed into the main area.

"How does roast beef sound?"

Kirk nodded and took the sandwich from Geoff's outstretched hand. "So, what exactly do you do for this *World Magazine*?" He opened the Coke and took a sip. He closed his eyes and savored each sip. It had been too long.

"Well, I get assignments to go wherever to investigate stories, take pictures, and interview people. Then I send the info back to our main office, where they compile it and print it. That is, if it's any good."

Kirk, who didn't seem much like talking, finished his hoagie roll and looked out the window.

Geoff felt like Kirk did not want to divulge any more information than he had to about his kidnapping. He didn't want to push him too much, but he believed with time he would open up—then he might have the story he so desperately wanted. He shifted in his seat, trying to get Kirk's attention.

"I just got off the phone with my editor, and it looks like I got about a month off. I was thinking. If you don't mind, I could help you try to track down the people responsible for your kidnapping." He could see Kirk start to reject his idea, but he butt in before he could say anything. "Everything will be off the record. I know my way around the Middle East, and Europe is a cinch. I'm a great researcher. I could help you."

Kirk held up his hand. "Okay, okay. You can help. If you are as much help as you've been so far, you might come in handy. Just know one thing: If I read anything about this in the papers or your crappy magazine, I'll personally hunt you down and kill you."

"No worries. I'll keep it just between us."

For the next hour, Kirk filled Geoff in on everything that

had happened, from the David's Island case to the hit he got on the head at the mill. He left out the part about his high-tech prison. Even a nice guy like Geoff wouldn't believe he'd been suspended on a disc one hundred feet in the air all those months.

The reporter made notes on his laptop and asked several questions, then shut off his computer and sat back in his seat. "So it seems the WJA group is behind the kidnapping as well as the poisoning. With the notes in the pillow cases and all, it's almost like they're daring people to find them. Have you cross-referenced WJA with any other cases?"

"Not yet, but I plan to get my friend Mooch on it as soon as we land in Detroit."

"From what I remember reading about the food poisoning in the newspaper, the authorities said it was caused by bad meat from a company that sold to the food supplier. It was ruled as an accident."

"So the FBI shut the case down." Kirk shook his head. "That means I'll need to convince my boss to allow me to investigate under his jurisdiction, and when we get solid proof, go to the feds."

"No worries. I'll get a hold of that CSI lady. What was her name? Oh, yeah. Cassy. I'll call her this week to see if she has anything new on that drug."

"Good idea. Maybe she found the partner drug. That would just be what we need. I wonder why the feds still thought it was accidental after what she found."

Geoff could feel the airplane start to descend. "We're here. You're home, bud."

"Great. After a shower, I'm going to sleep all weekend."

* * *

THE WEEKEND WAS JUST what Mark needed. Saturday morning, he and Maria ice skated in Central Park, then ate lunch downtown and looked at the Christmas displays in the store windows. The air was crisp and cool. Huge snowflakes began to fall as they walked back to his apartment.

Saturday night, they talked and watched movies at his place, drank eggnog and ate popcorn. It was late when they finished the last movie, and several inches of snow had piled up on the streets, creating a beautiful scene under the light of the full moon as well as slick streets. He insisted Maria spend another night on his couch, not just for her safety, he had to admit to himself, but because he enjoyed her company.

Sunday afternoon, he walked her to her car, his arm around her shoulders. "Thanks for helping me make it through what could have been a really tough weekend. You're a saint."

She smiled up at him, her golden eyes glinting in the sunshine. "My pleasure. Thanks for letting me sleep on your couch. And for loaning me a shirt."

He laughed. "It was more like a dress on you. Reminded me of my little girl when she played dress-up in her mom's clothes."

She stopped, studying his face. "You can't imagine what a privilege it is for me to be associated with your happy family memories."

He kissed her forehead. "And I am privileged to have a friend like you to help me create new happy memories. See you tomorrow."

He smiled and waved as she drove away. Maria was a special kind of lady. For the first time in a year, he felt truly happy again. Not all the way down deep in his soul, but as happy as he thought he could ever be without K and Sam.

Monday morning the sun rose in a cloudless sky over the piece of New York skyline he could see from his apartment. The snow had stopped but still lingered on the trees and his balcony, making everything look clean and untarnished. He called in to work to tell Hank he'd be late. He needed to go to the police station to talk to Detective Owens.

He smiled at the front-desk receptionist as she waved him back to Owens' office with a big smile. They'd seen so much of each other, she'd dispensed with formalities.

He stuck his head in the partially open door. "Hello,

Detective Owens. You got a minute?"

The detective looked up. A look of annoyance flashed across his face. "What can I do you for, Mr. Appleton? If you're here about the explosion, I told you months ago the case was closed."

Mark plopped into a chair in front of Owens' desk. "Remember the note I showed you last year? I just got another one, on Christmas Eve." He laid the envelope on the desk.

Owens stared at the envelope for a moment, then sighed and picked it up. He slid the note out, glanced at it, and said, "So where's this DVD?"

Mark rubbed his palms against his pants. "Uh, that's the bad news. I know this'll sound strange, but after I viewed it, my DVD player caught on fire and melted, with the disc inside."

The tall detective stood, leaned over the desk and handed the note and the envelope back to Mark. "Mr. Appleton—"

"Mark. You can call me Mark."

"Okay. Mark, I'm very sorry your wife and daughter were killed in the accident—"

"But, it wasn't—"

"Accident!" He glanced at the open door and lowered his voice. "… This case is closed. And no amount of notes or videos is goin' to change what happened." He rubbed his hand across his jaw. "If you're wantin' to obsess over this your whole life, you go right ahead. Just leave me out of it."

"I'm not—"

"Appleton, you need to stop... Just let it be. That's an order." He motioned toward his desk. "If you don't mind, I got work I should be doin'."

Mark swallowed a retort, stood and walked out.

"And if I catch you tryin' to investigate this," called Owens, "I'll arrest you for interferin' with a police investigation. Ya hear?"

He didn't respond, though a wave of rage flooded his body. He passed the effervescent receptionist, who—thank

God—was talking on the telephone. Interfering with a police investigation? How could he interfere in an investigation that's closed? Closed, despite the hundreds of citizens killed and the hurting families they left behind.

He unlocked his car and got inside. This was *not* over. He was supposed to protect his family, to be their guardian. But he'd let them die. Though the explosion was not his fault, it would be the same thing as killing them himself, if he let the monsters who bombed the building get away with murder.

He picked up his phone from the charger in the center console and dialed Maria's cell number.

"Hey, Mark, how'd it go?"

"Not good. Owens basically told me to leave it alone and threatened to arrest me if I did anything about it."

"Oh, I'm so sor—"

"I need you to find out whatever you can on this Pat Rotter guy. He's my only hope of figuring out who did this."

"Okay, I'll keep looking into it. We'll find him. I promise."

"Thanks, and be careful. Don't get caught. Okay?"

"I'll use my laptop in the Java down the street, so I can't be traced. On my lunch break, okay?"

"Great. See you in a bit." Twenty minutes later, he pulled into his space in the parking garage. He turned off the engine but sat for a moment, his hands clamped on the steering wheel. People had died in the explosion. Lots of people. How could the detective ignore evidence that it wasn't an accident. He got out, slammed the door shut and headed for the elevators.

Inside his office, he dropped his briefcase on his desk, then marched to Bert's office. The door was open. He tapped on the doorframe.

Bert looked up and smiled. "Hey, Mark. Did you have a good Christmas?"

"Yeah. How about you?"

"Great. It was really good to have a long weekend to relax with the family." He paused. "Looks like you have something on your mind."

"You still go shooting at the range?"

"Yeah, in fact, I'm going tonight. You want to meet me there?"

"If you don't mind. I need to blow off some steam."

"Sure. It's a great stress reliever. I'll bring an extra gun."

"Thanks." He needed to at least know how to use a gun, just in case the Pat guy proved to be dangerous.

All morning long, he fought to focus on his work and not obsess about the detective's comments. Like he'd supposedly *obsessed* over the deaths of his family. It was almost impossible to fathom that the police weren't interested in new information. If the gas line story was a cover-up, what were the police hiding? Were they involved somehow? What did they gain by blowing up a grocery store?

He glanced at the clock. Eleven forty-three. Maria had said she planned to go to lunch shortly after noon. He'd wait until he heard from her before he took a lunch break. Or maybe he'd skip lunch. His stomach was too jittery to be hungry, and he had plenty of work to do.

At five after one, his phone rang. He grabbed the receiver. "Mark App— Oh, hi, Maria. You find out anything?" A secretary passed his office, a stack of files in her arms. "Just a minute. I'd better close my door."

Maria's voice was hushed. "I hacked into the police database to see if his name popped up anywhere. But didn't get anything, so I moved to the DMV website and got a hit. Pat Rotter is twenty-two years old and lives in Manhattan."

Mark punched the air. "Great work!"

"There's more. I wanted to see if he had a criminal background and also find out what he does for a living. So I did a search of employment agencies. And guess where he worked two years ago."

"Where?"

"Manacore Manufacturing." She paused. "Guess what they make there."

"I have no idea."

"They produce C-4 and other plastic explosives for the U.S. Military. He was fired after suspicion of theft."

"You got to be kidding." He sat back in his chair. This was the break he needed. "Does he still live in Manhattan?"

"Not sure, but here is his last-known residence." She gave him the address of an apartment building in lower Manhattan.

He wrote it down and thanked her for her help. He would visit Mr. Rotter after he shot a few rounds at the range tonight. He could not go searching for Rotter as upset as he was at the moment. It might mean a slip in judgment, one that could put him behind bars.

CHAPTER ELEVEN

KIRK SLEPT MOST OF the weekend, only getting up to go to the bathroom and eat a donut or two in a dazed stupor. Geoff, he could see, had crashed on the living room couch. He vaguely remembered the two of them cleaning off old, rotten food wrappers and a pizza box that in the past year had molded and morphed into the size of a small animal.

Then there was the refrigerator. One look at the miniature city skyline of white and green fuzz—and one smell—had convinced him he'd be buying a new fridge.

But, though his place had been sitting empty for over a year, it wasn't in much worse shape than when he lived there. He had never cleaned the bathroom or washed dishes. If he wanted to eat off a plate, he just wiped it with his shirttail and called it good.

When he awoke, he discovered Geoff had picked up around the place and scrubbed the bathroom and kitchen. He didn't remember his place ever being so clean.

His answering machine had dozens of messages from his boss, which he deleted without listening to them, and one from his ex-wife, which he also deleted.

He'd always paid his rent a year in advance with his tax return, so he wouldn't have to worry about it. The utilities were included in the rent, so the place could run without human involvement for some time, which in this case it had.

He stirred from his hibernation on Monday morning to the smell of coffee and bacon drifting into his bedroom. He got out of bed with a moan and wandered into the living room in his boxers. "Good morning, Mr. Weston." Geoff looked at the wild tangle of hair that wrapped his head and face and laughed. "You look like a bear who just awakened from hibernation."

Kirk grunted. The guy was always chipper. If it was going to be like this every morning he stayed at his place, there could be a problem, like a slug in the jaw. He shuffled toward the kitchen. "I'm not yet sure if it is good or not, but it's definitely morning." He sat on a wooden stool that faced the kitchen counter and rubbed his eyes.

Geoff placed a cup of black coffee in front of him, followed by a plate of scrambled eggs and bacon. "You feeling better?" He sat on a stool next to him, sipping from a mug that said, "Don't Drink And Drive—You Might Hit A Bump And Spill Your Beer."

"Much better. I... Uh... Hey, what happened to my place?" He jumped up. Something was definitely wrong. He liked to live comfortably, but now the apartment looked as if it was a set for a television sitcom. Suddenly, he noticed the smell of bleach and pine, lemon and something else he could not place.

Geoff laughed. "I cleaned, and I must say it wasn't a pretty experience. You should get a maid."

"Cleaned!? My place was just fine the way it was. How am I supposed to find anything now?" Grumbling, he returned to his breakfast.

"I did your laundry and put your clean shirts in the closet. You'll find your pants folded in the dresser."

Kirk swore. "Man, you're some kind of nutcase. I thought my ex was bad." He wolfed down his breakfast, then reached for more eggs and bacon. "But if you keep up this cooking, I'll hire *you* to be my maid."

Geoff stood to wash his plate in the sink. "I don't think you have the money to hire me."

"What do you mean? I'm loaded." Kirk wiped his mouth with the back of his hand.

Geoff arched an eyebrow and began washing the skillet.

Kirk shoved a final forkful of food into his mouth. "Forget the dishes. We've got to get down to the station to see if we can give my boss man a heart attack." He headed for the door.

Geoff grabbed his coat and followed Kirk to the parking garage.

Kirk straddled a Harley Davidson motorcycle with a sidecar and grinned. "Geoff, meet Sandra, my woman." He loved the beat up old hog, and now he was back in the saddle with her.

He pointed to the sidecar and laughed devilishly. "That's where you ride."

Geoff eyed the small box for a moment, then stepped inside, folding his long legs like a lawn chair to sit.

Though the motorcycle had sat silent for over a year, it roared to life on the first kick. A cloud of thick, black smoke billowed from the tailpipe.

Geoff gagged and coughed.

* * *

MARK HEADED STRAIGHT FROM work to the firing range. After taking off-ramp 109, he checked the directions Bert had written on a piece of paper. He made a right and headed out of the city. Ten more miles.

He could not remember the last time he'd shot a gun, but it had been a long time. He'd hunted a few times in the Colorado mountains with his dad, but they never got much. It was more like hiking with a gun than hunting.

When he got out of the car, a cutting wind blasted him in the face and snatched his breath away. He shivered. Maybe this wasn't such a good idea in cold weather.

He heard a yell and saw Bert standing in the doorway, waving his arms above his head. He hurried toward his friend.

Bert pulled him inside the warm building. "I know what

you're thinking. This is crazy. But you'll be happy to know they have an indoor range in the basement. We're only allowed to shoot pistols there, but it's still a hoot."

Mark unzipped his coat. "Good. I was thinking we'd have to be insane to shoot in this cold."

The building was made of large logs, with cracked, white chinking between them to keep out the wind and the mice. A huge, deer-antler chandelier hung from the ceiling. Its flickering lights danced like candles.

The front desk had a gun case built into the front, with handguns under the glass. A stocky man stood behind it, polishing a pistol with his well-muscled arms. He looked like he could crush the gun like an empty pop can, but he cleaned the weapon with gentle precision.

Behind the counter was a wall full of rifles and shotguns of every make and model. A nearby sign indicated the guns were for rent but not for sale. He had a feeling they didn't want to bother with New York's strict gun laws.

Bert walked over to a sitting area by the fireplace and sat on a leather couch.

Mark stood nearby, letting the heat from the fire soak into his back.

Bert plopped a black case on the coffee table and opened it, revealing two handguns fitted into the foam lining. One was a silver revolver, while the other was black metal, and looked different.

"This one is a forty-five caliber Smith and Wesson. It packs a punch. And this is a three-fifty-seven Magnum. This guy could blow a person's head off his shoulders." He explained how the pistols worked and how to use the safety, which he said was the most important thing to know.

"So, which one do I get to shoot?" Mark asked as he looked at the guns gleaming in the firelight.

"I think you'll like the forty-five for starters. If you want, you can take your chances with the three-fifty-seven later." Bert grinned as he handed Mark the smaller gun and a box of bullets.

After they signed in at the front desk, they trotted down a flight of stairs that opened up to a big room with individual counters separated by half walls. Each lane was about thirty feet long with a target on a pulley at the end. Bert showed Mark how to draw the target back to look at it and how to set up a fresh one.

Mark hung a fresh target of an angry man pointing a gun at him. He pushed a red button, which activated the pulley and ran the target out as far as it would go, then looked at Bert.

With his dark hair slicked back and his hands clad in black, fingerless gloves, his coworker looked the part of a gangster wannabe. Mark eyed the three-fifty-seven he clutched in his hand. Definitely not someone he'd like to meet in a dark alley.

Bert motioned for Mark to shoot first, so he could watch for problems. Other than a few people a few lanes over, they had the place to themselves. Mark put on his earmuffs, then dropped one bullet at a time into the magazine until it was full. He slid the clip into place until he felt it click, then slid the action back and let it drop forward again.

He tried to remember if he'd ever shot a pistol before. He couldn't think of a time, but somehow the loaded gun felt natural in his hand. A sense of power came over him as he studied the silver weapon reflecting the lights of the room in his hand. The feeling of remembrance from a far away part of his mind was so powerful, for a minute he felt as though he was in another world. He noticed his hands were shaking. Was he scared?

Bert nodded at him from the other lane, as if waiting for him to do something besides stand there and look confused.

He lifted the gun with his right hand, his index finger on the trigger and his left hand cupping the right, just like he'd seen in cop movies. He closed one eye to focus and slow his heartbeat.

And just like that, it was over. He lifted his head. A whiff of smoke floated from the barrel toward the ceiling. He lowered the handgun and looked over at Bert, who was staring at him with his mouth hanging open.

Mark was not sure how many times he had fired the gun, so he dropped the clip. It was empty.

Bert stuttered, "What was that? In all the years I've been coming to this range, I've never seen anyone shoot that fast. That was awesome!"

"Was I only supposed to shoot one bullet?"

Walking around to his booth, Bert took the gun from his hand. He opened the barrel, examined the clip and shook his head. "Well, I don't know what to say. That was… was amazing. But it's one thing to shoot fast. Anyone can pop off a clip. Did you hit anything?"

Mark shrugged his shoulders and looked down the lane but was not sure what the target should look like. It looked the same to him. No huge, gaping holes. Maybe he'd missed.

Bert hit the button to return the target. As it got closer, light shone through the center like a golf ball had gone through it. Maybe he did hit it.

"No way." Bert shook his head, looking as much amazed as disgusted. "No way, man. You said you never shot a pistol before. You're a dirty, rotten liar."

"No, really, I haven't. I shot a few times when I was younger, but it was a rifle." He held up two fingers. "Scout's honor."

Bert eyed him for a moment. "Must be beginner's luck. Try that again. I bet you can't hit a thing this time."

"Bet's on." Mark held out his hand to shake on it. "Load me up, and let's see." He grinned, not knowing if he could do it again or not, but it was fun either way.

Bert filled the clip and slid it into place, looking sideways at Mark as if he suspected him of cheating somehow.

Mark took the gun and stepped into the booth. A man from a nearby booth moved behind Mark. "I gotta see this."

Slipping his ear protection back on, Mark looked at the new target at the end of the aisle. Closing his eyes, he pictured the enraged man, whose gun pointed at his chest. A wave of raw energy filled his body. He opened his eyes, saw the action slide back and then forward, sending a flash out the end of the barrel.

Click. A trail of smoke swirled from the end of the barrel.

Lowering the gun, he scrutinized it, thinking it must have jammed. He dropped the clip and stared in shock at the empty chamber. Mystified, he turned to Bert.

The two men behind him were staring at him as if he was a celebrity or something.

"Do it again!" Bert yelled.

And he did, hammering target after target with golf-ball size holes. Not only that, he emptied the clip in less than four seconds every time.

Soon, a crowd formed. They cheered as he brought in the last target and held it up for all to see. He could not explain his prowess with a gun. Each time he lifted the pistol, a surge of... of something flowed through him, and he just knew what to do. He lowered the paper and shook his head, watching Bert make fifty bucks off a newcomer.

After the others returned to their own aisles, Bert showed Mark how to clean the handguns. Then they put them back in the black case.

"That was something," said Bert. "You've got a natural gift, you know."

"Thanks. It felt easy, as if I instinctively knew what to do. I can't explain it."

"Cool. I wish I could shoot like that." He closed the black carrying case. Mark noticed a huge, hairy man sitting on the couch in front of the fireplace and whispered, "Who's that? He's been hanging around all night and looking over at us."

Bert glanced at the big man. "That's Fred. You want to stay away from him. Word is he sells black market guns on the street and is moving a butt load of drugs along with it."

"So he just hangs out here, trying to pick up new clients?"

"Yup, a lot of guys who come here want to buy a gun as soon as they try it. It's an addicting sport."

Mark nodded. He understood the desire. "What about the

cops? Doesn't anyone turn him in for selling guns?"

"Nope. Most people look the other way. It's not worth punching a guy that has crazy friends and contacts outside the law. He goes down—and whoever turned him in ends up at the bottom of some lake."

After they buttoned their coats, Mark thanked Bert and promised to come with him again.

Bert grinned. "It has to be on a weekend, so I can wager more bets."

Mark rolled his eyes, and they hurried through the cold night air to their cars.

Bert pulled out of the parking lot first, but Mark sat in his car with the heater running. He stared at the building, wondering if Fred had weapons with him right now. He shook his head and put the car into drive. *Don't be an idiot. Fred's guns are illegal.*

As he started out the exit, he saw the directions to Pat Rotter's house sitting on the passenger seat, like an omen prodding him to act. He pulled back into the parking space, turned off the engine, and got out of the car. What was he doing? He wasn't a hero or a detective. He was just an ordinary guy.

Inside the building, he weaved his way over to where Fred was sitting. When Fred saw him, he grinned, showing his blackened teeth, or what was left of them.

"You got a minute?" Mark sat on an overstuffed chair across from the large man.

Fred removed a fat cigar from his mouth. "What can I do for you this fine evening?" Smoke poured from between his lips as he spoke.

Mark lowered his voice. "I need a gun."

"Ah, I see. Now, what kind of gun are we looking for, I wonder." His voice rumbled from deep within his heavy chest. After a bout with a nasty cough, he shoved the cigar back into his mouth and took a long pull.

Mark leaned toward the obese man. "I need something for

home protection. Something that can take out more than one person at a time. You know—close up. Do you have anything like that?"

Fred's thick beard bounced like a mass of irritated worms as he laughed long and hard. He coughed after each laugh, which sent him doubling over for a few seconds, until he caught his breath. Finally, he sat up. "I think I got what you might be looking for. Follow me." Wheezing like a forge, he pushed himself off the couch and headed to a side door that led to the parking lot, bypassing the front desk. He led Mark to an old, paint-chipped car with a long nose and huge trunk.

Pulling a set of keys from his pocket, he opened the trunk and removed a black carrying case. The case looked a lot like the one Bert had, but it was much larger and heavier, judging from the way Fred grunted and groaned when he lifted it out of the deep trunk.

Mark zipped his coat to his chin and peered into the strange man's car, wondering what he might see, wondering if he was losing his mind. K would have had a fit and Maria would probably pass out if she knew he was not only standing in a cold, dark parking lot with a drug dealer but considering buying an illegal, unregistered gun from the man.

Fred scanned the parking lot, then turned to him. "This is a riot gun—or a modified shotgun. It holds nine shells and is semi-auto." He pointed to a little slide on the side.

Mark liked the look of the weapon. It had a short barrel and was a dull, black color with a light mounted to the side, so the shooter could see what he or she was aiming at in the dark.

"Now, the beauty of this baby," said Fred, "is that all you need to do is point it in the general direction of the target, and you'll hit it."

Mark took the shotgun. It felt good in his hands. "So how much do you want for it?"

Fred thought a minute and took another pull on his cigar. "Eight hundred dollars, and I'll throw in a box of shells."

Mark fired back, "Seven hundred, and I'll pay you cash

right now." He pulled bills from his wallet and held them up.

An evil glint crossed Fred's face. He grunted and took the cash. "You got a good deal, man." He placed the shotgun in the case and handed the case and a box of shells to Mark. "Now, get out of here before I change my mind."

"Thanks, Fred." He hurried to his car, which he had left running, put the case in the back seat and pulled out of the parking lot. He refused allow his mind to think about what he had just done. He had to do something. He did not have a choice.

* * *

KIRK WALKED PAST HIS coworkers at the station without being recognized. Fifty pounds lighter, with a bushy beard and long hair, he resembled one of the bums who lived under Ambassador Bridge rather than a DPD detective. He marched into the chief's office, Geoff trailing behind him, and caught his boss mid-sentence in a phone conversation.

"Gotta go. I'll call you back." As he hung up the phone, he stared at Kirk, then at Geoff.

The chief leaned back in his chair with his hands folded across his chest. "What's your story this time? You look like hell!"

Kirk could see his boss was in no mood to play catch-up, so he decided to get right to the point. "I'm going to need some time off to gather evidence against whoever kidnapped me. I think I might know who was behind it, but I need more proof."

"You're not getting any more time off. You already had over a year. You were kidnapped, so it's now an active case. You will report anything you have and any new information directly to me. You got that?"

Kirk nodded, but let the warning pass over him as he always did. He was not going to let this go, no matter what this old windbag said.

The chief let his chair fall forward. He landed with his forearms on his desk. "I know you want to keep looking into the prison case. But you'd better not even think about it. That case is closed, and I can't afford for the two of you to go chasing down ghosts. And who is this clown, anyway?" He looked at Geoff with disdain and waved his fist in the air as his neck bulged.

Kirk frowned. *I wonder what or who freaked him out.*

"But," Kirk stuttered. "I have—"

The chief glared at Kirk and raised his voice. "I mean it, Weston. Drop it."

"Fine, have it your way." He opened the door, let Geoff out, then slammed it behind him, sending the chief into a tirade of curses after them. Kirk grinned and went over to his desk to get a few things. He checked the drawers, surprised his desk was just as he left it, that they hadn't messed with the contents or given it to someone else. Opening the bottom drawer, he pulled out a forty-five and a box of rounds. "Might need these."

Geoff grimaced but did not say anything. The handful of other officers looked at them with concern and some paid no attention.

"Let's get out of here. We need to see if Mooch turned up anything." Kirk brushed past a large woman who glared at him through small, close-set eyes.

As they exited the station's parking lot, Kirk smiled down at Geoff, who was scrunched in the sidecar like Goliath riding in a Barbie car. He rather enjoyed seeing his companion's discomfort, but Geoff didn't complain.

They needed solid evidence. He was going to run out of time in a hurry, if his boss decided to put his foot down. He cranked the gas and tore up a freeway ramp. Out of the corner of his eye, he saw Geoff grab his knit hat with both hands and pull it down over his ears.

CHAPTER TWELVE

MARK ASSUAGED HIS GUILT over the illegal purchase by remembering the look on Detective Owens's face when he told him the case was closed, no matter what new evidence turned up or how much proof he uncovered. There was something going on. He didn't know what it was, but it bothered him, a lot. Rapists go free on a technicality, murderers get slaps on the wrist because they had bad childhoods or they didn't get to go to Disneyland, but hundreds of innocent people are murdered, and the authorities call it an accident.

He peered at the dark highway illuminated only by his headlights. He didn't care if it was after eleven, he was going to get answers, one way or another.

* * *

AFTER TWENTY MINUTES ON the expressway, Mark made his way into what appeared to be a lower-class residential area. He looked again at the address he'd written down, making sure he didn't miss the street he wanted.

East Bower Street.

He turned right onto a narrow car-lined road with tall apartment buildings on both sides. Seeing a sign marked, *The Birches* in the front of a large, brick complex, he pulled in and drove around to the back.

There it was. Building Eleven Forty-Seven, Apartment C. He pulled in a few doors down and shut off the engine. Even in the dim lighting, he could tell the red brick building had seen better times. Lights from scattered windows lit up the three-story complex like fireflies in a jar. He pushed the window button and rolled it down several inches. All was quiet in the apartment building, but not in his heart.

He swallowed. Now what?

He pulled the heavy case from the backseat, then set it on the passenger seat and opened it. After a quick glance at his surroundings, he loaded the gun until all nine rounds were in the magazine. After pumping it, he set it next to him on the passenger seat, opened the door and met a blast of bitter cold wind.

Apartment C faced the street, so he had to round the corner on the second floor landing to get to it. The porch light was on. He hoped that meant someone was home. As he knocked, his mind raced with possibilities, most of which were not good. Before he could scroll through them all, he heard the lock release. The door cracked open and a nose peeked out underneath the chain lock.

"Who is it?" The voice sounded like a woman's. It was weak and quivered when she spoke.

He ignored her question. "Sorry to bother you so late at night. I was wondering if Pat Rotter still lives here." A wisp of thin, white hair fluttered into the opening, like a stray strand of cotton.

"Oh, I thought you were Pat." She looked at him confused. "He's out right now, but he should be back in a little bit. Do you want me to tell him you stopped by?"

"No, I'll come back some other time." He thanked her and hurried away before she could ask any more questions. He pulled up his collar around his neck, shuffled back around the building and down the metal stairs toward his BMW.

Getting back into his car, he turned on the heat full-blast and sat there, rubbing his gloved hands together and thinking about what to do next. He could wait. He didn't want the old lady to warn Rotter that a strange man was looking for him. The guy might spook and run. He needed answers, and he needed them tonight.

* * *

AN HOUR PASSED. MARK listened to the radio and tapped his finger on the steering wheel in time with the music. It would be worth the wait if he got some answers. But, how would he recognize Pat? And what could he tell him about the explosion?

He was just about to call it a night, when he saw a car in his rearview mirror.

The crumpled compact slid on the ice and hit the curb as it bounced to a stop just a few spaces away. A kid in his twenties opened the door and stepped out. He was wearing a beanie cap and a thick winter coat. He pulled a backpack onto his shoulder and tried to lock his car door with the key, but the lock wasn't cooperating. Mark studied the college-age youth as best he could in the dim light. Judging from the flat skater shoes, the baggy low-ride jeans and thick, messy hair, he figured the guy was more likely to be a skateboarder than a student.

A surge of adrenaline pumped through his body. He quietly opened his door, slid out and started toward the man. He tried to stay calm, but it was too late for that. As he got closer, his body filled with rage and his mind emptied. It was as if he'd stepped through a looking glass and now was on the other side in a world completely foreign to him.

Coming up behind the kid, who was still fumbling with the lock, Mark grabbed the back of his jacket and spun him around. The kid staggered and his backpack fell to the ground. A look of shock, then fear, ran across his face. "Hey! What the—"
The kid tried to break free from his grasp, but Mark held on, shoving him against the side of his car with more force than he intended, but it worked.

"Are you Pat?" But just as he asked, he realized who Pat was. But it couldn't be. He died in the explosion. Nevertheless, here he stood, the youth who'd set the bomb, who'd run from the supermarket. His face was scarred, probably from skin grafts and surgeries. Half his mouth sagged on one side, like Batman's adversary, the Joker. But it was him, he was sure.

"You!" Mark dragged the terrified youth across the parking lot.

"What do you want from me? I don't even know you, man!" The helpless kid tried to squirm free, but a knee to the gut sent him sprawling across the ice-covered pavement. Mark opened his car door and reached inside. He grabbed the shotgun and swiveled toward the floundering boy-man. "One move—and it'll be your last." Mark was surprised at how calm his voice sounded. Inside he could feel his heart pounding faster and faster. Any minute, he expected a heart attack, but he hoped to God it wouldn't happen before he got his answers.

Pat froze when he saw the shotgun in Mark's hand. "Hold on, man. Don't shoot!"

"Get into the car, and you might live."

Pat slowly moved toward the BMW, eyeing the gun, hands in the air. Mark opened the back door and shoved Pat inside. "Scoot over!" He got in beside him, making sure to keep the shotgun leveled at the kid's head.

"Look, man, you can have my money." He dropped his hands and reached for his pocket.

Mark jabbed him in the ribs.

Pat's hands flew up. "Please, I don't want any trouble."

"Too late! You should've thought of that before you blew up the Super Mart!" He felt his heart rate start slow down and wondered if he was calming down or if he was just adjusting to the situation.

Even in the dark, he could see Pat's face pale. "Uh... I, I don't know what you're talking about."

"Don't you even try to con me. I have you on video from the store's security cameras. I was there, in the parking lot. I saw you run out of the store."

Pat clasped his head with his hands and cowered in the seat.

Mark shoved the business end of the shotgun in his neck, making him squeal in fear.

"You tell me everything you know, or I'll splatter your brains all over this car!" He felt his lip curl as he drilled the shotgun's muzzle into the kid's neck.

Pat started to whimper. Tears ran down his cheeks. His shoulders shook and snot bubbled from his red nose. "It wasn't me who made the bomb. It was someone else. I just supplied the C-4. They offered me fifty grand to get them some C-4 and fifty more if I put the bomb in the store. Please don't kill me. I needed the money. Please, mister."

Mark looked at the kid who should have died in the blast. "Who are they?" he demanded. "I want names!"

"I don't know. I swear I don't! They just call me on a cell phone they shipped to my house when they need something." He pointed to his jacket pocket. Mark reached in and pulled out a red cell phone.

"How do you get a hold of them?"

"They told me to sit on a park bench at First and Holly whenever I want to talk, or if I want to do a job." He blubbered and sniffed. "It has to be at nine a.m. on a Tuesday. If I'm there, they call me an hour later." His eyes had puffed, making his scarred face look even more hideous in the dim moonlight.

"Well, it's your lucky day. It's almost Tuesday, and that means I still need you. Now, you're coming with me, and if you try anything—I mean anything—I'll shoot you faster than it takes a bug's butt to go through his mind when he hits the windshield!"

Pat nodded, eyes wide.

Mark got out and pulled him around to the front of the car. Shoving him inside, he went around to the trunk and opened it up, pulling out three large zip ties from the supplies he picked up earlier. He got in the driver's side, told Pat to put his hands together, and slipped the zip ties around his wrists, pulled until they were tight, then bound the two together with the third. He searched the kid for weapons but found only an iPod and a small bag of pot.

Starting the car, he pulled out of the parking lot, holding the shotgun with his left hand on his lap aimed at the frightened Pat's midsection. He knew he would kill him if he had to. This was now officially out of control, but Mark was determined to go through with it.

* * *

GEOFF SAT IN THE warm coffee shop typing on his laptop. It was already getting to be late in the afternoon. He turned to Kirk and gave the thumbs-up, signaling he was online and good to transmit. Kirk was on the phone with someone named Mooch, and from the sound of it, he had something over him.

Kirk asked for the IP address of his laptop.

Geoff wrote it on a napkin and handed him.

Kirk read the numbers into the phone then whispered, "I hope this works. It's always hard to revive a dead case." He put the phone closer to his ear then pointed toward Geoff's computer. "Okay. You should be getting something."

Geoff squinted at the screen. "Looks like a video feed from a satellite." He saw a run-down building with a truck pulling in and parking behind it, just out of sight. "The picture is kind of choppy, like it's in stills."

"It is, but it's all we've got. Mooch, come on, give me something new," Kirk grumbled into the phone. "I've already seen this stuff."

Geoff could hear the voice on the other end saying Kirk would like the next shot. His screen changed to a single photo of a different truck, maybe a retired armored transport vehicle of some kind that had been repainted. The vehicle was white, with the words *Food Services* stenciled on the side.

Kirk leaned closer to the computer screen. "What's this? The other truck?" Mooch must have zoomed the view, because in the next instant, they could make out the shape of the driver. It was fuzzy at first but cleared as Mooch worked on the other end. It looked like a woman with dark hair and sunglasses.

"Can you get closer, Mooch?" The screen zoomed in once

more. After the pixels settled, they could see plainly what the woman looked like.

Kirk brightened. "Great job, Mooch. I'll check you later." He closed the phone and asked Geoff if he could save the image.

"Sure, I have my printer docked, if you'd like me to print it."

"Yeah. That would be great."

Geoff hit the print button and waited until the photo came out. He handed it to Kirk. "So who's the woman?"

"This, my friend, is our hard evidence. She's the only person I know of connected to this WJA group. Now we have a photo to prove I'm not crazy."

Geoff eyed Kirk's scraggly beard and hair. Weston didn't appear to have a clue how crazy he looked. He studied the picture. The woman appeared to be in her late twenties, maybe early thirties, and had long, jet-black hair. "She is beautiful, in a dangerous sort of way."

"Yeah, well, now we need to pay our friend Cassy Meyers a visit to see if she can find out who this woman is." Kirk waved the waitress down for a refill in a to-go cup. "Let's pack up and get going. I think we can get to CSI before it closes."

"Sure thing. But I've got one question for you."

"What's that?"

"Can we get a rental car? I'll pay."

Kirk laughed. "Sure. No worries."

CHAPTER THIRTEEN

THE SUN CREPT UP over the trees of a small park on the corner of First and Holly. Mark sipped the coffee he'd purchased from a street vendor a block down. The air was sharp and cold but not bitter like last night. The wind had stopped, and now the sun was glinting off the snow with painful brightness.

He turned to study his captive.

Pat jerked, like he did every time his captor made a move. He hadn't stopped shaking all night.

"Calm down. It'll be over soon, as long as you play along." He gripped the kid's arm and peered into his face. "You're lucky I don't just kill you now. Do you have any idea how many people you murdered in that blast?"

Pat glared back, his eyes dark orbs of fury mixed with fear. "They told me it was just to scare the store owners. I didn't know it would blow up the whole store."

"That, I don't believe." Mark stabbed his finger at Pat's disfigured face. "You *knew* it was a bomb! For all I know, you built it." Pat inched toward the door. "They tried to kill me too, dude. They're the ones who had the remote. I just activated the bomb."

"Well, now it's your turn to pay them back for using you."

Mark took a breath and sat back. "You help me, and I'll let you live. You try to run or do something stupid, and I'll take you out. You got it?"

Pat nodded and glanced at the car's digital clock.

Mark thought about what Pat said about the remote detonator. The people who hired him had to have been close enough to see the explosion. Someone had paid this numbskull to set the bomb and activate it but intended to get rid of him at the same time, the primary source of evidence against them.

He punched the radio button. "Gas prices are on the rise again, bringing the price at the pump to an all-time high. With the dollar weakening against the Euro, analysts don't expect it to go down any time soon—"

"Man, what a bunch of junk," Pat muttered. "They could pull all the oil we'd ever need from Alaska or Texas and drop the prices. But no. We've got to get it from overseas." He rambled on about the government and how they were forcing the prices up, how it was a big conspiracy.

"Shut up," Mark growled. He glared at the kid, trying to see if he had any brains. It was beyond him how he could kill hundreds of people and go on as if it didn't matter. He could have gone to the police and turned himself in or at least tried to implicate those who hired him.

Mark stared out the window. He was planning to have Pat sit on a bench under a tall oak tree, and then he was going to stroll through the park to see if he could spot anyone or anything out of the ordinary. It was a long shot, but at the moment, it was the only shot he had.

He reached into the backseat, pulled out Pat's backpack and rifled through it.

Pat stiffened. "Hey—" One look from Mark made him turn away in silence.

Finding a wallet, Mark pulled out a driver's license, several credit cards that would be useful in tracking the jerk, in case he decided to make a run for it.

He turned to Pat, cards in hand. "Okay, here's the deal. I'm keeping your license and credit cards. If you run, I'll report you to the police and give them your ID. I've seen a video of you setting the bomb. If you run, you'd better pray the cops find you before I do."

"I won't run, dude! Besides, I wouldn't mind giving those people a little piece of my mind. They tried to kill me..." He ran his fingers over the deep scars that covered his face. "Not like I can hide with this face."

"You lived, kid. My family didn't." He motioned toward the park. "It's almost nine. You go sit on the bench. I'm going to keep an eye on you from that bench over there." He pointed to a bench that sat about one hundred yards from the one Pat would be sitting on. "How long do you usually have to wait?"

"About ten minutes. Then I just leave, and they call about an hour later."

"You'd better be right. If we don't get a call, then you'll find out what it feels like to die." He opened the car door and went around to Pat's side and cut the zip ties from his hands.

Rubbing his wrists, Pat started across the street. He looked around, then brushed snow off the bench and sat on it.

Mark walked around the park on the sidewalk, taking the long way to the other bench. The old oak trees and trimmed shrubs made a beautiful picture with the fresh blanket of snow covering the ground, but he wasn't in the mood to enjoy the scenery. He stopped at a coin-operated news rack, dropped in a couple coins, opened it and pulled out a newspaper, all the while keeping an eye on Pat, who hadn't moved.

After he reached his designated bench, he brushed away the snow with the newspaper, shook it off and sat down. He glanced at his watch—two minutes to nine—and began to flip through the newspaper. He pretended to read and also watched a young woman walk her dog.

Peering over the top of the paper, he could see Pat huddled on the bench, his arms tight against his ribs. Across from him, a four-story apartment building looked down on the park. The windows had small balconies with wrought-iron rails. Mark inspected each window, searching for movement.

When he got to the third floor, he saw a man open a sliding door and step out to light a cigarette. He blew out a ring of smoke and appeared to scan the park. When his head turned toward the bench where Pat sat, he visibly stiffened and hurried back inside.

Mark's heart began to pound. The man returned to the balcony, but this time he had a phone to his ear. Mark looked at Pat to see if he was on the phone, too.

He wasn't.

The guy had to be talking with someone else. Pat just sat there hunched over, shivering with his coat collar pulled up around his neck. The window closed, and the stranger disappeared. Another five minutes went by. Nothing more happened.

Mark got up, rolled the paper up under his arm, and headed back to the car. He nodded toward Pat, who got up and walked toward him. A pair of joggers passed Mark and he nodded to them.

"Get in."

Pat climbed in the passenger side.

Mark started the engine and turned the heater on high. It was waiting time.

Pat didn't say anything. Just sat there shivering and holding his hands over the heater vent. Mark glanced at the gun in the back seat. "Do we need that anymore?"

Pat shook his head.

"Good."

Pulling out into the street, Mark turned left one block down to drive into the alley behind the apartment building. He stopped the car behind a large dumpster with thick, brown grime running down the sides. This end of the building had a carport, where tenants apparently parked their cars. From his vantage point, he could see eleven vehicles parked in a row.

Exhaust spewed from the back of a gray pickup truck about fifty feet from where they sat. He couldn't explain it, but he was positive the truck belonged to the man in the window. He was headed somewhere.

The truck backed out and started down the alley away from them, aimed at the street. He was sure it was the same man he'd seen standing at the window. His hair stuck up on one side and smoke trailed out from the cracked window of the truck.

Mark tailed the pickup through the city and onto the expressway. Neither he nor Pat spoke. Finally, the truck took the exit to Rockefeller State Park. Soon they were in the mountains, with trees thick on both sides of the road.

Pat's phone rang, making both of them jump. Mark handed the phone to Pat, screwing his face into the fiercest possible look.

Pat rolled his eyes. "I get the message." He opened the phone. "Hello."

"What do you want?" The gruff voice filled the car as Pat turned on the speakerphone.

"I need my money."

"What money do you think you're getting?"

"You said to set the bomb, then you'd pay me fifty grand. I want my money! Or we can talk to the police to see what they think about it."

Mark looked at Pat, half-impressed at his boldness, when just a short time ago he was cowering and snotting all over his leather seats.

"We thought you were dead. A year went by without hearing from you."

"I was in the hospital. Got out a few weeks ago. Don't think I don't know what you tried to do to me."

"Don't get all hot with me, kid. You just shut up and listen. I'll get you your money. Do you remember the KOA campground where you met us the first time?"

"The same one where you gave me the package?"

"That's the one. You go past that, and you'll see a dirt road off to your left. Turn in there and it'll take you to a cabin in about a mile. Meet us there in two hours, and you'll get what's coming to you."

Pat closed the phone and handed it back to Mark. "Yeah, I'll get it, all right."

"They'll kill you, you know."

"Yeah, I figured. So now what?"

"You see that sign up ahead?" Pat sat up and looked as a KOA sign came into view.

"Guess we'll be a little early."

"Yup." Mark saw a dirt road coming up on the left. The truck they were following turned and disappeared. "You'd better pick whose side you're on, because it might get ugly."

"You do what you've got to do. I'll stay in the car."

Maybe the kid wasn't as dumb as he looked.

* * *

KIRK LOOKED AT THE CSI building, which looked a lot different than he'd imagined it would look. A one-story, square, brick box with bad landscaping and a bent handicap sign, the plain structure's dullness was highlighted by a glass door with two narrow windows on each side.

He got out of the dark blue Mustang and started for the front door. They had caught an overnight flight from Detroit and had arrived a few hours before daybreak. Geoff was a handy guy to have around. He'd found them a good deal on airfare as well as the car and hotel rooms with the discount he got through the magazine.

The receptionist pointed them in the direction of Cassy's office. "I'll let her know you're on the way, Mister—Sorry, I didn't get your name…"

Kirk ignored her and turned toward the hallway she'd indicated, Geoff at his side.

The inside of the building was as bland as the exterior. The dim hall lights flickered constantly, and the pictures on the walls looked like they were from the seventies. They came to a door with *Cassy Meyers* posted next to the doorframe. Kirk knocked on it.

The door opened. "May I help you?"

"Yeah. We met several months ago. I wanted to go over an old case with you."

She frowned and peered at him like she was trying to remember who he was. Her blond hair was neat and had a touch of curl to it.

"Detective Kirk Weston." He shoved out his belly, pulled his hair back and smashed his beard down. "I lost weight. Plus, I need a shave and a haircut."

Her eyebrows lifted. "Oh, the detective from Detroit! You were on the David's Island case, right?"

"Yeah, that's the one."

"Okay, wow. You could use a shave and a haircut. For a minute there, I thought you were some bum looking for a handout. What did you do, go on some boot-camp diet thing?"

Kirk chuckled. "Something like that."

She pointed to the two chairs in front of her desk, motioning for them to sit down. "So, introduce me to your friend."

Geoff held out his hand and smiled, making his patchy beard crinkle. "I'm Geoff Martin, I'm a friend of Mr. Weston's. Good to meet you."

"And you." She turned to Kirk. "What brings you down my way, Detective?" She sat behind her cluttered desk in a big, black, high-backed chair. Pictures covered the walls around her, tacked up with pushpins and tape. They looked like something from microscope slides: blood samples, pictures of hair and fingerprints, and a few Kirk couldn't place.

"I'm trying to tie up a few loose ends in the David's Island case and wondered if you have anything on it still lying around?"

"Hmmm. I think I have still have the file, but I gave most of the information to the FBI after we were finished. I might have something, though. I'll look."

She got up and walked over to a tall file cabinet that sat in the corner of her small office. Opening up the second drawer, she flipped through the folders until she came to the right one.

"Yup, here it is—or at least my findings, anyway."

Closing the drawer, she sat down again, opened the file, and went through the papers inside. "I thought this case was closed. Did they reopen it?"

Geoff jumped in. "No. We have reason to believe something else is going on, though the FBI deemed it as an accident—food poisoning. We just wanted to find out what you think based on what you discovered."

She looked at Geoff, then back at the file. "I did find it odd, given all the evidence we uncovered, that they would still come to the conclusion it was an accident."

"What did you find out about the second drug? Did you ever find traces of it in the victims?" Kirk asked.

"No, but we did find something interesting about those notes that were sewn inside the pillows. They were made of a cloth we can't trace. It's some sort of disintegrating fabric. Most of our samples are gone. Last I knew, we only had a few threads left."

"Weird." Kirk stroked his long beard. "Is the fabric toxic in any way?"

"We didn't check it for toxicity, because it wasn't a food substance, but that's a good idea." She thought for a moment. "If the fabric puts off a gas or fume of some sort as it disintegrates, that could be the missing piece of the puzzle."

Jumping up from her chair, she asked Kirk and Geoff to follow her. They walked down the hall to a long staircase that led to a basement, which looked like it belonged to a bachelor, not a branch of the police force. Boxes were stacked along the walls, and the air smelled like mothballs and old dust.

Flipping on the lights, she hurried over to a small room off to the right filled with metal locking drawers. They looked like security boxes, but a little bigger in size. Scanning the numbers on the front of each one, she ran her finger down to one almost at the bottom.

"Got it."

She removed a small key from the file she'd carried down

with her, unlocked the drawer and pulled it out. Inside was a small plastic bag with a few strings of off-white thread. "This is all that's left of them, but I think I have enough to run a few tests."

"Great. How long will it take?" Kirk asked.

"A few hours. You can wait if you like, or come back. I'll run them right now."

"We'll stop by later. We still need to run a few errands." Kirk thanked Cassy, and they headed back up the staircase and out the front door to their rental car.

After they were on the road, Geoff asked. "What do you think?"

"It could be the break we need, but we still don't know how they died. And one thing confuses me."

"What's that?"

"If the FBI handed over all that evidence, why did they ignore all the signs that led to foul play? It doesn't make any sense."

"It is a little odd, with the note and all. You would think they would jump all over a thing like that." Geoff shook his head then looked out the window.

"I think we need to find out exactly who in the FBI had access to that CSI file."

"And how do you plan to do that?"

"Not sure yet, but I'll find a way."

CHAPTER FOURTEEN

A FRESH SET OF tire tracks broke a trail through the snow that covered the ground like a white blanket. The rolling hills boasted tall, thin pine trees and patches of quaking aspen running up the draws. The ruts in the dirt road were deep, but the snow was hard packed. The BMW was able to make it through without scraping the bottom of the undercarriage.

Mark drove slowly over the crunching snow, wondering what he was going to do if he found what he was looking for. If he did not hand-deliver the criminals to the police himself, the case would stay closed and be lost to the memories of the public. Then again, he wondered if something else going on, some sort of cover-up to protect someone or something. Pat sat in silence, fidgeting with the zipper on his coat.

He went over the items he'd put in his car right after he had the conversation with Detective Owens: zip-ties, a shovel, and some plastic. He also had a full gas can in the trunk plus a lighter in his pocket. He didn't smoke, but he'd bought a pack of Marlboro Lights just to make it look at least semi-normal to purchase both a lighter and a fill-up on a gas can.

He glanced over at Pat, who appeared to be in his own world. He clenched his jaw. Was he losing his mind? Driving the fool bomber to meet his evil bosses was insane. Bosses who thought it was okay to bomb a supermarket filled with innocent people.

The road crested a small hill, then dropped down to the other side, spilling out into a small valley. His adrenalin began to pump. A log cabin on the far side of the valley billowed gray smoke from the stacked-stone chimney. Several outbuildings stood off to the west side of the cabin. One looked like a storage shed and the other one looked like it was an outhouse. He found a wide spot in the road, turned around, and pulled the car off as far as he dared. This would not be a good time to get stuck.

Pat looked out the window and rubbed his hands together.

Mark sat for a moment, trying to gather his thoughts. He remembered how K smelled and that special smile she saved just for him, how it felt to hold her in his arms. He thought about Samantha and her blonde hair bouncing as she ran to meet him at the door when he returned home after a long day at work. She was so innocent and perfect, so full of life. Now she was dead, thanks to the jerk next to him. Nothing in the world would bring her back.

He flipped on the radio, tuning it until he found a station playing opera. He did not know why, but in times of stress, opera was the only music that could clear his head. He closed his eyes and listened as the rich sounds of La Boheme flowed through the car.

After a few minutes, he shut the car down, got out, and pocketed the keys. He walked around to the passenger side and opened the door, pulling zip-ties from his pocket. "Give me your hand."

"Come on," Pat squealed. "I'll be good, I swear!"

He grabbed one of the kid's wrists, slipped a zip-tie around it, and reached across the seat to attach his wrist to the steering wheel. "You'd better be here when I get back."

He slammed the door shut, popped open the trunk and grabbed a handful of shotgun shells, shoving them into his pocket.

The shotgun sat in the back seat He dropped more zip-ties
into his other pocket and shut the trunk lid. Then he opened the
back door to grab the shotgun. "How many should I expect?"

"Don't know—I only saw three, but there could be more."

Three.

He shut the door and started down the incline, keeping to
the trees and cradling the shotgun in the crook of his left arm.
After about ten minutes of hiking and moving from tree to tree
in the crisp snow, he could see the cabin backed up to the side
of a mountain that closed off the small valley. He made his way
deeper into the woods, where the snow was softer, and there
was more cover.

His heart was racing as he crouched behind a rock
outcropping, holding his shotgun in one hand. The cabin was
just beyond the next clump of pine trees. He could see the gray
pickup truck sitting next to a brown Chevy extended-cab that
was even more beat-up than the gray one.

The cabin looked like any other log cabin, similar to one
his parents took him to on summer vacations when he was
a child. The place was square and probably only had a main
room and one bathroom. A stack of wood was piled beside the
front door. Though he didn't see any movement, smoke poured
from the stone chimney and he smelled the faint odor of coffee
and hickory.

He pulled up the collar on his jacket and crept closer to the
cabin, angry, violent thoughts flooding his mind as he made
a dash for the gray pickup. He slid to the ground and crawled
under the truck on his belly in the snow. After a moment, his
heartbeat dropped to normal, his breathing slowed, and his eyes
sharpened.

In a flash, he rolled from beneath the first pickup, across the
gap, and under the second truck. One more roll, and he found
himself at the edge of the front porch. For a brief instant, he
laid on his back in the dirt and snow staring up at the clear,
blue sky.

He jumped to his feet and leaped onto the porch, where he

lowered his shoulder and crashed through the front door.

As he broke through the door, he hit the floor and sprang to his feet, his shotgun aimed at the two men sitting at the table.

They jerked to their feet, as a third man ducked behind a green leather couch.

"Don't move—or I'll shoot!"

Eyeing the shotgun, the two men at the table threw up their hands.

"Get up from behind that couch," Mark bellowed, "or this riot gun will go to work on your friends!" He was surprised to note his breathing was normal and he was thinking more clearly than ever before.

The third man raised his hands from behind the couch. "I got no gun. Don't shoot!"

"Sit at the table, and keep your hands where I can see them, all of you."

All three men sat down, arms raised above the bomb components they'd been assembling.

Mark leveled the shotgun at the thick man on the far left. "Now, here's how this is going to work. You're going to answer with a yes or a no. If any of you tries to move or does anything that sets me off, you'll all die. Got it?"

They nodded.

"You in the red, stand up and empty your weapons onto the table."

The man, who wore a red, tattered, flannel shirt, pulled a six-inch-long hunting knife from the back pocket of his tattered jeans. Slowly reaching down to his boot, he drew out a revolver and placed it on the table. After he was finished, Mark had the next man do the same, then the third, until the table was piled with pistols and knives.

"Now, if any of you feel the need, you go ahead and reach for one of those guns, but I would strongly advise against it." He fired a shotgun round into the roof, sending wood chips and dust raining on the three terrified captives.

No one moved.

He glared at the men. They looked like a bunch of wild hogs just waiting for the right moment to stampede. Out of the corner of his eye, he could see the door to the bathroom and the cook stove off to the left, steam rising from a pan of water boiling on top. The place stunk of burnt metal and sweat.

His gun still pointed at his prisoners, he walked over to the stove, pulled off the pot of hot water and held it in his free hand.

He turned toward the table and spoke in a calm, low voice. "First question, and don't bother lying to me."

The men glanced at each other.

"Did you have a kid named Pat steal C-4 for you?"

"No," said the slim man in the middle. He had a long-sleeved brown shirt on and a thick, black beard that made him look like a mountain man. He seemed to be the leader of the group, and from the size of his arms, he was probably a former logger.

Mark shook his head in disappointment as he moved over to the messy-haired driver of the gray pickup sitting closest to the kitchen. He pushed the shotgun barrel up against his neck.

The driver squirmed in his chair.

Mark's voice deepened, and he narrowed his eyes. "I'll ask again."

The man didn't even blink as he growled out the same response.

Without hesitation, Mark dumped the hot water on the driver's head.

The man screamed and fell to the floor.

Mark dropped the pot, grabbed his coat collar and yanked the writhing man back up into his chair. He flipped to the front of the table and pointed the gun directly into the face of the leader. "I'll ask one last time, and this time, you better tell me the truth!" He was yelling now, and his blood was thumping in his ears as he stared into the dark eyes of one of his wife's killers.

"Yes! Yes, we did," said the red-flannelled man, glancing at his scalded, whimpering partner.

"That wasn't so hard, now, was it?" He could feel his instincts taking over and felt like he could predict every move, as if he had done this before in another lifetime. The way it happened at the gun range, what he needed for each moment came to him like a sixth sense.

"Question number two. Did you make a bomb, then have the kid put it in the Super Mart?" Mark backed away from the table, shotgun raised.

The leader spit at Mark. "Screw you!"

Red Flannel reached for a pistol.

Mark pulled the trigger just as the man's fingers touched the barrel of the gun.

The heavyset man screamed and pulled his hand back, clutching the bloody stump. Blood spurted from his wrist like a ruptured pipe. He stared at it in horror.

"I told you not to push me!" Mark pumped another round into the chamber and stared down the barrel at the leader of the group. "You want to die?"

He shook his head, staring at his friend, who was fumbling to make a tourniquet with his belt. "Yes, we had him plant the bomb." His voice quivered as he gaped at the blood pooling on the table.

"Last question, and we'll be done." Mark walked behind the men, leaned down and whispered, "Who detonated the bomb?"

The room went silent. Even the panting from the handless fat man stilled, as the full weight of what was happening to them sunk in.

No one spoke.

Mark placed the cold steel against the back of the handless man's head. "Was it you?"

He moaned and shook his head no.

Mark slid the barrel over to the driver of the gray pickup and asked again, "Was it you?"

The man's neck had already blistered in great white boils.

One broke open as Mark shoved the shotgun against his scalded neck. He shook his head no and hunched over, trying to pull away from the still-warm barrel.

Mark grinned as he put the barrel of the shotgun to the back of the black-bearded leader's head. "So… it was you." Leaning down, he whispering into his ear, "You killed my wife. You murdered my daughter."

The room fell silent once again as Mark stood up. He turned the gun over and slammed the stock on the back of the leader's head.

The bearded man slumped over, and his face hit the table with a thud.

Mark returned to the front of the table and pulled zip-ties from his coat pocket. "Tie your hands, one to each of his." He pointed to the unconscious man.

They each tied one of their hands to the man sitting next to him, one to the right, and one to the left. The fat man had a hard time zipping the tie tight on his good hand without fingers on the other. The driver reached over to help him.

When they finished, they stared defiantly at Mark, hatred flashing in their eyes. The fat one, pale from loss of blood, was gritting his teeth in pain. One of the driver's eyes had swollen shut, and his messy hair hung in wet clumps over his blistered face.

Mark walked to the kitchen stove and ripped the gas line from the wall. A hissing sound came from the gas line as it filled the air with toxic fumes. He picked up the almost-finished bomb they been working on. Placing it on the stove, he looked over at the wide-eyed men.

"Justice will prevail."

He turned his back to the two conscious men and started for the front door, but caught a glimmer of steel out of the corner of his eye.

A third truck!

Through the shattered doorway, he saw the shadow of a man crouched on the porch. Dropping to the floor, he rolled across the rubble and grabbed the man's ankles. Pulling with everything in him, he wrenched him to the porch, sending a pistol flying into a snowbank.

The man grunted as he hit the ground. Mark leaped on top of him and punched him in the throat. He stood up as the man gasped for breath and clutched his neck, kicking his legs to get a lungful of air.

But it was no use. His muscles stiffened and his eyes bulged as a final wheeze escaped his lungs. He collapsed, eyes wide and lifeless. One leg twitched. Then nothing.

Dead.

Picking up his shotgun, Mark raced toward his car.

* * *

MARK FELT THE FAMILIAR heat on his back as the sound of the explosion pummeled his eardrums. The force of the blast nearly pushed him to the ground, even though he was a good hundred yards from the cabin, but he managed to stay on his feet. He turned to see a ball of fire roll out the front door and consume the three trucks. One by one, they exploded with a thunderous crescendo.

Panic overcame him as he raced for the BMW, fearing what he'd find. His lungs felt like they would burst, but he kept running.

He stopped when he saw the open passenger door and the blood stain in the snow. Pat's pale hand dangling from the open door like a white flag.

Falling to the ground, his head in his hands, Mark began to sob, so overcome with emotion, he didn't know what do. Relief and rage tangled in his head like the snarls in his daughter's hair. His mind reeled and his body trembled as he cried—cried for his family, cried for what he'd done, cried for his future. He even cried for Pat, whose stupidity had cost him his life.

The thought of what he had done began to creep into his mind but he pushed them back, not willing to take a look at who he was becoming. If he shoved it down, even if temporary, he could deal with it later. Emotions buried will always rise to the surface.

Struggling to his feet, he wiped his eyes and walked over to his car. Inside, he could see the gunshot wound oozing blood across the boy's chest. He was slumped over, almost falling out onto the snow, but held back by the zip-tie attached to the steering wheel.

Mark took a long breath. He had to get it together.

After he cut Pat loose, he dragged his body out of the car and onto the side of the road, where he covered it with snow. With any luck, wild animals would devour the body before the snow melted.

Cold and weary, he crawled into the car, started the engine and backed it out of the trees, then turned toward the main road.

CHAPTER FIFTEEN

THE TINY BELL ON the door rang as Kirk and Geoff left the barbershop. The air felt extra cold on Kirk's now-bald head and smooth face. He ran his hand over his head, then reached inside his coat and pulled out an old beanie. He pulled it low over his ears and hunched his shoulders against the bitter winter's frigid breath.

"What now, boss?" Geoff asked.

"We head back to the crime lab to see what Cassy found out. I think she might be able to tell us something about our mystery lady, as well."

The day looked warm, with the sun shining in the cloudless sky, but it was deceiving. A cold, knife-like wind cut through the boxed-in city streets as if barreling through a tunnel, snatching the breath from anyone who dared step out into its path. On a day like today, Kirk liked the rental car better than his open motorcycle, but he still grumbled about all the gas it guzzled.

The receptionist told them Cassy was in the basement. Once again, they traversed the long, dingy stairs downward.

Cassy had her eye glued to a microscope and did not look up when Kirk and Geoff walked into the lab.

Kirk glanced around the room, which contained several tables covered with test tubes, blood-sample testers and other objects he couldn't identify. Several white tables were lit from underneath, apparently illuminating objects of study. The place was jammed with boxes, file cabinets and plastic bins, but everything was in order—not messy, just in dire need of more space.

Kirk leaned over Cassy's shoulder.

She looked up. "Wow, when you get a haircut, you get a haircut! Feel better?"

He nodded.

She grinned. "You guys won't believe what I discovered." Her smile lit the room, which was noteworthy in the midst of the clutter and dim, blinking lights.

"Please tell me you have good news." Kirk said.

"I think you'll be pleased," she said, a twinkle in her eye. "The cloth sample had no poison or any other substance in it, but I looked closer and found that this string isn't cloth at all." She motioned to the single white strand that lay in a round dish on the slide under the microscope lens.

"Really? What is it?" Geoff leaned over to look in the microscope.

Cassy pointed at a stool for Kirk to sit on and placed an open book in front of him. "See this description here? It's a form of plastic mixed with an acid that eats away at cloth. When the material in the pillows started to deteriorate, it put off a gas that the inmates breathed as they slept."

Kirk frowned. "So this gas stuff is what killed them?"

"No. By itself, it's nontoxic, but I ran a few more tests. Guess what could be mixed with it to make it lethal?"

He shook his head.

"Botconie." She looked expectantly at the men, but they just shrugged. "Okay. I'll back up. Remember that theory we talked about last year, about how every drug has its partner opposite?"

He nodded.

"Well, Botconie is the partner to the anti-drug that was found in all the guards. It acts like a repellent to Dypethline.

Geoff looked confused. "I don't get it."

"I'll tell you what I think happened. The pillows somehow had this patch of material placed in them. Over time, it filled the prison with a gas that could not be smelled or otherwise detected. Then the antidote was administered to the guards through their coffee, if you will, seeing as the guards had their own coffee pot in a private break room that was inaccessible to the inmates. The food was injected with Botconie, and when it mixed with the gas, it caused anyone who had it in their system to go into instant cardiac arrest."

Kirk grinned. "You're one smart cookie, Cassy. How did you come up with all this?"

"Easy. I tested the note against all the food samples and nothing happened until I got to the samples of coffee. I found traces of Dypethline in the coffee."

"So the gas had been pumped into their systems, and the coffee drinkers were saved. I guess coffee does have its advantages." Kirk said.

"Yeah, and lucky for them, all the guards drink coffee or we would have a few dead guards too. Whoever did this did their homework. Not one guard, or any other staff member, was hurt. I do have some bad news, though. With all the tests I had to run, I don't have anything left of the fabric, which leaves us without any hard evidence outside of our own testimony."

Kirk scratched his head, trying to figure out a way to get something hard to nail the case shut. "What we need is a witness and to find out who is behind all this. That's the only way we'll get this to stick. Without something concrete, we're still standing with nothing more than a fancy story."

He pulled the photo of the mystery woman from his jacket and handed it to Cassy. "Could you check your computer files to search for a match?"

She nodded. "It's worth a shot." She scanned the picture it into the computer. "NCIC will pull up anyone who has any kind of criminal record. It matches facial structure and bone lines, so even if a person changes their looks, the program can tell with a ninety-four percent accuracy rate who they are—or were."

The original picture appeared on the left side of her screen, while others scrolled across the right side. The photos flipped onto the screen for almost an hour as the three watched, hoping for a hit. Kirk drank the last cup of coffee, so Cassy made another pot while they waited.

Kirk was reviewing the details of the case in his head for the third time, when a beeping sound jerked his attention to the flashing sign on the screen, which read *No Matches Found.* "Bah! That's not what I wanted to see."

Cassy sighed. "Sorry. Anything else you want me to look up?"

He drummed his fingers on the table. "Can you access all past and present government employees?"

She nodded. "Sure, hold on. I'll pull up everyone in the CIA, FBI or any other government program."

Geoff asked, "You think she might work for the FBI?"

"Well, the file was given to the FBI," Kirk said, "who did nothing about it, even though the evidence was clear that David's Island was no accident. Somewhere along the line, the investigation was compromised." He looked at Cassy. "Who did you give the file to, exactly?"

"I gave it to Jenkins. He works for me and delivered all our files to the FBI, but it couldn't be him. He's the last person in the world who would be in on some sort of cover-up."

"Why are you so sure?" Geoff asked.

"I've known him for at least ten years. I'd trust him with my life."

Kirk rubbed his chin. "Okay, but I still want to talk to him. I'd like to ask who he delivered that file to. I'd also like to get the names of everyone who had access to it in the FBI." He paused. "Is Jenkins here now?"

"No. He'll be in tomorrow. He had to go to the dentist

today, so I gave him the day off."

A beep sounded. They all turned to stare at the screen, which flashed the same message as before: *No Matches Found.*

Kirk tried not to show his mounting frustration. "What else can we try? She has to be there somewhere."

Cassy bit her lip and stared at her keyboard. "I could try one other thing, but it is a little on the—well, how do I put this—risky side."

Kirk perked up. "I can do risky. What do you got?"

"There's a top-secret project database we can run it against that will pull up any active or underground programs the government is running or has run in the past. But if they find out I hacked in, I'm dead meat!"

Geoff's forehead wrinkled. "It isn't worth it, Cassy. You could lose your job, whether we get a hit or not."

Kirk glared at Geoff then bent to look Cassy dead in the eye. "Please, I need to find this woman. She's our only lead left. Without her, we're finished."

Cassy straightened. "Okay, I'll do it, but you'd better cover me if the fur hits the fan."

Kirk nodded and sat on the stool beside her. "Absolutely."

Typing in a series of commands, she pulled up a page filled with file names and a search box and started running the list against the photo. As before, pictures flipped past the screen, but they suddenly stopped, and a green message flashed: *Positive Match.*

"Yes!" Kirk jumped to his feet to peer at the screen. "Isis Kanika—that's her. I'm sure it's the same woman!"

Cassy read the bio. "Looks like she used to work for the FIA, which is an intelligence agency based in foreign countries, mainly in Europe. They were disbanded about ten years ago. She was killed in action on a mission in Paris, but her body was never recovered." She lifted an eyebrow. "My bet is she went rogue, and no one knows who she's working for now."

Geoff kept reading. "This says she was an assassin with over thirty-five confirmed kills, that she has trained in hand-to-hand combat as well as heavy weapons. Boy, I'd hate to be on her bad side."

The list went on for twenty more pages, noting her assignments and the missions she completed. Kirk shook his head. "So we have a professional on our hands, who obviously isn't working alone." He frowned and stopped the scrolling. "It looks like she was born in Egypt and moved here to the States after she entered the program."

"What is the FIA supposed to do—what was it doing?" Geoff asked.

"As far as I know," Cassy said, "its agents would go in under the radar and carry out hits for the US military." She switched to another screen. "Let's see what else I can find." After a couple clicks, she read for a moment, then said, "The most unnerving thing about the FIA is that it was shut down for doing some sort of experimentation on soldiers."

Kirk leaned back on his stool. The FIA must have set her off somehow. Something must have gone wrong. "Can you print off Kanika's information for me?"

"Sure, and if you know a good hacker, you might want to have them research this so-called agency. According to the file, her code name is *Black Widow*. I'm not sure if that will help you, but it's a start."

Geoff shook her hand. "You've been a great help, Cassy."

Kirk took the papers from the printer. "Thanks for everything. I'll keep in touch. If you find out anything more, give me a call."

Cassy walked up the stairs with them to the front door. "No problem. I just hope you find out who's responsible for all those deaths. I hate to think what else they are capable of."

* * *

THE FIREPLACE FLAMES ROARED as they consumed Mark's clothing, his coat, his boots—and anything else that could contain blood or DNA to trace him to the cabin and the explosion. The heat drifted over his body as he lay crumpled on the floor in front of the fire thinking about absolutely nothing.

He had driven straight home and run the stairs up to his apartment to grab a bottle of carpet cleaner from under the kitchen sink. The blood came out with ease from the leather seats, but the floor mats were a different story. They ended up in the fireplace along with his clothes.

After thoroughly scrubbing his car, he dragged himself to the elevator and returned to his apartment exhausted and drained. But his mind raced, repeatedly replaying the explosion. *What have I done?* He tried to feel guilty, but couldn't. Though his retaliation was the only justice his family would ever see, somehow, he did not feel better. Yet, at the same time, he felt like a huge weight had been lifted from his shoulders.

Finally, he passed out in front of the fireplace and didn't wake up until the next morning. He looked around, trying to pull out of the nightmare, but it was not in his head. It was real.

Making his way to the kitchen, he started the coffee pot then headed for the bathroom to jump in the shower. The water seemed to clear his mind. As he thought about his uncharacteristic behavior and the things he'd done, he realized something about himself.

He stooped under the showerhead to rinse out the shampoo. *How did I take out those guys without training?* And where did he learn to turn on and shut off his emotions at will, as if he had an internal switch. His reactions had been quick and precise, like at the gun range. His movements had come to him like they'd been imprinted on his brain.

He turned off the water. Or maybe he'd watched too many Matt Damon movies.

Wrapping a towel around his waist, he wandered into the kitchen and poured coffee into a mug. As he sipped on the dark brew, he looked at his hand. No cuts, no bruises. He walked into the bedroom to look at his back in the mirror. Same thing—not a scratch or a mark anywhere on his body. He tried to think back. *Was I hit or punched at all through that?* He couldn't remember.

"Weird. Sheer luck, I guess." He put on a pair of jeans and a black shirt and walked out of the bedroom buttoning the shirt. Just as he finished the bottom button, he felt a presence and froze.

Someone was standing beside the fireplace. In two steps, he had the fire poker in his hand. One more step, and he'd shoved the tip against a soft throat. His hand was steady as he whispered in a dark voice that didn't even sound like his, "Who are you, and what do you want?"

CHAPTER SIXTEEN

"MOOCH." KIRK BARKED INTO his cell phone as he drove toward downtown Manhattan. "I've got a name for you. I need to know where to find this chick. Now."

"Hold on, man. I'm putting you on speaker."

Kirk could hear Mooch shuffling papers and muttering, "Sometimes I think I would've been better off going to jail."

"What are you doing?"

"Trying to find my chair. Hold on one sec."

Then Mooch yelled, "I heard you the first time, Mom. I'll take out the garbage when I'm finished with this call."

Kirk moved the phone away from his ear and pounded the car seat with the side of his fist. Waiting was one thing he did not do well.

Finally, Mooch said, "Okay, I'm back. Give me her name."

"Isis Kanika. First name spelled I-s-i-s. Last name, K-a-n-i-k-a. She's the woman in the drop-off picture. I need to know where she went or anything that will give me a last-known address, place of employment, family members, and if she has been or is married. I need everything you can find about her."

He could hear Mooch typing, so he clenched his fist and tried to be patient. He glanced at Geoff in the passenger seat. The reporter seemed engrossed with something on his laptop.

Probably his latest squeeze on Facebook. Kirk shook his head. Nothing made him angrier than all this techno garbage. Internet, cell phones, iPods, or pads, or whatever they were. What would they come up with next? Antennas to screw into the techies' dimwit brains? He liked it better before the world turned electronic and people actually had to talk to each other rather than constantly check Twitter and Facebook.

He put the phone back to his ear. "Got anything, Mooch?"

"Hold on. I'm tracking her from where she left the warehouse, following her truck. Okay, she turned into a parking garage on Forty-Fourth and Fifth Avenue. It looks like an office building of some kind."

"Great. Does it show her coming out?"

"No. Just going in. That's all I got. As far as a home address or anything like that, all I could find are files from something called the *Black Widow Project*."

"I got that already. Keep looking, and one more thing. Try to find out what that project was all about and why she left, if you can. They said she was killed in action, but we know better."

"Fine, but I want four large pepperoni pizzas delivered to my house. I don't work well on an empty stomach."

"Ha! Now you're pushing it. Just get to work, Mooch, or I might forget to be so nice to you." He hung up the phone and turned to Geoff. "Hey, I need you to send some pizza to Mooch's house. You think you can take care of that?"

"Sure. I can even order it online." He began typing. "So what did you find out?"

"There's an office building at Forty-Fourth and Fifth where we might find Isis. That's where she went after the switch."

"That's the Merc Building, I think." Geoff pulled up a website and was soon on the site of Merc, Inc.

Kirk squinted at Geoff. "How did you know that?" He raised his coffee mug and took a sip.

"I was an intern there before I got hired on at the magazine. They put out a publication that goes out all over the world about politics, third-world governments, ecology, global warming—stuff like that."

"Are you talking about the *Global Advisor?*"

"Yup, that's the one. It's a multibillion-dollar company and very big on saving the world." Geoff's face lit up as he talked about the huge corporation.

Kirk could tell he admired what they were trying to do, but he could not care less about the poor earth and its temperature. Not as if he could do anything about it, anyway. The environmentalists were all bent about carbon and cow farts, when China, India, and every other country polluted ten times what America ever thought of doing. *We can't build a nuke plant, so they do. And in the end, the world is polluted faster, but we sleep better at night, because we didn't do it.* "If they're involved in this," he said. "They'll be going against everything they claim to believe in."

"If you think about it,' Geoff said, "these people think they're doing the right thing. They killed the prisoners at David's Island, which were all convicted rapists and murderers, but they didn't kill innocent people like the guards. They did a good job of burying the truth, too, with the whole food poisoning thing."

Kirk rubbed his smooth chin. "I think we've got a vigilante group on our hands." Thinking about the case so far, maybe he'd been kidnapped to give the FBI time to close the case. That they spared his life fit the prison pattern. No innocents killed.

He turned to Geoff. "This isn't going to be easy. With the technology I saw at the prison I was in, and how good they are at covering their tracks, we might be neck deep into a highly-sophisticated underground operation."

Geoff nodded as they turned onto Fifth Avenue.

The Merc Building was made of brick and stone, with dark glass covering the windows. It shot up into the skyline like a crystal through solid rock. Kirk pulled into the parking garage, found a space on the fifth level and parked. He reached for his door handle. "You ready?"

"Ready as I'll ever be."

* * *

MARK'S HAND WAS SURPRISINGLY steady as he held the weapon at the intruder's neck. He could feel his heart rate slow until all he felt was the adrenaline pumping through his body.

"Hello, Mark." The voice and the face were those of a woman.

He stepped closer, cocking his arm, ready to thrust the poker into her throat. "What do you want? And how do you know my name?"

"I know what you're going through. I'm here to help you." She reached up and carefully touched the end of the poker. "If we could talk, I would explain everything."

He stepped back, weapon lowered but held firmly with both hands. "Start talking."

She looked up at him, her dark eyes shining as a shaft of sunlight cut across her face. "My name is Isis. I'm the one who left you the surveillance video, as well as the note in your car over a year ago. I'm also the one who knows the truth about the bombing that day."

"You drive a black Lexus, don't you?"

She smiled and laughed, her long, black hair swinging as she shook her head. "You're better than I thought, but he said you would be. And after seeing the cabin—"

His grip tightened on the metal rod. "How do you know about that?"

"I know more about you than you do, and that's why I'm here. We have been watching you. It's only a matter of time until you begin to wonder—"

"What are you talking about? Wonder what?" He knew something was happening to him, and he didn't know why, but maybe he didn't want to know.

"Have you noticed anything different about yourself? Have you wondered how you know how to shoot a gun without any training? Did you ever think you were capable of killing four people in a matter of minutes?" She cocked her head. "I know this is a confusing time in your life, but I need you to come with me. I can show you the answers you're looking for."

He scowled at her. The woman had enough evidence to put him in jail for the rest of his life. Why should he trust her?

"Who are you, anyway?" He ran a hand through his hair. What had he gotten into? What had he started by murdering four men—five, if he counted Pat. The way things were going, he would have eventually killed the kid, anyway.

"I'm with the World Justice Agency. I can provide answers. I can take you home."

* * *

MARK STRUGGLED TO PUT all the pieces together as Isis drove through downtown traffic toward Central Park. They were in the Lexus he'd seen many times but never seriously thought much of until now. She must have been watching him for months, maybe even years.

The traffic brought them to a crawl as they hit Forty-Fourth Street. He looked around, trying to implant everything about the woman and the car in his brain. The car was spotless, nothing out of place. He could smell the faint scent of a subtle perfume. She looked confident as she drove, though she didn't say a word. But every now and then, he saw her looking at him out of the corner of her eye.

She steered the car into a parking garage attached to a tall building and drove up one level. The moment they got out of the car, she started toward an elevator at the end of the aisle.

He hesitated.

She stepped into the elevator and held the door. "You coming?"

Here goes. Without a word, he walked to the elevator. The door closed. Isis pushed the buttons for floors nine, five and two all at once, and the elevator began to descend.

It didn't stop until they had gone at least six stories down. At least that's how it felt. When the doors opened, he saw a large foyer-like room.

Isis stepped out and motion for him to follow her.

He couldn't stop staring at the glass floor beneath his feet. A shark swam by the starfish attached to the underside. It was a huge aquarium, so deep he couldn't see the bottom.

The receptionist, an older man, looked up at them through his reading glasses. He smiled when he saw Isis and stood up to greet her.

"Hello, my dear. It is so good to see you this fine day." His voice shook a little as he took her hand and held it in-between his bony fingers. He turned to greet Mark. "And who is this young man?"

Mark felt like he was on a first date and was about to meet the father.

Isis introduced Mark to the old man. "This is Mark Appleton. Mark, this is Mr. Able. He's been with us since the beginning."

The older man stared at Mark's face, as if trying to remember. "Mark, it has been a long time—great to see you again." He grabbed Mark's hand and shook it, grinning around his false teeth.

"Uh, yeah. Good to meet you, too." He frowned at Isis. *Again? What did that mean?*

Mr. Able ushered them to a nearby couch. The white leather couch was so smooth that he hesitated to sit on it. He guessed it was imported. When he finally sat, he knew from the feel it was Italian.

He looked at Isis, who was watching him, an amused expression on her face. "So, now what?"

"We wait for the boss. He's in a meeting, but he'll be finished shortly." She leaned back into the soft cushions.

He tried to relax, but it was hard when his mind raced with questions. Resting his forearms on his knees, he watched the exotic sea life that floated under the floor. The fluid movements of the sea creatures calmed his mind.

He pulled himself from the mesmerizing scene to study his surroundings. The room had to be at least twenty-five feet round. The front desk was made of a metal that had a soft shine to it but didn't look like anything he'd ever seen. On the wall behind and above the desk, big, bold, silver-and-black letters declared the establishment, or whatever it was, to be *WJA*. In small print below that were the words *World Justice Agency*. Maybe it was some sort of government agency.

The corner where they sat had a big couch with an enormous plasma screen on the wall playing CNN, a beautiful Persian rug on the floor, and a weird-looking coffee table made of metal and wood.

To the left of the front desk was what appeared to be a large door, except it had no handle. Suddenly, it slid down into the floor, and a huge black man stepped through. He wore a black suit and held a cigar in the corner of his lips

He smiled as he entered the foyer, his bald head reflecting the light as he walked. He looked at Mark, and a big smile crossed his face. "Mark, my man. How ya doing?" Holding out his giant hand, he grabbed Mark's hand and pulled him to his feet. "I'm Brian—or, as I'm called around here, Big B."

"Good to meet you." Mark tried not to cringe at the power of the man's grip. "I suppose you know me, too."

"No, man, but you've been the topic of many conversations." He laughed with a thunderous noise that sounded from the bottom of his belly. "Come with me. I'll lead you to—well, you'll just have to wait and see. Come on, Isis, my little lady. You're invited, too."

Isis followed them through the sliding door, which led to a long hallway with unadorned white walls. A door at the end had a keypad on the doorframe. Big B punched in a code, then a retinal scanner flipped open, and he stared at it for several seconds before the door retracted into the ceiling, and the three of them walked through.

The next room had an X-ray machine and fingerprint center. The people working the stations carried sidearms and wore wide belts loaded with batons and walkie-talkies. Mark and his companions rode through an X-ray machine on a conveyor belt. All the while, Mark imagined what it must look like to watch a full, live scan of the human body, to see the action beneath the skin.

He had to put his thumb on an electronic pad that a tall guard held out to him. It made a beep as he did. The guard motioned him on. Big B and Isis were waiting on the other side in front of a set of three elevator doors.

"You ready?" Isis asked.

"Sure. Not like I have much choice." He shoved his hands into his pockets and looked at Big B, who could not stop smiling. "What?"

"Nothing man. Don't worry. You'll be okay as long as you do everything we say." He laughed and slapped Mark on the back. It hurt and just about knocked the breath out of him but he ignored the pain. *Just what did that comment mean?*

Like the two previous days, his circumstances seemed surreal, but he knew it was really happening, so he decided he might as well enjoy it. The place so far was amazing and seemed to be safe. With all the security, it was probably better fortified than the White House.

The single arrow by the elevators pointed down. Isis pressed it. The doors opened, and they entered. Like the foyer, this elevator was made of glass, even the floor. He could see all the way down the very deep elevator shaft. He decided WJA must have a thing for glass, because it seemed they used it a lot in the construction of this building.

As they descended, he could see a huge room with people sitting at desks, some standing. It looked like a command center. The far wall was covered with screens that ran from floor to ceiling. The room had to be two stories tall. He tried to get a closer look, but they continued descending, and the room disappeared from view.

Looking down, he saw that they were almost to the bottom of the elevator shaft. They came to a stop, and he nearly fell over when the elevator began to travel sideways through a tunnel. When it turned, he could see a light ahead of them. As they came closer, he felt the machine slowing down.

"This is our stop." Isis smoothed her long hair and waited for the doors to open. This floor was different from what he'd seen so far. The walls were made of brick and had lights embedded into them. The curved entry ceiling was amazingly high for how far underground they were. A beautiful crystal chandelier hung from the center.

Beneath the chandelier was a desk with a short, dark-haired man sitting behind it. He looked up from his computer as they walked in. Mark noticed the room had two exits—the elevator and a set of wide double doors made of thick wood. *Must be the boss's office.*

"Welcome to the WJA, Mr. Appleton." The man stood, shook his hand, and pointed to the double doors. "He's expecting you."

Big B walked over to the heavy door, turned the handle, and opened it for Mark. He looked at Isis, who nodded for him to go in. He hesitated for a brief moment, then walked through the open door into a large office.

In contrast to what he'd seen so far, the room was dimly lit and had bookshelves on all the walls. It looked like an eighteenth century library. At the far end of the large room, he saw an old, oak desk piled with papers. A computer monitor sat off to one side. A large, black chair was turned away from him, but he could tell someone was sitting in it, reading a leather-bound book that looked to be over a hundred years old. The bookshelves looked like the same ones in the DVD.

"Mark Appleton. It's been a long time."

* * *

GEOFF AND KIRK WALKED into the main lobby of the Merc Building, which was everything one would expect from a billion-dollar company. The floors were covered with marble, interwoven with a globe of the world. The elevators they'd ridden ran along the east wall, with six different stations, and they were lined with intricate engravings of letters which Kirk couldn't read.

184 | AARON PATTERSON

A huge, glass dome covered the whole lobby area. Sunrays streamed in, making the place glow with natural sunlight.

Geoff stopped to examine twenty-foot-tall palm trees that stood in the middle of the entryway. "Wow, some place, huh?" he said as he looked at the tall palms.

"Yeah, real fancy. Let's see if anyone remembers our lady friend."

The large front desk curved in a half-moon shape was big enough to host three receptionists. The one in the middle was talking on the phone, trying to give driving directions to someone. Kirk made eye contact with a shorthaired blonde girl who couldn't be older than twenty. She smiled and asked if she could help them.

"I'm Detective Weston, and this is my partner. We're trying to track down this woman." He showed her the photo of Isis. "Have you ever seen her here before?"

The girl shook her head. "No, can't say that I have." She turned to the receptionist next to her, who had just hung up the phone. "Hey, Barb, have you ever seen this woman before?"

Barb took the photo from Kirk.

"This picture is a year old," Kirk said.

"Hmmm, she looks familiar. Does she work in this building?"

"We were hoping you could tell us that."

Barb sat down at her computer and began to type. "Do you have her name?"

"Yeah, but she would probably be under a different name. Do you keep surveillance tapes of the parking garage that far back?"

"A year ago? No. Sorry. We only keep them for six months." She held up a hand. "Hold on, I think I have something. I looked up employees who are female and ethnic and came up with Katrina Meskhenet. She sure looks like the same person." She swiveled the screen.

Kirk leaned over the counter to look. "Bingo—that's her. What floor does she work on?"

"She's on the fourteenth floor in Suite 102. She's the supervising field officer for the Middle East division."

Kirk smiled and thanked them for their help, then hurried to the nearest elevator. He could feel his heart start to race. *Middle East.* Did she have anything to do with his kidnapping?

"Easy, man," Geoff whispered. "Let's just question her and not fly off the handle."

The elevator stopped on the fourteenth floor. Kirk sucked in a deep breath and stepped out. The floor had a long hallway with suite doors approximately fifteen feet apart on each side of the hallway. They found 102 at the corner and were greeted by a young, dark-haired man. "How can I help you?" His tone was friendly enough.

"We're looking for Katrina Meskhenet." Kirk looked around. The room was filled with Egyptian décor, from pictures of pyramids to a tall, half-dog, half-man statue that guarded an office Kirk assumed belonged to Katrina.

"She's out to lunch. If you like, you can wait. She should be returning shortly."

"Thanks. We'll wait."

"Do you have an appointment with her?"

Kirk held up his badge. "She has an appointment with me."

"Very good, sir. I'll show you to the waiting room." He ushered them to a small waiting area with a couch and a TV in the corner. Kirk plopped down and tuned the television to ESPN to see what was going on with the Lions—if anything.

CHAPTER SEVENTEEN

"HELLO, DETECTIVE. I'M KATRINA. I hear you're looking for me." She motioned toward her office. "We can talk in my office."

After the two men sat down in the two chairs across from her desk, she took a seat in a sleek leather chair behind the desk. She remembered Kirk Weston from pictures and surveillance videos from the MAG Chamber. It seemed this man was not one to give up easily.

"So, Detective, what can I do for you?" She folded her hands and looked at the two men across from her. Detective Weston was dressed in a white T-shirt and blue jeans. His leather jacket was tattered and in dire need of replacement, but he looked better than the last time she saw him.

"We just want to ask you a few questions." Pulling out a photo, he placed it on her desk and slid it toward her. She picked it up and looked at it without expression before handing it back to him.

"Is that you, Miss Meskhenet?"

"May I ask what this is regarding, Detective?" She avoided the question, hoping he didn't notice her evasion. The trail to her was cold, and the case was closed, but something in his eyes told her this would not be the last time she saw him in her office asking questions.

"That's confidential, Miss Meskhenet. But I have other photos of a woman who looks a lot like you driving away from a crime scene and into this very office building. Can you explain that?"

She could tell this would get out of hand if she didn't give him something he thought was a help. Or maybe she should shut him down so hard he had no reason to ever come looking her way again. She was a smart and complicated person, but she was not careless. Quite the opposite, in fact. She was detailed and covered her tracks in every situation. Now, with a cop poking his nose in a high-profile investigation, she was glad she was so thorough. "When was this taken, might I ask?"

The detective looked over to his partner then back to her with a knowing look in his eye.

She knew now he knew he was chasing a cold case and had nothing on her other than some blurry satellite pictures. "Last year in October. October fifth, to be exact. Can you tell me where you were on that day?"

"I'm not sure where I was a year ago. Do you remember where you were a year ago Detective Weston?"

Kirk grinned and nodded. "Actually, yes. I can tell you exactly where I was."

Isis mentally kicked herself. Wrong thing to ask. "Let me see what I can do." She pushed a button on her phone. "Biba, please pull everything on my schedule from October fifth of last year." She smiled at Kirk. "We keep very good records, due to how much I travel with the company."

The intern came into the office a few minutes later with a folder marked *October*. He glanced at the two men sitting across from his boss, handed the folder to Isis, and left the room without speaking.

"Okay." She flipped through the folder until she came to the fifth. "Here it is. You said the fifth of October, right? I was in Baghdad working on a story about oil drilling and its effects on our environment. Here's my hotel receipt plus a few from a local restaurant." She smiled politely as she handed the contents to the detective.

* * *

KIRK TRIED TO HIDE his disappointment as he looked through the folder. Everything was signed and date stamped for the fifth of October. She was his only real lead, but maybe this woman wasn't Isis Kanika. He thought back to her file. Did it contain fingerprints?

He returned the folder. "Thank you, Miss Meskhenet. Apparently you're not the woman we're looking for. Do you have any idea who the person in this photo is?"

She glanced again at the photo. "It is a little fuzzy, but I can understand how you could mistake her for me. Same hair color and skin tone. The fact she drove to this building is very strange, but this is a big parking garage. Maybe she just came here to drop something off."

Kirk looked at Geoff, who hadn't spoken the entire time, hoping he had something to offer, but got nothing extraordinary from his expression. He turned back to Isis. "Thanks for your time."

"Not a problem. If I can be of any further help, just let me know." She stood and walked them to the door.

As they were about to leave, Kirk asked, "Oh, one other thing. Does the name Isis Kanika ring a bell?"

She thought for a moment. "It sounds Egyptian in origin. But, no, I can't say that it does."

He nodded. "Thanks, anyway." As they made their way down the hall toward the elevators, Kirk thought about the interview. Everything fit so well. The picture leading them to the building. This woman and the Isis lead... "Geoff, I think we're being played."

"How so, boss?"

"Everything fits too well—the picture, the building, and this Katrina woman looking like our suspect. I think we were set up to think it all came from here. Something is definitely going on, and we need to find out what it is."

190 | AARON PATTERSON

"So we're back to square one, huh?"

"No, we ruled out this Miss Meskhenet woman, which leaves us with one other option."

Geoff looked confused, but then his face lit up. "Follow the file, right?"

"Yup, the file was sent to the FBI. From there, the case was ruled as a freak food poisoning accident. Something went wrong—or should I say some*one*. We find who touched that file, we find our guy."

* * *

ISIS SHUT HER OFFICE door and sighed in relief. That was too close for comfort, but at least she convinced them. Or did she? She sat in her leather chair and spun around to look out the window. The sun was shining on the frost-covered ground, which sparkled like gems in a clear stream. She could see the outline of Central Park with the trees, the faint glint of light as it hit the water. Picking up her phone, she dialed Big B.

"They're gone. Can you text me when Mark is out?"

"Will do."

She closed her eyes and leaned back in her chair to let the sun warm her face. How much of her story did the detective believe? Was he on a vendetta now that he was free? Was he out for blood? She hoped he wouldn't be a problem and made a mental note to bring it up in the next meeting. They might need to intervene again in Detective Kirk Weston's life.

* * *

THE MAN SWIVELED HIS chair to meet Mark's gaze. He wore a tailored, black, pinstriped suit and wire-rimmed glasses.

Mark gasped when the older man rose from his chair. It was as if he knew him, knew him well, but couldn't remember who he was or when he'd seen him before. The thought bothered him. This was happening a lot these days. Was his memory going? Or was he in some sort of twilight zone, where everyone knew him—but he couldn't remember them?

"Who are you?" His simple question broke the silence and made him feel like he had some sort of control, as slim as it might be. The man, who had thick, silver hair, appeared to be in his late sixties or seventies. The cane that leaned against his desk had a bright-red ruby on top. It sparkled and glimmered, looking like an all-knowing eye.

"That's a loaded question, Mark. In time you will know everything." The older man stood, reached for his cane and walked to where Mark stood. He held out his hand.

Mark took his hand. The man's handshake was firm and warm. Somehow, that made him feel a little better, despite every cell in his brain telling him something was wrong, dangerously wrong.

"My name is Solomon. I'm the leader of the World Justice Agency. I'm sure you have many questions, which will be answered in due time. Just be patient with us, if I might be so bold as to ask." Pointing to a chair, he motioned for Mark to sit down.

Mark walked over to the wood-lined chair, sat down, and watched this—boss—or mastermind, or whatever he was— pace in front of the desk, his cane clicking. From the looks of it, Solomon didn't need the cane. Mark wondered why he used it.

For a moment, the gray-haired man stood with his back to him, stroking his neatly trimmed beard, as if to gather his thoughts.

Mark looked around the room, marveling at the tall bookcases, wondering what wisdom they held and the years it must have taken to build the collection. He'd never seen so many books in one place. There had to be thousands, maybe hundreds of thousands covering every wall, floor to ceiling, all around the great room.

Solomon leaned with both hands on the cane. "I'm going to tell you who we are and what we do. After I'm finished, you may ask any questions you like, and I will answer them. Is that acceptable to you?"

Mark nodded.

"The world is filled with violence, evil, hate." Solomon

began. "For thousands of years, justice was meted out by kings and judges. In our current era, it is the duty of government. In centuries past, citizens have sometimes been driven to rise against their governments to restore justice when it was lost." He stepped to the nearest bookshelf and pulled out a leather-lined book that looked like it was about to crumble.

"This great country was founded on the rights of the people. The people ruled themselves because everyone had the same basic values as to was acceptable, what was considered a crime, what was sin—if you will. Today, we are losing more rights every day with each perverted laws Congress passes in the name of saving us from ourselves. The Supreme Court houses judges who crave power and overturn whatever laws they are not paid to support. We have lost the passion and the common sense to see the difference between a *what* and *why*."

He leaned toward Mark, looking deep into his eyes.

Mark felt like Solomon was looking into his very soul. The feeling unnerved him so much he wanted to turn away—but he couldn't.

"Do you see the murder, the rape, the evil going on all around you? Do you feel the fear of dark alleys where women are raped and killed without retribution?" He straightened. "I do, Mr. Appleton. I see that our justice system is not doing what it should. I see where it is understaffed, unable to keep up with the amount of hate that is splashed across our streets every single hour of every single day."

Standing tall, he raised his voice as he paced the room. "Throughout time, there were groups of people who were appointed judge and jury. In Bible times, it was the Levites. In the reign of the British Empire, it was Parliament. In our great country, it's the Supreme Court."

He slammed his cane on the floor, his eyes blazing with passion. "WJA is here to bring balance to the court system. We, the World Justice Agency, carry out justice. We are here to uphold the law that says if you kill, you will pay with your own life. Eye for eye. Tooth for tooth. Life for life. This is our country, and we are taking it back.

"We have two choices. We can sit by and let our country burn under the flag of tolerance, or we can recreate a world where our children and grandchildren can live in safety." Once again, he slammed the cane against the floor.

Mark swallowed. The guy was serious.

Sitting down in the oversized chair behind his large desk, he turned his back to Mark and sighed. "You see, Mark, WJA is the last thing holding America together. We are involved in every part of government and in every agency, and the reason you are here today is because of us." With a soft voice, he finished. "I'm your father, Mark."

Mark clutched the arms of his chair as he tried to remember his childhood. His parents had died in a plane crash when he was a baby. As far as he knew, he'd lived with foster parents most of his life. He didn't have many memories before the age of twelve.

"What are you saying?" He choked on the words.

Solomon turned his chair, rested his elbows on the desk and steepled his fingers together. "I'm not your blood father, Mark, but I'm the one who rescued you after your parents died. You lived down here with me until you were eleven years old. I taught you and trained you up as a child."

Mark opened his mouth, then closed it. "I don't believe it. If it was true, I'd remember you. I'd remember this place." This was crazy. He had to get out. Get back to the real world. He tried stand but was too dizzy. He plopped back down in the chair with a thump, feeling his stomach turn and a lost, confusing loneliness wash over his soul.

"Just relax. It will all come back to you." Solomon stood and walked over to a dial on the wall. He turned it, and the room filled with music, strong voices of people singing opera. He closed his eyes and leaned back in his chair. It was so soothing, it felt like... like home.

The music filled his ears and his mind, making everything come into focus. The fear and confusion left him and a sense of peace wrapped him like a warm blanket. He thought of his wife and daughter, but this time, he remembered more than just the recent past. Memories buried deep within his subconscious began to surface. Yes, he remembered Solomon.

It felt like a movie in fast-forward. The images of his childhood flipped through his mind, skipping from one event to another, taking him back to a world he'd forgotten. He opened his eyes to see Solomon standing in front of him with a kind smile on his face.

"Welcome home, son."

* * *

MARK SPENT THE EVENING walking through the underground buildings with Solomon, Isis, and the rightfully named Big B as his guides. Solomon was gentle, almost tender. Isis was quiet but obviously taking it all in, not missing a thing. Big B was loud and cheerful in a rather intoxicating way. Mark laughed at his jokes and fought to remain upright each time the giant man pounded his back.

The Merc Building served as a physical home for WJA, and a media company was the front organization that the agency used to cloak its activities. The Merc was the ops base for most of their field agents. The front organization allowed their operatives to penetrate otherwise inaccessible areas, such as the Middle East, and even other areas where nothing but traditional press credentials would do.

He was astounded by the maze of training rooms, which provided everything from hand-to-hand combat to classes on reading satellite maps to French, Chinese and ancient Greek language instruction. The organization appeared to be far from a group of hell-bent assassins who traveled the world dealing out revenge. They were trained and organized in a way that made the CIA and the FBI look like a bunch of schoolyard kids playing hide and seek.

Mark learned that there were four classifications of assassins. The first was the *Avenger Class.* This group was comprised of people who came to the organization through some sort of family crisis. Like Mark, their families were killed or somehow taken from them. They were enlisted to avenge someone or something. Trained to take on the deadliest missions, they jumped when no one else would. They had nothing to lose.

The second was the *Co-op Class*. These agents were trained in highly sensitive missions that involved stealth and agility. Most of these killers were women, due to their ability to blend in. Isis, Mark learned, was a CC assassin. Their missions involved chemical warfare and had to be carried out with absolute accuracy and discretion.

The third was the *D Class*. Those agents were trained in all aspects of explosives and heavy weapons. They were called in when the WJA got involved in a combat operation and in situations where multiple targets or buildings were to be eliminated.

Then, there was a fourth and very rare classification. Only a select few advanced to that level. These elite belonged to the *Sniper Class*. Highly trained snipers, they were also schooled in the curriculum of the three other classes, including hand-to-hand combat. The SC class could only be held by a born assassin, one who was brought up by the WJA and trained from birth.

Mark rubbed his forehead. That was it. He was a trained assassin. The thought made him cringe, but as his past came flooding back, he knew deep down that was what he'd been born to do.

They walked through the main command center, where people scurried from one place to another. Screens were lit throughout the room.

Solomon swept his hand over the scene. "Each person in this room is responsible for a single operative. They are making sure the people in the field have everything they need. Plus, they monitor their progress." He turned to Mark. "You've been awfully quiet. Any questions."

"Why is it I don't remember all the training I supposedly

had as a child? I remember bits and pieces, like maybe some martial arts, but not everything." The memories were jumbled and seemed to come in slow bursts.

"We use a process that buries the information deep within a child's subconscious. It was taught to you before you could even talk. The mind before the age of three years of age is like a sponge. We simply programmed the information into you using a machine I created. I'll show you."

They followed a walkway that wound its way around the command center. It ran next to the wall, about forty feet in the air, and was suspended from the ceiling by large cables. Along the way, they passed five doors—all closed—with no windows through which he could peek. When they reached the last door, Solomon opened it, and they went inside.

The room was dimly lit, but from there, they could see into a second room through one of the large, rounded windows on the south wall. It appeared to be a small computer room with three men in head-to-toe medical suits working at a machine.

Mark could see a small chair apparatus suspended from the ceiling like a giant robot's hook. It had a rounded bottom with a soft, padded lining and a pillow at the top. Round pads dangled from it like spider legs.

"We have one of my children here now." Solomon pointed to a woman dressed in ordinary clothing holding what looked to be maybe a five-month-old baby. She held the sleeping child close to her body and looked down at it with love. He could tell she cared deeply for the baby.

After the child was put in the bed, the woman placed small electronic pads on the baby's feet, then pulled down a clear plastic top and locked it in place.

After everything was set, the men at the computers began to work.

"What are you going to do?" Mark asked. He felt a little sick and for a brief second wondered if he was about to witness some sort of evil sacrifice or a mad-scientist moment where the crazy old man yelled for Igor to "pull the switch."

"Don't worry. We won't hurt him. Just watch."

The baby woke and looked around, content as could be, as if in a baby swing. The clear plastic top apparently acted like a computer monitor, flashing images so fast Mark couldn't tell what the pictures were. He watched the baby, expecting it to cry out in fear, but he—or was it she?—just sucked his thumb and watched the images with an indifferent expression on his face.

"What's happening?"

"Right now, that child is learning everything there is to know about hand-to-hand combat. When the image is beamed through the electronic pulse, it sends a signal to his brain and makes a muscle memory of it. So his brain retains the information, and the baby's brain thinks it is actually performing the actions, like taking apart a weapon or pulling the trigger and so on." Solomon's voice grew excited as he talked.

"Does it hurt him?"

"No, no. Everything's on a subconscious level, so the baby is just sleeping or watching the screen and will not remember anything. And the best part is, if the child grows up and doesn't want to be a part of the WJA, they won't have any memory of it."

"How is that possible? I mean, I remember some things about this place."

"Yes, but you only remember me, or maybe a room, or when we played catch in a park. You remember places, people and experiences but not any of your training. It will only come to you when you need it. And with practice, you'll be able to turn it on and off at will."

Mark gaped at him.

"You don't believe me?"

The next instant, he felt the cold steel of a knife blade on his throat. Before he could even think, he grabbed the back of the knife with his hand and twisted it downward as he dropped to one knee. As the attacker was thrown off balance. Mark flipped around, and in one swift movement, threw the attacker to the floor and straddled him, holding the knife to his throat.

"Hold on!" Big B yelled. He touched Mark's shoulder. "It was just a test. Don't kill him, buddy."

Mark looked up at Solomon, who was laughing, and released his attacker, who got up and pulled off his ski mask. He was one of the men who had been standing at the first checkpoint on the way in. He offered Mark a nod and walked away.

"So, Mark, how did you know how to do that?" Solomon asked. "Have you ever had any training or experience with someone holding a knife to your throat?"

Mark thought a moment. "I don't know. I just reacted with my instincts."

"Exactly. That is what we do here, in this lab. We create instincts. You don't remember them until you need them."

Mark folded his arms and thought about the explosion and the men at the cabin. He'd done what felt natural. He'd known what to do, how to talk, what to say—and how to keep the situation in his control, as if he'd done it a thousand times.

"Oh, and one more thing," Solomon said. "All the children in this program are either orphans or children of current employees. We make sure the orphans are placed in good foster care at around age eleven. All the employees' children are free to come in for training and go home afterward, if they like. Anyone who lives here is cared for and assigned to a current family already in the program."

"So I was in the orphan program?"

"Yes, and that older man you saw on the way in was your caregiver. He and his wife tried to give you as normal a life as possible. They loved you very much."

"I thought he looked familiar. Mr. Able, right?"

"Yes. His wife passed last year, but he's still here with us." He patted Mark's shoulder. "Big B will take you upstairs to get checked in and run through all the rules and legal information. I'll see you later tonight, after dinner, and will try to ease your mind over a drink."

Big B walked Mark back to the main lobby area. Mark glanced back as they entered the elevator. If this was a wild dream, he didn't know whether he wanted to wake up or not.

CHAPTER EIGHTEEN

"CASSY, WHERE'S THIS JENKINS guy?" Kirk glared at her, his fists balled. He was frustrated and tired, but most of all, he was a sore loser. The meeting with Meskhenet was a bust, and now he found himself back in Cassy's office.

"Jenkins? Why? Do you think—"

"Is he here? I need to talk to him."

"He's running some errands and won't be back until late, but I'll give you his home address and phone number." She checked her computer records, wrote down the information, and handed it to him. "Just for the record, Detective, he's clean."

"I'll be the judge of that." He took the note and turned to leave.

"What got you all grumpy? You hit a dead end with the woman?"

He rolled his eyes. "You could say that. We have nothing but a witness who seems to be invisible. The other one has an airtight alibi." Kirk ran his hand over his smooth head and cursed. "And all I have is a fuzzy picture with no fingerprints or any witnesses."

"Didn't you shoot your last witness?" Cassy's voice had a glint of steel in it. She shot a tight look at Kirk then broke into a cheerful *I'm just joking* smile.

He could tell she meant to sting his ego. "Fine. I'll be taking my depressing mood elsewhere." He knew she was being flirtatious, but he didn't care. This whole thing stunk to high heaven. He knew it and they knew it, but someone was covering it up.

"Glad I could help." Cassy giggled, which irritated him even further. He marched out of her office, not bothering to respond when she yelled, "Next time, a thank-you would be nice!"

He opened the Mustang door and dropped into the seat.

Geoff was staring at his laptop, like always. Didn't even look up.

"In case you're interested, we got an address." Kirk pounded the dash. "It better lead us somewhere worthwhile, or I might just shoot someone. This is our last real lead, so you might want to cross your fingers. If it's a dead end, it'll shut us down."

Geoff typed the address into his laptop. "We're about ten minutes from this location. Do you want to go tonight or in the morning?"

Kirk looked at his watch. Almost ten. "Let's pay him a little visit. I won't be able to sleep, if we don't. Besides, he's sure to be home at this hour."

As they pulled onto the busy street, Kirk had an uneasy feeling someone was watching them. He looked at the headlights in the rearview mirror. The car was almost on top of the Mustang's rear bumper. From the classic dark Ford sedan, he knew it had to be his friends from down at the station—or worse, the feds.

"We have company." He spoke in a voice barely above a whisper, as if the occupants of the other car might hear him.

Geoff started to turn around, but Kirk backhanded his chest. "Don't look, you numbskull. Just keep an eye on the car in your side mirror."

"Sorry, man," Geoff muttered as he rubbed his chest. "I'm a

little new to this detective thing."

Kirk switched lanes to see if the tailing car would follow, and it did. He sighed and parked in front of a doughnut shop. "Hey, you want a coffee or something?"

"Yeah. I'll take a bottled water and a plain bagel, no cream cheese."

Kirk rolled his eyes and got out of the car. He walked into the shop muttering, *"Only sissies drink bottled water."* At the counter, he peeked through the window to see if the boys in blue were following.

Just as he suspected, they had pulled in a few cars down and turned off their headlights. After getting a twenty-ounce black coffee and a coconut-covered doughnut he asked the man behind the counter where the back door was.

"Right there." The clerk pointed to a door down the hall just beyond the bathrooms.

Kirk grabbed his items, tossed the man a twenty-dollar bill, and ambled out the back door. Making his way to the rear of the building and circling around, he came up behind the Crown Victoria. He set the coffee and doughnut down on a nearby newsstand.

Ducking down, he pulled out his forty-five, crawled beneath the driver's side window, and took a deep breath. The next instant, he jumped up, smashed the glass of the driver's window and pointed the gun at the stunned man's temple.

The man jerked back as glass hit him in the face, showered across his body, and landed in the lap of his passenger. "Hey! What—?" He reached into his jacket to draw his weapon but stopped short when Kirk shoved his pistol against his head.

"Easy, pal," Kirk said. "Don't do anything you'll regret. I've got an itchy trigger finger, so move nice and easy. Place your guns on the dashboard, and no funny business, or I might slip and make a mess of your faces." He motioned to the man sitting in the passenger seat, his belly hanging over the seat belt.

The two men slowly took out their handguns and placed

them on the dash. The man in the driver's seat was thinner than his partner, but not by much. He grimaced, his lips disappearing into a thin line. His face was flushed. Kirk knew he was furious as well as embarrassed that a washed out cop got the drop on them.

"Now, hand them over nice and easy-like."

As soon as he had their side arms, he brushed aside glass and leaned into the window. "So, what are you boys doing tailing me?"

"We're FBI. If you know what's good for you—"

"What's good for me is you two to stay off my bumper, unless you want it shoved down your throats."

"You'd better watch yourself, Detective," the guy in the passenger seat said. "And drop this case or—"

"Or what?" Kirk demanded. "What, pray tell, do you think you're going to do to me? Run to your daddy and tattle on me?"

He pulled a knife from his pocket and slashed the front tire. It deflated with a loud hissing sound. The two feds yelled, but were quieted with a wave of Kirk's gun.

"You two sit tight, and I'll be on my way. Next time, I won't be so nice." He grinned, showing them all of his teeth. The driver managed to turn an even brighter shade of red. Kirk laughed in his face, daring him with his eyes to try something.

Walking back to the newsstand, he grabbed his coffee and doughnut and returned to his car.

"You okay?" Geoff asked.

"Yup," Kirk sipped his coffee. "Had some business to tend to."

"Where's my water and bagel?"

Kirk hit his forehead with his palm. "Right, water—uh, want a doughnut?"

* * *

MARIA WAS WORRIED. NEITHER she nor anyone else had heard from Mark in days. She tried to be cheerful at the office, but it was hard when her anxiety level increased exponentially

with each day he didn't show up at the office or call her or
Hank or Bert—or someone she knew.

She'd tried calling his cell phone several times, but every
time, she got his voice mail.

Watching but not seeing the game show on television, she
sipped a cup of herbal tea and tried to believe he was okay. But,
where was he? Why hadn't he called her back?

The more she thought about his disappearance, the sicker
she felt inside. Christmas without his family had been hard for
him, but he seemed to cheer up with her there. They'd had a
wonderful time. At least that's how she thought the weekend
went. But maybe his loss had finally gotten to him. And
he'd… She didn't dare think about what he might have done to
himself.

Picking up her cell phone, she dialed his number again and
listened as it rang—and rang.

* * *

MARK SAT IN FRONT of the warm fire staring at the flames.
Solomon's office was a comfortable place, much like his own
living room. The firelight flickered on the dark bookcases and
reflected off Isis's black hair. The four had talked into the early
morning hours, the others filling Mark in on his past as well as
the wonders of WJA.

Solomon was a wonderful host. He made them any drink
they could dream up. Beautiful Isis talked in smooth, soothing
tones that would have lulled him to sleep, if she hadn't been
so interesting. Big B could wake the dead with his laugh and
his energetic presence. Mark found himself bonding to the big
guy as if they were long lost brothers. But as he sipped his iced
coconut mocha and looked around at his new friends, he still
wasn't sure yet what to think of it all.

The orientation had taken just over two hours. It included
a new driver's license and ID that couldn't be traced, plus a
fingerprint laser transference, which was, amazingly enough,
painless. The new credit card was what he liked the most
and what he was to use for any and all transactions. It was

untraceable. The money came directly from the WJA, not through any bank, and routed through hundreds of cities to throw off the scent, if needed.

His credit card bills and student loans had been paid off with a simple phone call. Everything that made him Mark Appleton was placed into a vault in the lower security room. His name stayed the same, but any past records, including his Social Security number, were erased. On paper, he no longer existed. No birth certificate, no traceable fingerprints, no identity. Everything old was replaced with the new, which indicated he worked for *Global Advisor* as a consultant.

He thought about how he was going to break the news to Hank that he'd found another job. It would be hard, but he knew Hank would understand. Then he thought about Maria. They had grown close, but he had to commit himself full-time to the project. Would she would accept a friend who could never tell her where he was or what he was doing? Mark took another sip of the coconut mocha and smiled. He could change who he was to a point, but he'd always love his mochas.

He didn't return to his apartment until late and crashed onto his bed fully dressed. For the first time since his K and Samantha's deaths, he slept undisturbed.

When he awoke, he rolled onto his back, wondering if the morning would bring more amazing experiences or something from a horror novel. Opening his eyes, he gazed at the ceiling, trying to get his brain to wake up. A beep from his cell phone brought him into reality. He pushed the past few days from his mind.

Rolling out of his bed, he shuffled into the living room and picked up his phone.

"Hey, Mark, just wondering if you want to do anything tonight. I'll call you later." Maria.

He hit the *next* button.

"Mark, just wondering where you are—"

She sounded more urgent with each message. One was from Hank, who was wondering if he was going to come into work this week. He said with the New Year coming up, that he could take the next week off as well, if he needed it.

He dialed his office, hoping Maria would answer. When he heard her sweet voice, his heart jumped into his throat.

"S-E-D, how can I help you?"

"Hey, kiddo."

"Mark! Where have you been? I've been worried sick!"

"I'm so sorry I didn't call. I had to go to a long meeting and got tied up."

"It's been three days, Mark. I thought you might have gone off and done something stupid. You were in a funky mood the other night."

"I just had some business to deal with. But it's taken care of now. I need to talk to you about some things. Do you want to go out to dinner tonight?"

"I have to work a little late to get ready for the weekend. If you'll pick me up at eight, I'll be ready."

"Okay, eight it is. Hey, can you get Hank on the line? I need to talk to him, too."

She transferred him to Hank, who seemed pleased to hear his voice. "Hey, bud. You okay?"

"Yeah, I just wanted to see if you could break away for lunch. I'd like to talk to you." He tried not to sound nervous. He loved working at SED, but his life was now headed in a totally different direction.

"Yeah. I'll meet you at Hugo's at eleven."

He pushed the end button. Hank was not only his boss, he was a good friend. It was going to be hard to quit. He hoped Hank would understand.

He jumped into the shower. It was past ten. He would need to leave soon to get to the deli on time. After the shower, he pulled on his favorite pair of blue jeans, then he grabbed his wallet. It felt lighter than normal. He flipped it open and remembered the switch.

Everything personal had been replaced with identification only WJA could track. He pulled out the credit card they'd

given him. He flipped it over and stared at the strip on the back.
It looked just like any other card, but this one had no limit—or
so they said.

He smiled. It was like winning the lottery, but without the
exposure. He wondered if it really was unlimited. Maybe he'd
test the limit later today.

* * *

THE STREET WAS LINED with cars and a few trashcans
rolling in the road. Kirk drove slowly as Geoff read house
numbers. The houses were jammed close together. Almost all
of them were two-stories tall with no yards or privacy. Tall and
skinny, like living on top of each other.

"Next one, I think." Geoff checked the number on an old,
black mailbox. "On the left."

The house was stucco, with concrete steps leading up to
the front door, which was painted blue and needed another
coat. The dirt yard featured a small doghouse with the name
Fluffy stenciled over the opening. The few patches of grass left
indicated the yard had once been green and lush—probably
before Fluffy arrived.

Kirk touched the butt of his gun as he stepped from the
Mustang. He had *that* feeling again, which was never a good
sign. He waited for Geoff to get out of the car and follow him
up the sidewalk to the cracked, peeling, blue door. Through
the half-drawn curtains, he could see a man in a lounge chair
reading a newspaper by lamplight. He knocked and tensed
when he heard movement.

The deadbolt clicked and a chain rattled as the door cracked
open. A middle-aged man peered out. "Yeah?" he barked.
"What do you want?" A quiver hovered beneath his gruffness.

Kirk held up his badge. "Detective Weston, and this is my
partner." He pointed over his shoulder to Geoff. "We just want
to ask you a few questions Mr. Jenkins."

Jenkins sighed and opened the door. He waved them inside,
a frown on his face. He indicated the sofa. "Have a seat. Want
somethin' to drink?"

"No, I'm okay. My partner would like a glass of water, if you've got one." He smirked at Geoff, who rolled his eyes.

"Sure, I'll be right back."

Kirk looked around. The house was decorated with photos of family and simple trinkets that might be found in an old spinster's house. He could see by the photos on the mantle above a white, brick fireplace that Jenkins was married—or at least had been at one time. The morning paper lay open on the coffee table next to a book on criminology.

"Here you go." Jenkins handed Geoff a glass of ice water.

"Thanks." Geoff smiled and took a sip.

"So, what can I do for you, Detective?" Jenkins sat down in his recliner and peered at them through his thick glasses.

"We're trying to get some information on a case you and Cassy Meyers worked on a year or so ago."

"Oh?" Jenkins raised a single eyebrow and settled back in his chair. He folded his hands on his lap.

"The prison, David's Island. I was on that case. I had some new evidence come to my attention recently that made me curious. I was told you delivered the file to the FBI?"

"Yeah, I probably did. Meyers and I work on many cases together. I'm the spokesperson to the FBI. That was a weird case, as far as I remember it." He took off his glasses and started chewing on the earpiece. "I'm not sure, but I think the lead person on that case was a Jacob... uh... yeah, Jacobson."

"Captain Jacobson?" Kirk remembered the tall captain, who so passionately encouraged them to investigate the case his way.

"Yeah, that's the one. I delivered it to him, and I went over everything we found in detail."

Kirk rubbed his chin. That didn't make any sense. Jacobson seemed to know it wasn't an accident from the very beginning.

"Why are you still interested in that case? It's been closed for a while now, hasn't it?"

"It's been reopened. We're just following the evidence. So far, it leads back to Jacobson."

"Well if there's anything you need, just let me know."

Jenkins was a little too helpful for Kirk's liking. "Thanks. We'll get out of your hair." Geoff thanked Jenkins for the water and his help as Kirk got up and headed out the front door.

The moment they got in the car, Kirk asked, "Well, what do you think?"

Geoff scratched his head. "He seemed on the up-and-up, but it is a little fishy that this Captain Jacobson would have anything to do with covering up anything."

"Yeah, I know what you mean. I have a feeling our friend Jenkins is lying to us, that he knows something. Now I have to figure out how to interview Jacobson. The last time I saw him, he kicked me off the case."

Geoff looked out the window. "Why am I not surprised?"

"You." Kirk pointed at Geoff.

"Me?"

"Yeah, you can get an interview for that magazine of yours. You could say you're doing a story on the case."

Geoff nodded. "I guess I could do it."

"There you go."

"No worries. I'll get a story out of this yet."

Kirk laughed. "You deserve it, man. After this is all over, you'll probably have more story than you bargained for."

* * *

JENKINS WATCHED THE DETECTIVE'S car drive away. He put on his glasses and went into the kitchen, where he picked up the phone. He dialed.

The call was answered in two rings. "I told you never to call me at home."

Jenkins tried to calm his shaking voice. "I know, but I just got interviewed by Detective Weston."

The man on the other end went silent.

"I didn't tell him anything he didn't already know. He wanted to know who was in charge of the investigation. I told him Jacobson."

"Good. Now, you stay out of this, or you can kiss your

pretty little wife goodbye." The gruff voice gargled and coughed as if he had a bad cold. Jenkins was glad his contact was on the other end of the phone, not standing in his kitchen.

"I won't say anything. I was just a delivery guy."

"I'll take care of Weston. You make that file disappear on your end, you hear? I don't want anyone else poking their nose into this."

"I'll take care of it." Hanging up the phone, Jenkins hiked the stairs to the bedroom. His wife was asleep with the lamp on the nightstand still on. He leaned over, kissed her on the cheek, and stopped to look at her as she slept before he clicked off the lamp.

Grabbing his car keys, he hurried downstairs and out the back door. He needed to get that file from Meyers' office. His old Ford Escort smoked and sputtered when he started it. It didn't like the cold weather any more than he did. He opened his glove box and pulled out his service revolver, checking it to make sure it was loaded. He set it on the seat next to him and pulled into the vacant street.

The parking lot was dark and empty, which gave him a creepy feeling of being watched. The back door was locked and had a sign reading *Under Video Surveillance*. He knew where the camera was and pulled his hood over his head as he made his way across the icy asphalt.

He unlocked the back door and went down the hall toward Cassy's office. Her door was locked, but he had a key and was in without any trouble. Muttering, he flipped through her file cabinet. "Not here."

He took off his glasses and looked around the dark office littered with pictures and papers. There, on the desk.

He recognized it right away. The file was open, sitting out on the desk like a mocking, staring judge, looking at him with sharp, knowing eyes. He unzipped his coat and slid the folder inside, then zipped his coat over it and shut the file drawer.

In the hallway, he turned to lock the office and hurry down the hall to the back entrance, where he pulled his hood over his head and relocked the outer door. He held the file tight against his side, under his coat, and hurried across the frozen parking lot. He drove back toward his house wondering why he'd done what he'd done. He never thought he'd be mixed up in something like this, but he needed the money. However, he was beginning to think it wasn't worth the stress, no matter how far in debt they were. He could have saved and paid it all off. But the easy way out had looked so good. Now it was turning on him, like a snake lusting for his blood as well as repayment. He took a breath and told himself to stop worrying. It would all be over soon.

His car was still cold when he parked it in the alley behind their little house. The stupid heater would only work when it felt like it. He sat in the dark, shivering, trying to think. Should he get rid of the file? Or keep it? He might need it, just in case things got bad.

Walking up the stairs to his bedroom, he ducked into the closet and opened a small safe that sat on the floor in the back under a box of Christmas wrapping paper. He placed the file inside, closed the safe, undressed and quietly got into bed, being careful not to disturb his wife.

He stared at the ceiling, trying not to think about everything that had happened. Nevertheless, his mind would not let him rest. He could feel dark eyes staring at him, waiting...waiting for his soul.

CHAPTER NINETEEN

"MARK, IT'S GOOD TO see you!" Hank shook Mark's hand
and pointed to a nearby table. Hugo's Deli was family owned
and operated. Though the place looked as if it was about to
fall in on itself, the food was famous and delicious. He'd eaten
lunch here many times with his boss and friend. It made Mark
a little sad to know this was probably their last time to eat
lunch together.

"Hi, Hank." Mark sat down and looked around. The deli
was small, with only six round tables, all of which were filled.
The waitress brought them two glasses of water and a menu.
He picked up the menu but didn't see the words.

"So what's been going on, Mark? You haven't called in for
days. We've all been worried about you." Hank took a sip of
water, then took off his long, gray trench coat and draped it on
the chair next to him.

"Sorry. I've been a little preoccupied lately. Actually, for
the last year, I suppose. That's what I wanted to talk to you
about." He took a breath and placed his hands on the table.
The only way to do this was head-on and fast, or he'd lose his
nerve. "Hank, you're a great boss and an even better friend."

Hank's forehead creased. "I don't like where I think this
is going." He leaned back in his chair. "I know you've gone

through a lot this last year, but just hang in there. It'll be better. These things take time to heal."

Mark looked at the menu again and tried to focus on what he knew he had to do. "I know, and I'm thankful for all the help you've been to me. But I need a change. I need to regroup and start my life over."

The waitress came to take their orders. He didn't feel hungry, but he ordered a club sandwich anyway. "I'm taking another job. I'll be traveling a lot and might even relocate." He sat back. "I know it's hard to understand, but this is something I have to do."

Hank leaned on his elbows and stared out the window. His silence was unnerving. Finally, he turned back. "You've been there for me every time I needed you, Mark. If this is what you feel you need to do, then I support you in it. Just don't go crazy on me and do something stupid, okay?"

Mark smiled, thinking about the cabin and the last few days touring the Merc Building and the secret WJA city underneath. Hank didn't know how close he was to the truth. "I'll be okay. I just need new scenery, fresh air, and a place where I don't have to fight off old memories, if you know what I mean."

Hank nodded. "So what is this new job? Are you going over to the enemy?" He laughed.

"No, nothing like that. It's somewhat of a government-type of job. I'm not too sure of what it all entails, but I think I'll like it."

The food looked great and suddenly he found that he was hungry—very hungry. As they ate, he looked around the room and, for the first time, noticed a woman in the back reading a newspaper. A second look told him it was Isis. He nodded. She smiled and got up, leaving a tip on the table.

"Hank, excuse me for a minute, I need to hit the men's room. I'll be right back."

He headed toward the back of the deli. Isis's table was the last one before the hall to the restrooms. He saw a folded piece of paper sitting on top of the tip and slipped it into his pocket as he walked by.

Closing the restroom door, he locked it and took out the note, which only had three words: *Answer the phone.* He heard a phone ringing in one of the stalls behind him and opened the door. A slim, black cell phone sat on the top of tank. He flipped it open. "Yes?" He smiled as he heard Isis on the other end.

"Sorry for the runaround, but I needed to talk to you in private."

"No problem. What is it?'

"We have a case for you, and we need to meet. One hour, at the bookstore on Second Avenue."

"I'll be there."

Slipping the phone into his pocket, he threw the note into the toilet and flushed it. Back at the table, he bit into his club sandwich and sighed as the sweet juices mixed and tingled his taste buds.

Hank talked about the new high-rise SED was putting in a few blocks away. He'd begun talks with Trump Enterprises and it looked like they might reach a deal.

Mark listened attentively. He liked working for SED. The people were great, the work was interesting. The whole experience was something he wouldn't trade for the world. He was going to miss it, but at the same time, he was excited to begin this new chapter in his life—to see what his future held, and to learn more about his past.

He handed the keys to the BMW to Hank before he paid for the meal. Hank protested, but Mark insisted, saying he had a company car. As they parted, he held out his hand and thanked Hank for everything.

But Hank pulled him close. "Come on, man. Friends hug." Then he shoved him away. "Now get off me, I've got work to do."

Mark laughed and said he'd keep in touch.

Hank headed back to the office, Mark hailed a cab. He told the driver to take him to Second and Seventh. The cabbie nodded and flipped on the meter.

The bookstore was almost empty. Mark wandered over to the fiction section and flipped through a Stephen King book.

"So you made it."

Isis was good at sneaking up on people, but this time, he didn't even turn. He could smell her perfume and knew she was close, if not right behind him. "Yeah, books are becoming a thing of the past with the internet and all, but I still love the way they smell and the feel of holding one as you read. Those are sensations you'll never get with a computer."

"True. Are you ready for your first assignment?"

"I guess. I hope it's an easy one. I'm new, you know."

"Yes. The job was handpicked by Solomon himself." She pulled out a small white card from her pocket, handed it to Mark and smiled. "Good luck."

He looked at the card as she walked away, her dark hair swinging. The only notations on the card were the letter M and the number 359. He thought it might be the number on the back of a book in the bookstore. He looked around and found that every book had a letter and a number on the spine, so he searched. After twenty minutes he found one marked M359 And titled, *Systems of Governments and States*. He slid it from the shelf and walked over to a private reading room, where he stepped inside and closed the door. Not very imaginative. Maybe they picked a book that was sure to be shelved because no one would be interested in its contents.

Sitting down at the desk, he opened the book and flipped through the pages. Noticing a bookmark, he turned to the page where it was placed. The heading read *Law and the Government*.

He examined the bookmark and noticed a small earpiece attached to the back of it. Pulling it off, he placed it into his ear and heard the voice of a woman. It wasn't Isis's voice but one much harder, maybe a woman who had been with the organization a long time.

"Welcome to the agency. This is top secret and will only be played once. Pay close attention."

Mark relaxed in his seat and listened.

"The daughter of an important government official in Pakistan has been kidnapped. Her name is Alexis Moritiff. She was taken two weeks ago from her school and is being held in an abandoned office building just outside of Islamabad. Your mission is to extract her by any means necessary and bring her back to the point of origin. You will be instructed upon completion where to take her. You are to immediately go to the shop on the corner of Twenty-Third and Forty-Second, a smoke shop, where you will be given further instructions. You are to meet your contact at eleven p.m. today. Good luck."

He removed the earpiece from his ear and placed it in his pocket, his excitement rising. He was supposed to go half way around the world to rescue a kidnapped girl tonight. Easy assignment, huh? He'd expected it to be a simple look-and-tail job or something like that. But, no, they were sending him to a volatile, war-torn, treacherous place.

Leaving the bookstore, he jumped in a taxi and told the driver to go to the nearest car dealership. He needed a car, and he wanted to make sure that this was all on the up-and-up before he flew across the world trusting his life to the so-called World Justice Agency.

* * *

SOLOMON WAVED ISIS INTO his office. He smiled as she entered. "I want you to keep an eye on Mark on this one. He might need some assistance. Stay back unless he gets in a jam."

"Sure thing. This is a big mission for the first one, don't you think?"

"Yes, but I need to know if he can handle it. We're running out of time. I need him to be fully operational as quickly as possible. He was the first, and we have never seen anyone respond like he did. I believe he will exceed our expectations."

"I'll stay close to him." She opened her cell phone. "Hey, I need my gear ready by eleven, and get me a Taxi to Islamabad."

* * *

KIRK MOANED AND ROLLED over, desperate for a few more minutes of sleep. His head pounded from lack of sleep and too much coffee the night before. He reached for the snooze button on the hotel's radio alarm clock, which was spewing the morning news way too loud for his headache. But his hand froze over the button.

"A local crime scene investigator was found dead in his home this morning. He was shot in the head. His wife was also shot and killed. The NYPD and the FBI have not yet released a statement or the names of the couple."

Kirk jumped up, ran into the next room, and flipped on the TV. "Geoff, get up. We have a problem."

"Bugger!" Geoff, who was sitting on the edge of the bed in the main room, pulled on a pair of cargo pants, wandered over to the couch and sat down.

"This is not good, man." Kirk paced the room in his blue boxers. "First, we're tailed by the feds, then the guy we interview is shot. And the creeps killed his wife, too." He held his head with both hands, trying to think.

"Get your stuff. We're going down there." Kirk hurried back into his room, threw on a pair of blue jeans and a t-shirt that said *Pink Floyd* with a rainbow arching out of a prism on the front. When he walked out, Geoff was waiting, his laptop and camera in hand.

Kirk grabbed his jacket and was about to open the door, when they heard a knock.

Both men jerked and turned toward the door.

"FBI—open up!"

Kirk cursed, took out his forty-five and slowly opened the door. "What do you want?" He'd considered jumping out the window and taking his chances running, but knew that would only make things worse.

"We need to ask you a few questions." The first suit had on a pair of dark sunglasses. His partner was shorter and just as boring. They stood with guns drawn, as if they expected an army on the other side of the door, instead of a sleepy reporter and an ugly Detroit cop.

Kirk holstered his weapon and waved them in. "Come on in." He opened the door wide.

Geoff folded his arms. "We would like to see some identification, please."

Kirk raised an eyebrow but said nothing.

Both agents showed their badges and asked for ID. Kirk flashed his badge. Geoff pulled out his press card.

"Your supervisor informed us you're on suspension. We also have two agents who told us you assaulted them and destroyed government property."

Kirk rolled his eyes. "Come on, guys. You guys were tailing me, and if you think that's assault, then you haven't ever been assaulted."

The first agent stiffened. "You're on thin ice, Detective. I suggest you cooperate."

"Fine, fine. But I have a few questions of my own."

The taller agent pulled out a pad and a pen. "We have you two going into the home of Jefferson Jenkins last night at about ten-thirty."

"Yeah, he was a contact. We interviewed him about an investigation." Kirk had a bad feeling things might get out of control if the agents followed the line of questions they seemed to be on.

"Investigation? But you're suspended. What could you possibly have to talk about with a CSI agent, and what do you mean, *was*? You said he was your contact. How did you know he's dead?"

Geoff jumped in, holding up his hand. "We just heard it on the news. We talked with Mr. Jenkins because I'm doing a story about the prison poisoning last year for my magazine. Detective Weston is assisting me. Mr. Jenkins was one of the agents who handled the case. We talked with him to find out if he remembered anything about the case, which he didn't."

The agent in charge looked at Kirk, then back to Geoff. "So you don't have any idea who shot him and his wife last night?"

"I got an idea," Kirk muttered under his breath.

"You have something to tell us, Detective?" the agent in charge demanded.

"Yeah, I do.' Kirk placed his hands on his belt. "Why are we being tailed? What business is it of yours who we talk to?"

The agent arched an eyebrow. "You're a suspect."

"Suspect to what? You've got nothing on me." Kirk glowered at the agent and envisioned pulling his forty-five and shooting the pompous jerk right between the eyes.

A red flush crept up in the agent's neck toward his ears. "For starters, you killed a key witness to the prison case a year ago. Then you disappeared for a year, only to come back and just about blow our case out of the water with your questioning." The second agent remained alert but didn't say a word.

"What case? I thought you said it was closed! And I was kidnapped and held for a year." Kirk shook his head. "But I bet my crabby old boss didn't tell you. I lived in a cell the size of your bathroom and saw things you could never imagine."

The two agents looked at each other without saying a word.

"I was investigating the prison case when I got too close to the—whatever is going on here." He slammed his fist into his palm. "Then I find out the case was closed and I've got the feds behind me at every corner. You think I wanted to kill my only witness! *He* shot at *me* first and gave me no choice."

The short agent took off his dark glasses. He motioned for Kirk to sit down. "We didn't know you'd been taken. We assumed you fled. Why didn't you report it?"

Kirk remained standing. "I told my captain. He said I could look into the case on my own, as long as he couldn't be tied to what I was doing."

"I see. Well, if you'll come with us, I'd like to get you up to speed on what we've got going on here."

The men ushered Kirk and Geoff to a waiting car. It was the same model of sedan the last two FBI agents had driven, but they were nowhere in sight. On the ride to the FBI building,

Kirk went over and over in his mind everything he could remember about the evidence. He knew there was a mole in the FBI somewhere, so he had to be careful. For all he knew, these two men could be with them, or working for them.

Once they'd parked, checked in and were cleared, the agents led them to a small room with a table in the middle. He sat down in a metal chair and Kirk sat in the one across from the table, sighing and rubbing his head. The second agent took Geoff. Kirk was sure they had him in another room very similar to this one. *Divide and conquer*.

"Okay, this is one-hundred percent top secret," said the agent. "What I'm about to tell you will not leave this room." He waited to get an answer from Kirk.

"I understand."

The agent placed a large file on the table filled with photos and papers. "My name is Agent Goodwin. I'm placing you under my command. You will now be working with the FBI as a liaison. I cleared it with your supervisor, who offered me his sympathy."

Kirk grinned.

"To begin with, we never shut the David's Island case down. We just renamed it *Operation Justice*. As you probably know, David's Island was no accident. But what you may not know is that we're certain a group that calls themselves the World Justice Agency is behind this and many other crimes detailed in this file."

"World Justice Agency—that's what the symbol means. I found their mark everywhere. They're the ones who kidnapped me."

Goodwin's eyebrows lifted. "Interesting." He slid the file to Kirk, who began to flip through it.

Goodwin clasped his hands behind his head. "What we know is this. WJA is highly funded and extremely well-organized. We suspect they have infiltrated every branch of the government, including the NYPD. They consider themselves to be the judge and jury—as they see fit—over wrongs our justice system has missed or not dealt with. In other words, they take the law into their own hands."

Kirk rifled through the photos and papers that filled the file. Murdered rapists and killers, brutalized mafia bosses, corrupt politicians irrevocably damaged by scandalous news leaked to the media. On and on the stories went. Some cases went back twenty years. "As you can see, if WJA is not stopped, they'll change our justice system back to vigilantes and lynch mobs. The FBI has had an elite task force on this group for the last ten years. We believe we know who their leader is, a well-connected multi-billionaire. But we can't prove it. This operation is invisible."

"What are you talking about?" Kirk hefted the heavy file. "You have these photos and case histories."

"Yeah, but every suspect and every person we interview has an airtight alibi, some of them impossible to refute. Credit card receipts and witnesses that place the suspects somewhere else. We don't have a single matching fingerprint. Their covers are always perfect. But that's what is suspicious—they're too perfect."

Kirk could hear the frustration in Goodwin's voice and realized this was personal to him. He sensed he could trust this man. "One thing that still confuses me. Why did they let me go? One day, they just up and let me walk out the door. Why?"

"As far as we can tell, they try not to kill anyone they consider to be innocent. They'll detour a person from finding out who they are but will never kill an innocent. They apparently believe in justice, not murder for revenge."

Kirk nodded. "The guards at David's Island were left alive. Only the guilty were punished." He leaned back in his seat and sighed. "Of course, the million dollar question is, why stop them? They're doing good and making sure they don't hurt innocent people. What's the big deal?"

"Every one of us wants to see bad guys get their day of judgment, but I believe in our legal system. If we let this go, then all over the country vigilantes will spring up. Groups will take the law into their own hands, and the country will tear itself apart. We must stop WJA before the public finds out this is going on."

"So you've been covering their exploits, making their work look like accidents to keep the public in the dark?"

"Yes, and hopefully we'll make the WJA think that we've given up on trying to find them. We need them to think they've won."

Kirk rubbed his chin as he looked through the last of the file. "So, what can I do?"

"You hit on something they didn't like, enough so that they took you out of play for a whole year. We need your help tracking them down. You can continue your investigation with the full help of our task force."

"The first thing we need to find is this mole you've got inside your organization," Kirk said. "We find him, we find the WJA. Trying to track them the usual way won't work. They know every scheme, every place we'll tree them. They even know the sound of our bark. We need to gain their trust. We need to get close to them and take them down from the inside."

"So you'll join us?"

"Only if you let me do it my way. And stay out of my business."

"Done."

Kirk shook his new boss's hand. It was going to be interesting working for the other side. But, hey, maybe he could catch this mole and make him squirm a little. It would bring joy to his heart to see an FBI agent in the hot seat for a change.

CHAPTER TWENTY

"YOU LOOK WONDERFUL, MARIA. And your hair is, as usual, well, uh—unique." Mark stood at the door to Maria's apartment. She wore a dark-brown dress that highlighted her olive skin. She had a messy bun off to one side of her head with two stick-like things crossing through it like swordsmen fighting to the death.

She smiled and grabbed her coat before taking his arm. "I like to mess around with it, but never mind about my hair. It's so good to see you again, and all in one piece."

"Yeah. Sorry again for disappearing on you. It was a crazy time. I just couldn't get away to call you."

"It's okay. You're here now, and that's all that matters." She relaxed her grip on his arm and tried not to show how much she cared for him. With what he'd been through, it could be years before they could have a real relationship.

"I have something to show you." Mark's eyes sparkled.

Maria smiled, happy to see him excited about something.

They stepped out of the elevator and into the dark parking garage, and Mark hit the fob on his keychain, then led her toward the lights that flashed in the corner to a sleek sports car.

She looked at the silver car, then back at Mark. "It is so cute!"

He laughed. "Cute? No way. An Ascari KZ1 is not cute. You can say it's cool, amazing, beautiful... but not cute."

She laughed. "Whatever you say. Take me for a ride in this amazingly beautiful, cool, wonderful car of yours."

He opened the passenger door and helped her get in. As they drove, she tried to ask how he got the car, but Mark hushed her, telling her one day he would tell her the whole story. He winked at her. "But for now, just enjoy the ride."

As Mark drove, Maria checked out the car's interior, playing with every button and light she could find. She giggled when she pushed a button and the monitor for the DVD player flipped out.

"You're having way too much fun with that."

"Well, it's not every day I get to ride in a fancy sports car."

She eyed Mark, wondering if it would be proper to tell him how good he looked in the dark suit with silver pin-striping, red shirt and a matching tie. He looked like he was ready for the red carpet on Oscar night.

Just as she was about to speak, he pulled up to the front door of the restaurant, where they were met by the valet, who took the keys with eager fingers and smiled a huge smile.

Maria grinned. There was one man who was glad he didn't call in sick tonight.

Though she'd never been to *Le Cirque,* she'd read it was an elegant restaurant with an exceptional selection of French food plus a great view of the city. Mark took her arm and escorted her up the stairs and into the restaurant. The waiter showed them to their table, which overlooked downtown New York. The brightly lit skyline glimmered in the evening air, transforming the dirt and grime of the city into a beautiful, sparkling gem.

After the waiter took their orders, Maria leaned toward Mark. "So, Mystery Man, tell me what you've been up to lately."

He looked away for a moment, then back at her. "Well, to sum it up, I think I finally dealt with my past and with the death of my family. It's something I can now put behind me, so I can move on with my life."

Maria straightened. "Wow. With the state you were in the other night, I was wondering if you were going to take off and do something stupid. I'm glad you got away and thought things through."

He looked down at the table. "You're a great friend, Maria. More than a friend, really." His face flushed and he rubbed at an invisible spot on the tablecloth. "I couldn't have gotten through this last year without you." He looked up. "So what do you think of the car?"

"It's a little small for my liking, but if you like it, I guess—"

He laughed. "You're a hard one to impress."

"I'm not really into cars. All I need is something to get me where I want to go and back." She folded her hands and rested her chin on her knuckles. "You said you wanted to talk about something. Is this a good time?"

He tented his fingers together. Eyebrows arched, he asked, "Will you promise you won't get mad?"

"Promise."

He hesitated. Finally, he said, "Okay, I got a new job."

Her heart fell, and she couldn't help but sigh.

He held up his hand. "But, don't worry. It's a good thing. If we're going to be seeing more of each other, then it'll be better if we don't work in the same office."

"Well, if you put it like that." Though she was still disappointed she wouldn't see him every day at the office, she smiled. "Tell me about this job. If the car is any indication, it has good perks."

The waiter appeared again, this time with water and drinks.

After a sip of wine, Maria said, "Well, mister? Are you going to tell me about the job? I'm dying of curiosity."

He sighed and lowered his glass. "This is the hard part. Maria, I don't want to lie to you. I want to be always open and honest with you."

She nodded. "Same with me."

"That poses a problem with my new job. I, uh, you see..." He looked around then took her hands. "Look... do you trust me?"

"Of course I trust you. Why?" She didn't like the way he was hedging.

"I can't tell you what I'll be doing. But I promise you it isn't anything evil. I'll be doing just the opposite."

"But—"

"I know it doesn't make any sense, but this is who I am now, and what I will be in the future. I just want you to know up front what kind of relationship you're getting into."

She looked into his blue eyes and could tell he was telling her the truth, as much as possible. "You could've lied and made up some job that doesn't exist. I appreciate you telling me the truth. I only ask one thing."

"What's that?"

"Please be careful."

"I promise."

* * *

GEOFF SAT OUT IN the waiting area while Kirk talked with the stubby agent. He wasn't surprised that he was taken out of the loop, being a reporter and all. He pulled his phone from his pocket and opened it up. He had a text message from his boss. He opened it and read it. Oh, great. His editor wanted something from him, soon, and he wasn't even close to being ready with a story. He sent a cryptic message back and closed the phone.

He retrieved his laptop from his shoulder bag and logged on to the FBI website. He wanted to look up the director, get any information he could.

The director was Shaun M. Nichols. Next, he opened up a search on Captain Jacobson, trying to see what division he worked with.

Geoff stopped a man who looked like he might know what was going on and asked if he knew Jacobson.

"Captain?"

"Is he here somewhere?" Geoff asked.

"Yeah, his office is on the fifth floor. Just ask for him at the front desk."

"Thanks."

He put away his laptop and slid the bag's strap over his head and onto his shoulder. At the elevator, he hit the up arrow. He should try to get an interview and do something useful while he had inside access to the FBI offices.

The fifth floor was open, with offices around the perimeter of the building and a center area filled with cubicles. The woman at the front counter asked him how she could help him.

He stood tall and tried to keep his voice firm, in spite of his nerves. "My name is Geoff Martin. I'm with *World Magazine International*. I'd like to speak with Captain Jacobson, if I could."

"Do you have an appointment?" She didn't wait for him to answer. "No, I didn't think so. Tell you what—you leave me your card, and I'll have him call you, okay?"

Geoff could tell he wouldn't get any further, so he took out a business card and handed it to her.

"Can you tell him it's about his special task force?"

She nodded, put on her glasses, and went back to typing on her keyboard.

He took the elevator back down to the main floor and waited for Kirk to finish his meeting.

* * *

AFTER COVERING EVERY ASPECT of the operation they could think of, Kirk got up, shook Agent Goodwin's hand, and started to leave.

"Oh, before you leave, what's the story with your reporter friend?"

"He's cool. He knows almost everything about the case involving the prison. I left out some parts about my kidnapping, since they're a bit unbelievable."

"Don't let him in on too much. The last thing we need is for this to get out to the media."

"No problem. He knows I'll kill him if he tries to cross me."

The agent laughed, then saw the look on Kirk's face. "Okay, then, uh, you need anything, just ask."

"One more question. What can you tell me about Captain Jacobson?"

"He's the lead man on this task force and handles all the sensitive matters as far as the cover-ups go. He's the one who started the operation ten years ago."

"I'm just curious as to why Jacobson was given the file from Jenkins. Then after we talked to Jenkins, he ends up dead."

"We're looking into it, but I can assure you Jacobsen had nothing to do with the Jenkins' death. The file was doctored to try to preserve the operation and keep a low profile."

Kirk found Geoff in the waiting area typing away on his laptop, as usual.

"Hey, how'd it go?" Geoff asked.

"Good. I got new information that changes everything. First, I want to go out to the Jenkins place to see what's up."

The second agent who had brought them walked by just then. "I'm going out there now. You two can ride along if you like."

Geoff squinted at him. "Really?" He turned to Kirk for an explanation.

But all Kirk said was, "Great, it'll save us a cab."

* * *

MARIA WAS WATCHING FROM her second story window as Mark drove away. He waved and smiled. She was a wonderful friend and person. He just hoped he could keep her in his life. At this point, he wasn't sure of tomorrow, let alone what was going to happen next week or next year.

He made his way to the smoke shop he'd been told to visit and pulled up to the curb in front of the store. He looked around. This side of town was dingy, and if a guy didn't keep

his wits, he would be a prime target for a mugging or worse.
All of a sudden his shiny new sports car felt like a trouble
magnet.

As he opened the shop door, he heard a tiny bell bang
against the glass. The place was dim, almost dark, and filled
with choking smoke.

The solitary customer was looking at cigars. A grey-haired
man stood behind an old-style till with a short, fat stogie
hanging from off the side of his mouth.

"Can I help you?" he grunted, as if it he was a bit annoyed
by Mark's presence.

"I'm here to meet someone. Uh, I was told to be here at
eleven." He glanced at his watch and saw it was eleven, right
on the nose.

"You Mark?"

"Yeah."

"Take your car around the side, in the alley, and Mario
will tell you where to go." He puffed a thick cloud of smoke
into Mark's face before turning back to the television that sat
behind the counter.

Mark drove behind the shop and down a dark alley. A short,
heavy man wearing a beanie on his head, a scarf around his
neck and an expensive trench coat stepped out from a dirty
doorway and held up his hand.

Mark rolled down his window, and Mario leaned in. "I see
you got yourself a new ride. Nice. All the newbie's buy top of
the line." He laughed and held out his hand. "I'm Mario."

"Yeah, thought I would see who I was dealing with, you
know?"

"You'll take it back before you know it. You've got no idea,
pal. You ready?" He looked at Mark, a knowing smirk on his
face.

Mark nodded and looked as confident as he could, even
though he was terrified.

"Hold on to your hat—here we go."

Mario pulled what looked like a cell phone from his coat

pocket and hit a button. The ground shook, then opened into a huge, gaping hole with a ramp leading downward.

Mario pointed toward the hole. "Just find a spot and meet me at the office inside."

Mark drove down the ramp, which led to what looked like a lighted parking garage.

He aimed for a door in the corner of the underground parking garage and parked next to a red Porsche 911. He looked a few rows down to see an Aston Martin sitting sideways, filling up two spaces. He shook his head. That's how those sports car owners were—always worried about dents and scratches. Not that he was any different.

He followed Mario into the small, simple office. Several computers sat on a counter on one wall, but that was all, other than chairs. Mario took off his coat and led Mark through another door, which opened to a room that had a familiar look about it. This was definitely a WJA operation. Between the gadgets and gauges and the wall with a large glass case, it looked like something in a science fiction movie. Hanging in a row in the case were what looked like wet suits.

"You've been briefed," said Mario. "I'll go over the details. First thing is, you'll find your weapons and equipment at the safe house. If you have any questions on how to use them or what to do, you can access the mainframe computer in any safe house. They're all voice-activated. Watch this."

Mario put his hand on a wall sensor. After it apparently scanned his fingerprints, a screen came down from the ceiling. Once it was in place, the screen flashed on, and a voice welcomed him, asking what it could do for him.

"I need information on suiting up for the Taxi," Mario said with his Italian accent.

The droning electronic voice seemed to come from everywhere yet nowhere. "The suit is located inside the glass case and will mold to your exact dimensions and body density." The computer went on to explain how to operate the Taxi and the importance of using it correctly. The female-sounding voice was calm and devoid of emotion.

"Cool," Mark said. "So the Taxi is how I'm getting to Pakistan?"

"Bingo. The Taxi, as we call it, is a device that connects our safe houses by a series of sealed, underground tubes controlled from the main station you see in front of you."

He pointed to a control panel mounted to the wall. "It has settings for the place you want to go and the time you want it to get you there. A list of cities and safe houses will come up, like so." He punched in Pakistan, and five cities appeared on the screen. He highlighted Islamabad. With an audible click, the computer locked the location in place.

"It's around ten in the morning in Pakistan, so you'll need to get there as soon as you can. We'll set it at top speed."

"How fast is that?"

"Uh, you really don't want to know, pal." He chuckled and went on. "Next, you punch in your weight and height. I'd say you are just under six-feet tall and, what, a buck eighty-five?"

"One eighty. Why do they need all this information?"

Mario tried to explain without going into too much detail.

Mark grabbed a chair and sat down, striving to take in everything he'd just heard. "So, it's like a bank with the tubes and the canisters. And I'm the sucker inside the canister." A sucker in more ways than one...

"The suction picks the capsule up and sends it to the bank teller. It's like that, but much bigger and far more involved, right? It's an underground network based in just about every country, leading to multiple stations called safe houses."

Mario nodded.

Mark shook his head. "You can't be serious." But, from the look on his new friend's face, he could tell he wasn't joking.

Mario hit a key on the keypad, and part of the wall opened up with a grinding sound, revealing a round, metal, pill-looking machine.

Mark got up to take a closer look. It had a small, glass window on the top. Apparently, he would lie on his back. The lid opened from the side, like a clam. The interior looked like was made of a soft gel. He noticed it had a five-point harness, probably to keep passengers from shifting as they shot through the bowels of the earth.

"So I put on this suit, and then I get inside this thing and strap in?"

"Yup. When you close the top, a nontoxic sleeping gas will fill the capsule and put you to sleep. Believe me—you don't want to be awake for the ride."

"I see. And when I arrive at my destination, the capsule will send in fresh oxygen to wake me up, right?"

"Yup. You'll be fine. You might feel a little sick for an hour or so, but you'll get used to it." The little man giggled. "The first time is always the hardest." His slick black hair bounced out of place and he pulled a black comb from his pants pocket to run through his shiny helmet.

"And the suit. What does it do again?"

"It stimulates your blood by pumping your muscular system to keep the fluids flowing evenly. You'll be experiencing a whole lot of Gs."

"So, without the suit?"

"Well, let's just say… it'd be messy."

"Ah."

"When you arrive on the other side, you'll be met by your spotter. He'll get you lined up and ready to go. If you've got questions, he'll answer them. Okay?"

Mark nodded, stripped down, and pulled on the suit. It was soft, except for the cables and lumps from the small pumps imbedded in the fabric. He zipped it up and pulled the hood-like piece over his head. Now he knew what Spiderman must have felt like. He could barely move as the fabric suctioned tight against his body.

"You ready?"

"No time like the present."

Mario helped him into the small capsule and hooked him in, making sure the straps were tight. Before he closed the lid,

Mario wished him luck with a thumbs-up. Mark looked out the little window as Mario pushed him into the round tube, which encased his little projectile body like Spandex.

He heard a beep just before the same mellow, female voice filled his confined space, counting down from ten. The wall went back into place and Mario disappeared from view. A final thump made it feel like he'd just entered his own casket.

"Nine."

The sound of rushing air could be felt as the seal was sucked against the lid, making a *snap* as it locked into place.

"Eight."

Mark's heart raced as he imagined himself shooting beneath the surface of the earth and traveling under the ocean. Regret teased his mind. Part of him wanted to scream for Mario to let him out.

"Seven."

Tiny pumps began to massage his body. Now it wasn't so bad. He could use one of these at home. It felt like a Swedish massage, but as the pressure increased, the sensation was more like a python squeezing him to death.

"Six."

The sound of rushing air grew louder; he could feel the force of it compressing as it hit the tiny vessel. The air at the foot was pulling, and the air at the top was pushing–yet the machine stood still.

"Five."

He heard the hiss of gas. It smelled like vanilla and strawberries. Mmmm. The final numbers rang in his ears.

"Four...three..."

CHAPTER TWENTY-ONE

KIRK LOOKED AT THE two bodies that lay in the queen bed. He nodded to the coroners—who nodded back. They were thinking the same thing. This was the calculated work of a professional.

Jenkins lay on his stomach, a single gunshot hole on the back of the head. His pillow was soaked with blood, and bits of his skull were embedded in the pillowcase.

His wife was on her back, a horrified look on her face, staring with wide, lifeless eyes at the ceiling fan that spun in lazy circles above them. She must have awakened when her husband was shot, just in time to see the killer standing over her. She had probably been killed before she could even let out a scream.

The CSI agents took pictures of their coworker and dusted for fingerprints. They powdered everything, even though Kirk knew and they must have known they wouldn't find the slightest careless fingerprint or casing. The room was just as it should be. Other than the bodies lying in pools of tacky, gelling blood, nothing was out of place.

Kirk rummaged through the closet, touching the suits and dresses. The owners would never wear them again, unless one was suitable for a funeral. His foot hit something hard, and he bent over to get a closer look. It was a small metal safe, similar to those found in hotels, where guests kept personal items.

He motioned for Geoff to help him move the heavy box. "Know anything about getting into one of these?"

"I think I can do it," Geoff said.

Kirk didn't show any surprise at this bit of news. He was getting used to the idea that his friend had many hidden talents.

Kirk snickered. "I s'pose you're gonna tell me you were a locksmith in high school."

"No. Just a bad kid—you know, cars and the occasional quickie mart. My dad put a stop to it as soon as he found out. No worries, though. I'm retired now." He gave Kirk a half grin.

Kirk watched as he leaned down, put his ear to the small safe, and slowly turned the dial. In a few minutes, it was open. Geoff sat up and shrugged. "It's a simple safe lock. Anyone could do it."

Kirk smiled. "Thanks. Just remind me not to leave my wallet around your sticky little fingers." Inside the safe, they found a file, a few savings bonds, and a clip from a service revolver; however, the gun was missing. Kirk scanned the file, then shoved it in his coat and called one of the investigators over to look at the safe. He couldn't wait to get out of the house to look at the file.

A thin woman wearing a blue CSI ball cap came over to their side of the bed and stooped down to look at the open safe. She began dusting for prints. He decided now would be a good time to leave, before the questions started coming.

"Let's get out of here." He strode out the front door, Geoff right behind him. Something else was going on, something other than WJA. He knew from the file the FBI gave him that the WJA people would not kill an innocent man, let alone his wife.

"What was in that file?" Geoff asked.

"You're not going to believe it. It's the David's Island file from Cassy's office, the only file left outside of what the FBI has."

Geoff raised an eyebrow. He turned to look at Jenkins's house, which was now crawling with FBI and NYPD. Two officers were taping off the crime scene with bright yellow tape. "What are you thinking?"

Kirk looked at Geoff as he called a taxi. "I think we have a mastermind who is hiring hit men to do his dirty work, who works for the FBI, or worse, the CIA. He wants this to look like it was done by the WJA group, but maybe he has other plans as well."

A yellow taxi pulled up about ten minutes later and parked at the curb. Kirk told the driver to take them to the hotel. He needed to get a hold of Mooch for some more unconventional computer work. The FBI mole was getting on his nerves, and he was itching for the kill.

Even if it killed him.

* * *

MARK BOLTED UP OUT of a deep sleep, sweat dripping from his forehead and neck. His heart felt like it was going to burst through his ribs. He looked around, trying to see in the dark. He had a bad feeling in the back of his mind that something was wrong. Did the Taxi crash and kill him? Was he still asleep and just dreaming?

Then he smelled the faint, sweet scent of K's perfume. His heart leaped into his throat and for a moment, he thought he was going to cry. It was so real, just like he remembered it.

Where am I?

His thoughts spun as his eyes adjusted to the darkness. He rubbed the sleep from his eyes, saw the nightstand to his right, and had to look again at the old, black alarm clock and black touch lamp on the stand. A book hung lopsided over the clock. It was Ted Dekker's *Kiss.*

Then he realized where he was. He was in his bedroom back home, in the room he'd shared with K. *How did I get back here?*

He reached out his hand, sliding it along the sheets to his left hoping, praying he would find what he so desperately wanted to find—and he did. His fingers touched the warm, soft skin of a sleeping woman. He could feel the slow rise and fall of her gentle breathing and closed his eyes, praying the dream would not end.

Was it Maria? But they'd never—

He could not remember where he was or even what day it was. Confused and shaking, he reached up to the lamp on the nightstand and clicked it on. His head felt light and his heart began to beat even faster, making him feel like vomiting. But lying next to him was K.

The room was just as he'd left it, as if he'd never left the house. Rushing to his feet, he ran to the bathroom and threw up in the toilet, shaking uncontrollably.

What was going on? Was this a dream?

His whole body ached from the top of his head to the bottom of his feet. Every muscle tensed as he stumbled back into the bedroom. He just about made it back to his bed, when he stumbled and fell to the floor, twisting his wrist as he hit the carpet.

Get a hold of yourself. K is dead. This is not real. The more you hold on to the past, the worse off you'll be. This is a dream. A very vivid dream—but still, a dream.

Pulling himself to his feet, he stared at K's outline as she slept on her side. Her blonde hair flowed across her shoulder, one curl falling on her cheek. His brain fought to pull him back into reality. *But which reality?*

Hot tears streamed down his face as he watched his beautiful wife sleep. She was so perfect. He felt his heart tear open, the old wound rip apart, blood gush out anew.

I have to wake up. He slapped himself.

Nothing.

Again.

His nose began to bleed, dripping down his bare chest. He wiped it away with the back of his hand and tried to focus. *How can this be?*

He tried to stop his mind from bombarding him with

questions. He needed to go with this. This dream was more real than he'd ever thought a dream could be. *There must be a reason for this, something I must see and learn.* Now he was thinking clearly, all eight cylinders firing, and felt wide-awake, or as awake as was possible in a dream.

His bare chest was wet from sweat and blood, and his damp hair clung to his scalp. Walking over to the bed, he slid between the sheets. K rolled over and reached for him. Moaning peacefully, she put her arm across his chest.

Mark turned off the lamp and wrapped his arms around his wife. He pulled her close. Tears ran down his face as he sobbed quietly, knowing that in the morning she would be gone.

The feel of her next to him was the only thing he wanted, had ever wanted. He felt like cursing God and demand to have his life back, to take His old, wise face in his hands and make Him see what kind of pain coursed through his veins because of Him.

Then he quieted and thanked that same God for this brief moment, this space in time, where for one night, no matter how short, he had her back in his arms. He knew that tomorrow she would be gone again.

His world was perfect right now, at this moment in time. His beautiful wife lay in his arms, and his daughter slept soundly down the hall.

* * *

THE SOFT SUNLIGHT STREAMED through the window and danced on Mark's closed eyelids, but he kept his eyes closed, knowing that when he opened them, he would be alone.

The sheets were still damp from the night before. Finally, he slid his hand across the bed, longing to touch the warm body of his beloved K.

Nothing.

His fears were confirmed. It *was* just a dream. But he loved her more than ever after the dream. What was he going to do without her?

"Honey, you better get up, or you'll be late for work."

He gasped. K!

His heart stopped, but his mind whirred. He could not think or feel past the ringing in his ears.

He opened his eyes, looking down at his toes and past them into the bathroom. He could see his wife pulling a blue shirt over her blonde ponytail.

He pinched his leg, hard."Ouch." He wasn't dreaming.

Kay walked into the room buttoning her pants. "Honey, you okay? You must have had a bad dream. You soaked the sheets last night."

"Uh, yeah… I had a really, really… bad dream." The room spun, and his heart ached with a mixture of pain and joy.

"I'm sorry, baby. Maybe you'll forget it in the shower." She knelt to tie her shoes. "You'd better get ready before Sam wakes up."

I am not crazy. This is just an incredibly realistic dream. He threw back the covers and stood.

Time stood on end as he walked toward his dead wife. She was dead, yet here she was, all of her. Living, breathing, smiling K. His K. No matter how much he told himself that this couldn't be real, he could not deny how real it felt.

"Honey. You look terrible!" K reached up to brush his hair off his forehead.

Her touch triggered chills that shot from his scalp to his bare feet.

"Are you feeling okay?"

He grabbed her hands—her wonderful hands—and held them against his chest. "I feel a little sick to my stomach." Was this how shock felt?

"Why are you looking at me like that?" She scrunched her eyebrows. "You look surprised to see me this morning."

He wrapped his arms around her and pulled her close. He kissed her neck, kissed her lips, kissed her forehead, all the while sobbing. His whole body shook.

K clutched his jaw, one hand on each side of his face. "Baby? What's wrong? You're scaring me."

He tried to answer but couldn't. He just clung to her and cried until he finally managed to pull himself together.

She peered into his eyes, her forehead knotted with concern. "Tell me. What is it, hon?"

He dropped his head onto her shoulder. "My dream…it was so awful, and so real. I thought… thought you and Sam were dead. It was terrible, so—" He couldn't put into words the agony swirling in his head and heart.

She kissed him and whispered in his ear. "I'm right here, sweetheart. Forever."

He hugged her tighter and returned the kiss, tasting her sweet lips, drinking in the life he'd lost but was now found.

"Daddy!" Sam came bounding into the room, her hair sticking out every direction.

"Baby girl!" Mark took her in his arms and kissed her all over, making her squeal with delight. Her laughter filled his heart with incredible happiness as he tickled his darling little girl. He didn't know why he had dreamed such a horrible, vivid dream, but he'd discovered he loved his family far more than he'd ever showed them.

While K bargained with Samantha to eat her eggs, Mark called in to work to take the day off. He needed to recoup from his dream—or whatever it was. He could not put it all together. It was as if he had lived a year in a different world. Or was that world real and this one different?

K was overjoyed to learn he'd taken the day off. Sam had a play date that morning. After her afternoon nap, she was going to K's parents' house to spend the night.

Mark looked at the calendar, then turned on the news. It was the day before their wedding anniversary. Friday. He sat in his recliner and watched but didn't hear the news anchor talk about the weather. K and Sam had died on a Saturday. But that was a dream. It wasn't real. He shook his head, trying to talk some sense into his brain.

What if it was real but just hadn't happened yet? *That's impossible—you can't see into the future.* He didn't believe in that sort of thing. A guy could pay some crazy woman at the fair to read his fortune for him, but this—this was something completely different.

He tried to recall the dream, but all he could remember was that his wife and child had died, and that was enough for him to know it wasn't good. He remembered he was planning to take K to The Leaf on Friday night for their anniversary and that he'd reserved a hotel room as well. He wondered if the reservations were still active. He scratched his head. They had to be, because as far as he could tell, nothing had happened.

"K, I'm going to run into the city for a few hours today. I need to run some errands before we take Sam to her grandparent's house."

K answered from the kitchen. "Okay; I'll be a couple hours at the park, then she'll need a nap. I'll call Mom and Dad and ask if they can come over here to pick her up."

"Sounds great. Are you excited about your hot date tonight?"

"You know it, baby."

"Hot date!" Sam's little voice was muffled. Evidently, K had managed to shovel some scrambled eggs inside. "I hot. Me, hot date!"

K laughed. "Yes you are, kiddo. You have a hot date with Grandma and Grandpa tonight."

Sam giggled and hollered for her grandparents. She loved to be with them, but who could blame her. They always had plenty of candy and a bottomless supply of hugs.

CHAPTER TWENTY-TWO

MOOCH WAS WAY TOO perky for this time of night. Kirk was not a night owl, yet he was on the phone at midnight with a corn nut-crunching motormouth. He pulled the phone away from his ear and scowled at it, hoping to transfer his feelings to the annoying geek on the other end. But he needed Mooch, so he endured the assault on his eardrum and asked him to research Operation Justice.

"What is this? Some FBI thing?" Mooch asked.

"Yeah, I need to know everything about anyone who might be involved in the project. Also check out anything you can find on the World Justice Agency."

Mooch laughed in Kirk's ear. "The WJA?"

"Yeah, why? Do you know who they are?"

"Yeah, they're the thing of myths, man. You know, kinda like Robin Hood. They hunt down the bad guys, then disappear into the woodwork. They're kind of like X-men, but for real—not mutants—but pretty cool. If they were real, that is."

"Do you know who runs the organization?"

"No, man. It's just an idea, a concept. A bedtime story. If you think they're a real group, dude, you might want to check to see what's in your coffee."

"This is the real deal, Mooch, and they're a real

organization. I need to know who's in charge and where their headquarters is located. If the FBI thinks they exist, I'll take their word for it over yours. Besides, I have it from a secondary source that they do, in fact, exist." *I was there, or at least I think I was.* His imprisonment was becoming more and more like a bad nightmare every day.

"I'll do my best, but you'd better cover my butt on this. If I get caught hacking the feds, I'm in deep doo-doo."

"Just get me the information. According to what you say, you're the best. Here's your chance to prove it."

Kirk hung up the phone, set it on the breakfast bar, and stared off into space. They needed to find the mole and his or her connection to the WJA.

Kirk looked over at where Geoff had been watching TV. He was passed out on the couch, his mouth wide open and a guttural snore vibrating his chest. It had been a long day, and Kirk was getting tired himself. Tomorrow they'd get an interview with Captain Jacobson, one way or another.

* * *

GEOFF WOKE UP WITH a start and yawned, stretching his arms above his head. The TV was on, but the rest of the apartment was dark. His watch read two thirty a.m. He felt good, and his mind kicked into gear, reminding him why his internal clock had brought him back into the land of the living.

Getting up, he leaned back, popped a couple vertebrae, and let out a sigh. He went to the fridge to grab a Pepsi. Nothing was as good as an ice-cold Pepsi. Of course, at this hour, it might keep him awake for awhile, but he wasn't planning to go back to bed anytime soon anyway.

He looked at the door to Kirk's bedroom. It was half-open. He could see the detective's leg sticking out from under the covers like a dead branch on a very old tree.

It's time.

Walking over to his shoulder bag, he pulled out a nine MM and screwed on a silencer. He opened the curtains and studied the gun in the moonlight. It was a beautiful weapon. The stainless steel caught the moon's white light and bounced it back at him. Too nice of a gun, really, to waste on an old geezer like Weston. He sighed. It was a simple chore, one beneath his skill level, but he was a professional, and he had a job to do.

He tiptoed into the other bedroom, pointed the gun at Kirk Weston's chest, and fired.

* * *

MARK HEADED INTO THE city, trying to clear his head as he drove. This dream or vision, or whatever it was, had shaken him to his very core. Maybe he was dreaming now and what he thought was his dream the night before was reality.

He laughed.

Stop over-thinking this, Appleton. You're here, and your family is alive. But then, maybe they weren't. Maybe his mind was so broken he'd imagined K and Sam were alive, but he was really asleep somewhere, lost in a dream world of his own making.

The radio played in the background, filling the car with the distinctive voice of Glenn Beck, who was rattling on about gas prices. He sounded real enough. Mark stopped by a small coffee shop and found a parking spot right in front, which was a rare, if not unheard-of, experience. Maybe he was dreaming, after all. He ordered a coconut mocha, picked up a newspaper and found a comfortable chair.

"Cindy, are you there?" The morning news sounded from a television that hung in the corner just above a rounded counter filled with straws, creamer, sugar and everything else one might want to add to his or her cup of Joe.

"Yes, Tom. I'm here at the New York City maximum-security prison on David's Island. We don't know what exactly is going on at this point, but we've been told some inmates have suffered from food poisoning. The Center for Disease Control is already at the prison investigating the apparent outbreak."

Mark stared at the screen, mouth open. He'd heard the same report a year ago while stalled in traffic. He remembered how he'd anticipated his date with K all day and how anxious he was to get home to her.

This can't be. It was a dream. Or was this the dream?

He looked back at the paper in his hand and saw a "buy one, get one free" ad for Campbell's latest chunky soup at the Super Mart.

He jumped to his feet and ran for the door. He hit the fob button and climbed into his Honda Accord, trying to remember all the details of that day. He'd gone to work, returned home after work, took K out to dinner—and then they went to the hotel.

Nothing unusual on Friday. What happened next? He had to think.

We got up late, then we picked up Samantha, then... Then went to the Super Mart...

"Pat. I have to find Pat Rotter."

* * *

KIRK RUBBED HIS HEAD, which felt twice its normal size and throbbed as if a thunderstorm was brewing between his ears. When he tried to sit up, a bolt of pain shot across his left side. Feeling under his shirt, he could tell several ribs had been broken.

But he didn't remember how—or why. All he could remember was going to bed, then waking up here, wherever here was. He looked around. Light was coming from under a door in front of him.

He swore. Kidnapped for a second time. Either he was an easy target or he was making someone nervous. These WJA people were beginning to get on his nerves.

He could tell from the primitive cell that he was in an old prison. The floor was concrete and the walls were made of rough bricks. The thick wooden door was wrapped with metal around the edges.

He grunted and sat up, ignoring the pain in his side. Was this a WJA prison? Couldn't be. This wasn't their style. Too rugged and out-of-date. No magnets. No flying saucers.

He heard a key slide into the lock, then a click, and the door was shoved open. He covered his face with his hand to shield his eyes from the bright light and see who was standing in front of him. But all he saw were dark shadows.

Two masked men yanked him to his feet. He almost passed out from the pain as he was dragged out of his cell and down a hallway. He kicked his feet and fought for footing without success.

Other doors lined the wide hallway. Most of them were shut. Who knew how many more victims were waiting for their fate with broken ribs, or worse, in a cold, dark cell, wondering if they would ever see the blue sky again.

The men threw him onto a cold metal chair and tied his hands behind his back. His feet were strapped to the legs of the chair.

One of the masked men knelt before him. "You might be wondering why we brought you here, Detective Weston." The deep, thick voice had a hint of Russian and was tinted with contempt. He leaned close. "You have information we need. You are going to tell us everything you know. Understand?"

Kirk looked into the man's dark eyes, instinctively memorizing everything about his interrogator and realizing the large, muscular man could tear him apart without breaking a sweat.

He grinned at the Russian, then spit in his face. The man backhanded him and sent him toppling to the hard floor with a loud crash. His skull bounced against the cement and blue-and-yellow stars floated across his vision.

Ow—that hurt.

The two masked men pulled him upright.

His ribs rebelled, but he refused to cry out.

The big man folded his arms and looked at him as if examining a piece of fruit. "So, you think you're tough. We will see, Mr. Weston."

With that, he turned and left the room. The two other men followed him without a word. The door shut with a clink of the lock.

Kirk surveyed his surroundings. It looked like he was in a washroom. Clumps of hair clung to the rusted floor drain. The tiled walls were so dirty he couldn't tell the color. A naked light bulb hung from an cord in the center of the room.

He could hear someone talking outside his door and had a feeling his captors weren't planning ways to make him more comfortable.

The door flew open, and one of the masked men marched in. Pulling out a knife from his pocket, he cut away the rope, freeing Kirk's hands.

It's now or never!

Jumping to his feet, he spun around, sending his legs and the chair crashing into the masked man's face. He fell to the floor with his legs on top of the now-unconscious man. He frantically searched for the knife, then spotted it on the floor a few feet away.

He dragged his body toward the knife, the chair scraping the cement floor. He heard his attacker begin to stir.

One more foot.

With a final lunge, he grabbed the knife and spun onto his back, pulling his legs to his chest. He cut his feet loose from the chair and rolled to his feet, ignoring the scream rising from his ribs.

He jumped on top of his assailant, who was on his knees spitting blood onto the tile floor. Kirk shoved the knife beneath the man's chin and drew the blade from one side of his throat to the other. The guard made gasping, gurgling sounds and dropped to the floor. Kirk stepped over his body and walked toward the door, which was half open.

Kirk peeked into the hallway and could hear voices coming from the other end. He clutched his side with one hand and gripped the knife in the other.

What did they think he knew? And what did they think he would do—lie down and take their garbage?

He tried to ignore the questions that ran through his mind,

but he was a detective, and it came naturally. His anger was
rising, and he could feel his primal instincts kicking in as he
leaned out to get a clear view of the hall.

Just get out of here alive, Weston. No heroics.

The hallway was clear, but he could tell someone was in the
room to his right. He looked for a place to hide, but all he could
see was a large crate beside the door where the voices were
coming from.

He looked back to the room he'd just come from. *That's it!*

Returning to the washroom, he set the metal chair upright,
then lifted the masked man and balanced his limp body on the
seat. Taking off the man's mask, he pulled it over his own head
and tied the attacker's hands behind his back.

He looked to be Kirk's height and weight. *This might just
work after all.* He loosened the light bulb that hung just above
his head, then frisked the dead man's pockets for weapons.

Nothing.

A voice behind him suddenly demanded, "Hey, what are
you doing? You're supposed to take him back to his cell." The
man had a thick, Russian accent.

Kirk froze and waited for the man to get within striking
distance. He knew he would only have one shot at this.

"You! Hurry up!" The man stepped into the room.

Whirling around, Kirk lurched forward and slid the sharp
blade into his target's abdomen. The man gasped in pain, but
before he could react, Kirk yanked the blade out, and in one
sweeping motion, slashed it across his throat, spraying a stream
of blood onto his chest.

A confused look flashed across his face before the Russian
fell to his knees, blood spewing from his neck. He was dead
before he hit the floor.

Kirk removed the man's mask and searched his second kill
for weapons. He smiled when he found a Glock. After checking
to make sure the clip was full, he stepped into the hallway, his
pulse pounding in his ears. Despite the throb in his ribs, he
crouched and crept down the long hall, gun in hand.

The only way out appeared to be the door at the far end. He ducked behind a crate, rested a moment, then jumped from his hiding place. Almost running, but still hunkered as low as possible, he worked his way to the end of the hall.

Hearing voices, he stopped by a closed door, feeling like a sitting duck as he squatted in the open. He heard whispers and moans on the other side of the door. At least two people were in the cell.

That was all he needed. He'd be lucky to make it out alive on his own, let alone trying to drag other people with him.

He tried the cell door. Locked.

He crawled to the next door and twisted the handle, which gave way to pressure. He pushed the door open and slipped inside. The cell was dark and smelled like a sewer, but it made a good place to hide and think.

It didn't take him long to decide to go for help then return for the others, whoever they were. He looked out into the hall, wondering what to do next. He needed to draw out whoever was on the other side of the door—the door that could lead him to freedom. He needed the element of surprise, if he was going to make out of this place alive.

CHAPTER TWENTY-THREE

PAT ROTTER GRUNTED AS his jaw was slammed into the side of his apartment building.

"Hey," he squealed, "what d'ya want?"

Mark held him firmly against the wall, his forearm digging into the back of his neck. "You're coming with me, or you'll die!" Mark was determined not to lose K and Sam again, even if it meant killing this poor sop before he actually did anything.

"Easy, man! I don't have any money."

"I don't want your money," Mark growled. He pushed Pat toward his car, shoved him into the passenger seat and shut the door, still pointing the fake gun through his coat pocket.

He walked around the other side of the Honda and got in, thinking fast. The kid would soon figure out he didn't have a gun. He had to figure a way to keep the edge, no matter what.

He started the car then turned to Pat. "I want you to listen, Pat Rotter, and listen hard. I know who you are and what you're doing. I'm with the FBI. We know you're involved with a terrorist organization that is planning to blow up a grocery store tomorrow morning."

Pat's eyes grew big and round. "Uh, how did…" He stuttered and looked away, avoiding Mark's gaze. "I don't know what you're talking about."

254 | AARON PATTERSON

Mark sucked in a deep breath. "I'll give you two choices, Rotter. You can cooperate with me and tell me everything you know, or you can spend the rest of your life behind bars. Who will take care of your grandmother while you're in prison?"

Pat jerked his gaze toward Mark and ogled him, as if testing his resolve. Finally, with an exasperated huff, he nodded and began to talk, fast.

"All I did was sell them the C-4 I took from work." He raised his hands. "I swear on my grandma's Bible, that's all I did, man." He gripped his thighs and gazed straight ahead, eyes wide.

Mark tapped the steering wheel. "We have good Intel that you're the one who's going to plant the bomb. What is this about you *only* sold them the C-4?"

"I swear that's all I did. They haven't even paid me for it yet. I'm supposed to meet them today to get my fifty grand. I don't know anything about a bomb."

Mark studied the nervous youth's face. His contacts were probably planning to hold the cash until he promised to plant the bomb. Once he placed it in the store, they'd incinerate him along with everyone else.

He suddenly turned to Pat and barked, "Get out of the car."

Pat jerked. "Yes, sir!" He reached for the door handle.

"If you contact those people again, or I catch you getting into any more trouble, God help you!"

Pat shook his head violently. "I won't go back. I'll stay away from those people. It was a stupid thing to do." He clenched his fists. "I'll stay out of trouble, I promise."

"Good." Mark squinted at Pat, trying to give him his sternest stare. "I'll be watching you."

Pat jumped from his car, slammed the door and ran up the stairs to his apartment without looking back.

Mark sighed. Maybe he'd scared the kid good enough to avoid any more stupid situations. He started the car and pulled out of the apartment complex parking lot. It was time to pay a little visit to a few bomb makers.

He dialed directory assistance as he drove. He needed a gun
to make his point at the cabin. He could feel his instincts taking
over, just like in his dream. He didn't know how much of his
dream was true or how much was going to come true, but he
wasn't going to sit around when hundreds of innocent people
were about to be killed.

The computerized operator came on the line. "City and
state, please."

"New York City, New York."

Finally, he was connected to the American Gun Club.
"Yeah, is Fred there?"

"Uh, Fred? No one by that name works here."

"He's the fat man smoking a stogie over by the fireplace."

The voice on the other end went silent. It was a long shot,
but Fred was the only person he knew in the whole city who
could supply weapons on short notice.

"Hold on one second."

After what felt like forever, he heard Fred wheeze and
cough as he picked up the receiver. "Yeah, who's this?"

"Hey, Fred. I've got eight hundred dollars, cash, and I need
a gun—today."

"Uh… I don't know what you're talking about."

"Yes, you do. Meet me in half an hour at the old train depot
out in Brooklyn. You know the one?"

"Yeah."

"Half an hour."

He hung up the phone and tried not think about how crazy
this was. The depot was about an hour from the cabin. He was
going to change his own future and the future of hundreds of
other families, whatever it took. He could ask forgiveness later.

* * *

HUNCHED IN THE DARK, empty cell, Kirk waited. He
could hear what sounded like a child crying softly in the cell
down the hall. How could he live with himself if he left a
child, and who knows who else, to suffer what he could only

imagine? This was no preschool. But he worked better alone. He'd come back later.

He started to leave the cell but sighed. What if there was no *later*?

He slipped out of his hiding place and found the door where he could hear the child. It was another heavy, wooden door wrapped with old, rusty metal, like the one he'd been trapped in earlier.

He shot a glance up and down the empty, open hallway. If one of the Russians appeared, he'd have no place to hide. He was totally exposed.

He tapped the door and whispered, "I'm a cop. Anyone in there?"

"Yes, me and my daughter. Please help us!" The shaking voice sounded female.

"Okay, hold on. I need to find a key to unlock the door."

"Be careful!"

He tiptoed to the door at the end of the hall, where he heard loud snoring. He took a deep breath, and pushed the door open and peered inside, where he saw a desk topped by computer monitors and a small television. A sleeping guard was slumped in his chair in front of the television, his back to the door.

Kirk opened the door just enough to crawl through. Seeing no one else in the room, he snuck behind the sleeping guard, then stood with his gun drawn, adrenaline flowing, ribs screaming.

The foyer in front of the desk was empty. A guard walked past the glass windows on the outside of the building, but no one was nearby. He glanced at the marble floors and the rounded curve of the huge lobby.

He raised his gun over the guard's head and smashed it against his left temple. The guard grunted and fell to the side.

Kirk propped him so that he looked like he was watching the television, then took the keys from his belt.

Back in the empty hallway, he hurried to the woman's cell. Before he unlocked the door, he whispered, "Got the keys."

He could hear movement inside as he shoved one key after another into the lock. Finally, one fit. The lock was old and rusted and made a grinding sound as the key clicked the deadbolt open.

The door swung open and hit the wall with a bang. A slender woman and a small girl were standing just inside the opening. They squinted as bright light streamed in from the hallway.

Though the woman looked beat up and dirty, he could tell she had light-blonde hair. The little girl, who had similar hair color, was hugging the woman's leg, her eyes wide with fear and her face smudged with grime. A small cut above her right eye was caked with dried blood.

He motioned to the child, put his finger to his lips and whispered, "Be very, very quiet."

She nodded.

"Follow me and do as I say."

He wasn't sure how he was going to get out of the prison with a woman and a child in tow, but he knew he had to try. He led them to the end of the hall and had them wait outside the door.

Stepping behind the still-unconscious guard, he scanned the lobby. This time, he noticed three elevators on the left. But the expanse between the desk and the elevators was vast and windowed, with no place to hide. The guards, who were making their rounds on the other side of the glass, would see them for sure.

He looked around the desk, hoping to find something, anything that would help. *Ah, a radio!* He shoved at the fat guard's spare tire to maneuver the two-way radio from his belt. *Here we go.*

He hit the talk button. "Intruder! Intruder at the rear of the building. Every available man, run to the southeast end of the building!" He ducked behind the desk as guards rushed past the windows, then poked his head back into the hallway and motioned to the two frightened females. "Let's go."

He hurried across the lobby and out the main door, thinking they'd use the elevators only if they needed to retreat. It was dark, and he didn't know if it was early morning or late in the evening, but it didn't matter. They were out of the building.

The woman, carrying her daughter, followed directly behind him without a word. The air was cold and sharp as they made their way across the lawn that fronted the building. He could see his breath puff out in front of him as he ran hunched over.

They reached a large bush and hid behind it. They could see bouncing beams of light from flashlights as their captors searched for the intruders.

"Stay here. I'll be right back."

He moved behind a tree to get a feel for the complex's layout. They were in the middle of the woods. A dirt road on the left led to a gate flanked by guard towers. The glow of a cigarette stood out like a tiny spark against the dark sky as one of the guards took a drag. For some reason, the tower guards didn't seem too concerned by the alert.

Now what?

Between them and the guards, a double fence acted as a dog-run. The dogs he could see sniffing around looked like pit bulls. Other dogs were motionless, probably sleeping.

He heard a vehicle and ducked behind a bush. A Jeep was headed toward them with a gunner on top holding a machine gun and a spotlight.

He looked over to where the woman and child were hiding, and a sick feeling came over him. The Jeep stopped a few feet from them, and a guard stepped out, pulled a cigarette from his pocket and lit up. The flare from the lighter made his face look sinister.

Kirk willed the two females to remain motionless. He could barely make out the woman's form ten yards ahead. He cursed himself for leaving them alone, and his heart jumped into his throat when the girl started crying.

No!

He jumped up, yelled, and ran toward the Jeep waving his arms. The guard dropped his cigarette and leveled a gun at Kirk. He dropped the Glock on the ground behind him, hoping the girl and her mother would find it and have something with which to defend themselves.

"Stop or I'll shoot!"

He raised his hands in the air, stealing a glance at the two, who were crawling under broken pallets piled in a twisted heap.

The guard shoved Kirk into the Jeep and drove him to a loading dock, where he was dumped on the hard, concrete floor and soundly kicked before being dragged back to his cell. The door slammed with a loud thud, and, once again, he was alone in the dark.

* * *

THE WOMAN RELAXED HER grip on her daughter's mouth when her silent sobs stopped and she fell asleep. But she didn't relax her vigilance. She'd never been so scared. If her captors found them, she was sure they'd kill both of them for trying to escape. They were hateful, evil men.

She tried not to cry. She needed to be strong for her little girl. But the whole complex was swarming with guards, and she was terrified.

They'd stay hidden until morning. Then she'd decide what to do. She thought of their rescuer and shuddered at the thought of what he was enduring for their sake.

Who was he? Why did he help them? She pulled her little girl close. It would be morning soon, and she would have a completely new situation to deal with. The cover of the pallets wouldn't be enough for them to be able to escape detection in daylight. She saw a small outbuilding about a hundred feet away. Maybe it was an electric building or a pump house of some kind. Whatever it was, something told her they had to get inside.

CHAPTER TWENTY-FOUR

THE RIOT SHOTGUN WAS just like the one Mark remembered in his dream—down to the black stock and the way the cold metal felt in his hands. He paid Fred and left.

The road was paved with graying blacktop. Fall leaves shone in bright colors, making the hills come alive with bright reds, oranges, and yellows. Better than the snow. Then again, had that really been snow?

He wasn't sure what to think. The dream, or whatever he'd gone through, had taken him through a year of life he had no desire to repeat. His future was in his own hands now. For better or for worse, he believed what he dreamed or saw was real—or would be real, if he didn't act.

He glanced in his rearview mirror. He couldn't remember why, but he had a feeling he was supposed to see someone.

A car, maybe, or a woman. Yeah, a woman. Bits and pieces of that day were coming back to him as he drove the dangerous path toward the cabin.

Just past a KOA Campground sign, a dirt road on the left called to him like some spirit pulling him to his fate. He glanced in the mirror before swinging his Honda onto the road. He almost didn't recognize the hard eyes that stared back at him. He looked away before he lost his nerve and hurried home to his wife and daughter, who would be killed tomorrow.

He found the wide spot in the road where he'd parked before. For a moment, he stood on the hill staring at the valley below and the cabin at the base of the mountain. The shotgun was loaded and ready. He edged into the trees with it cradled in his left arm.

Up close, the cabin looked the same, but without a pile of wood stacked on the porch.

Two trucks were parked in front—the same two he remembered. A chill ran up his spine, making him shiver. The men inside were going to see someone other than Pat Rotter today, someone who didn't want money.

He crouched behind the old, gray Chevy and could hear what sounded like an intense argument inside the building. Peering around the front bumper, he could see that one of the men was standing with his back to the front window, waving his arms and yelling.

Time to make history. He shifted his feet, his heart pounding. But then, like a machine, he seemed to downshift a gear. He could feel his heart rate slow and a sense of control and knowing surge through his body.

He jumped from his hiding place and bull-rushed the door with his shoulder down, shotgun ready. The door splintered with a cracking, groaning sound and gave way as he crashed through it, landing on his side.

The man at the window swung around, yanking a pistol from his hip holster.

Mark rolled to his feet and pumped a shell into the man's chest.

The big man doubled over, and his gun clattered to the wood floor, sliding away in a spin. He landed in a bloody heap, a huge, red stain covering his chest.

The other two men, who'd jumped to their feet, guns in hand, froze.

"Anyone else care to try me?" His voice was calm, almost conversational.

They did not hesitate this time. Like obedient children, they dropped their weapons in unison.

"Sit down with your hands in the air. You drop 'em, you die." He waved the shotgun toward the table, and they did as they were told.

He saw the shell of a phone sitting on the table with a black remote transmitter next to the detonator. He picked the transmitter up.

The blond, scruffy-haired man twitched in his seat.

"What will happen if I push this button?" He moved his finger over the red button. The two men exchanged nervous glances. One started to rise in protest.

"Sit down." Mark dropped the phone and jacked another round into the chamber. His mind was racing. Bits of information processed too fast for him to grasp what it all meant. He'd sort it out later. Tactical details flashed through his head, providing information—the cabin layout, windows and doors locked or open, possible hiding places.

The bomb had apparently been wired and was about to be placed into the phone when an argument had ensued. He presumed the disagreement was about who was going to detonate the device. The poor sap who activated the bomb would die in the explosion, and they all knew it.

Walking over to the scarred wooden table, he found a button that looked to be the right one, the one that had been on the top of the phone casing. He pushed it.

The two flinched as the red light came on.

"It's ironic you should have this bomb in this very place at this very moment." Walking around behind them, he shoved the end of his shotgun against the hairy one's head.

But the guy, who was gaping at the bomb that was now activated and sitting just a few feet from him, didn't seem to notice.

Mark pulled four zip-ties from his pocket and tied the men's hands together. Then he hooked their free hands to the table legs, so that they had to sit with their heads on the table.

264 | AARON PATTERSON

The shorter man spit at Mark and cursed.

Mark wiped the saliva off his face and strapped the phone bomb to the spitter's back with the duct tape that was sitting on the table. Despite their cursing and kicking, he managed to tape both men's mouths shut.

Finished with the job he came to do, he walked out the front door and was struck by the fall hues that colored the mountainside. How could something so ugly exist in the midst of such beauty?

When he arrived at his car, he turned to look one last time at the little cabin sitting at the edge of the valley like a painting in an expensive hotel lobby.

He pressed the button.

A mushroom cloud rose to the sky, and the screeching squeal of ripping wood filled the little valley. A rush of wind charged up the hill and blew past his face, rustling through the trees and lifting red and yellow leaves from the forest floor in a brilliant kaleidoscope whorl.

Better here than in a crowded supermarket.

The simple thought did not justify what he'd just done. But he felt no guilt. He climbed into the Honda, anxious to go home, to kiss his wife and hold his daughter again. He had a feeling he would not only never feel guilt, but that he might even think of this day as the day he saved his family.

* * *

KIRK COULD FEEL BLOOD caked to his eyelids, which made opening them difficult. He carefully pried them apart and looked around. He was in a different cell, though it was the same as the last one—dark and cold.

His body shrieked in agony with every movement. Even breathing hurt, but he didn't have a way of not doing that. Sitting up, he could see light coming from under the door.

Is it morning, or is it still night?

He couldn't tell. All he knew was that he had to get out of there, because this time they would kill him. They would not be as stupid around him again, knowing he'd killed a few of their men already. He shivered as he remembered the woman and the little girl and hoped they were alright.

A plan. I need a plan. He didn't know where he was, or even what country, for that matter. However, one thing he knew without any doubt—if he stayed much longer, he would die.

Pulling himself to his feet, he dragged himself to the door and began to pound and yell for a guard. He threw in a few remarks about their mothers and the stench that surrounded them, although he was not entirely sure what he was going to do if one of the Russians came.

The yelling worked. Loud footfalls announced an arrival. He backed away from the door. A masked guard carrying a machine gun burst into the room.

"I want to talk to the person in charge—your boss, the main pig leading this pack of swine. You understand, tough guy?"

The guard whipped the butt of his gun around, hitting Kirk across the jaw and sending him to the ground.

Spitting blood out onto the concrete floor, Kirk looked up from his knees at his attacker, who stepped aside when another guard came in with a chair. They tied him to the chair and blindfolded him like before. He clenched his throbbing jaw as every broken rib made itself known.

Okay, this could be good. At least I can die in peace.

A third set of footsteps resounded as someone else entered the room. Kirk could hear the sound of another chair as it scraped on the concrete, and it made him cringe.

"Detective Weston, you have been trouble for me. You killed some of my men, and you took two very important prisoners." The voice came with an accent, but Kirk couldn't place it. It was very familiar, but something was not right with it.

He smiled and felt his lip bust open. That meant the woman and child were still out there, hiding somewhere.

"What do you want from me?" His voice cracked.

The man chuckled. "You should have figured it out by now, Detective. Unless you are dumber than I thought."

"You're the mole."

"Ah, yes. Then you have been paying attention."

Kirk thought as fast as he could. This had to be an FBI or CIA agent. "What made you turn against your own kind? You some sort of religious wacko or something?"

"No, no." He chuckled again. "Religion is for weak people. I don't need God. I want his power. And soon I will have it!"

Kirk tried not to laugh. He needed more information before he was executed, and the guy seemed ready and willing to talk to his dying prisoner. "Let me guess, you're one of these World Justice Agency freaks who thinks they can decide who lives and who dies, and it all went to your head. Am I close?"

By the silence in the room, he figured he hit on something. He could feel anger rising in the room.

"The WJA is a drop in the bucket compared to what I am capable of. They betrayed me. They left me, and now they are trying to kill me." His voice rose as he stood up and paced in front of Kirk. "You're one of them, aren't you, Detective? You're here to kill me?"

This time Kirk laughed out loud. "No. I'm trying to catch the WJA and the mole who works with them. I'm not a big fan of vigilantes, myself."

He was beginning to put the pieces together. This man used to be in the WJA and now worked with the FBI. He was their inside guy. But now he was rogue, out killing and doing whatever else on his own. The WJA must have dropped him when he went psycho, and now he was trying to bring down the WJA.

"I gave top-secret information to them, but they tied everything back to me and tried to set *me* up. No one sets me up!" He leaned down to yell in Kirk's ear. "Then you come along and mess everything up with your investigation. You stuck your nose into places where it doesn't belong."

"You killed a cop and his wife!"

"He was a liability, it had to be done. I'm going to take down the WJA by bombing every supermarket and school in this country—in their name—if that's what it takes. The FBI, CIA and every other government organization will hunt them down without mercy."

"So says you."

Kirk felt the man's harsh breath on his face as he screamed at him. "Who's going to stop me?"

The three marched out of the cell, and the door slammed with a loud bang before he heard the sound of a key being shoved into the lock and turned. He was still tied and blindfolded, and he could taste blood as he licked his lips. But he had to stop the lunatic before he killed any more innocent people.

* * *

THE TERRIFIED WOMAN AND her child finally made it to the door of the small outbuilding, which was more like a shed than a building and unlocked. She breathed a sigh of relief as they slipped inside without drawing attention to themselves.

Several electrical boxes lined one wall and two large machines, which she thought were pumps, sat in the middle of the floor like sleeping monsters, making a loud droning sound. They found a spot behind the larger of the two pumps and cuddled together in the warm room. After a few short minutes, they fell asleep.

The silence woke the sleeping woman when the pumps turned off. The lack of sound seemed almost louder than the noise. She yawned and rubbed her eyes, trying not to disturb her sleeping daughter. She ran their escape options through her head. As far as she knew, the gate was the only way out, but she didn't know how she could get herself and her daughter through two sets of fences and guard dogs, especially in broad daylight.

The door rattled, and her heart jumped into her throat. She froze as a short guard with a submachine gun slung over his shoulder came into the little shed. He took out a cigarette and lit it, then took a long drag and blew out a puff of smoke.

When he finished the cigarette, he dropped it and ground it

into the dirt with his heel. Then he leaned against the wall, slid to the floor and pulled his hat over his eyes. Within minutes, he was snoring. His loud breathing was erratic and choppy, but he was definitely out.

She looked down at her daughter, who slept with her head on the floor, then back at the guard. His gun rested against the wall next to his shoulder. She waited a few minutes, then slipped off her shoes and stood.

Barely breathing, she watched the sleeping man, trying to get up the courage to take his gun. From the look of the small pile of cigarette butts on the floor next to where he slept, he did this on a regular basis. Her stomach turned when he moved his arm.

She hesitated. *I can't do this. What if he wakes up? Then what?* She swallowed. *I've got to get it together, for both of us. I have to do what I have to do.* Inching closer, she bent down and grabbed the weapon.

She pulled it to her chest just as the guard's eyes blinked open. She tried to bring the gun around but couldn't. All she could do was stand there, frozen. He didn't move, either. Instead, he stared through her as if trying to plan his next move.

Then it hit her. He was asleep. His eyes were open, but unresponsive and empty. She slowly backed toward her daughter, who smiled in her sleep.

Sweet dreams, honey. Sweet dreams.

CHAPTER TWENTY-FIVE

MARK LOOKED AT HIS wife sleeping next to him.

She was so beautiful.

He didn't know whether he was in a dream world or in the real world. And his mind wouldn't stop trying to figure it out. Though it was the middle of the night, he'd awakened just to see if she was still there next to him. She was. He touched her soft shoulder, feeling the rise and fall of her breathing.

Time had a way of working out details. This gift, or curse he didn't yet know which it was—had given him something. He now lived life full throttle, with a lust for living he'd never before known. It was as if he'd been given a second chance at life. He was not going to waste one minute of it.

A year had come and gone since he blew up the cabin, with life changing for him in ways that would make most men shake in fear and others turn green with envy. He now worked fulltime for the World Justice Agency and every day retrieved more missing parts of his memory.

It was as if he had a new instinct, a second set of instincts. He could see and feel what was going to happen in a situation and react with incredible speed. Not that he was psychic or anything like that. It was just an overwhelming sense of knowing. If a good thing was about to happen, he would feel it, feel the emotion before anything happened.

He'd shocked Isis by following her downtown and into the Merc Building's underground parking garage, then into the elevator. "Hello, Isis. Going down?"

She tried to act innocent.

"Nine, five, two, huh? Clever. Spells WJA on the keypad of a phone."

"I take it your memory has returned." A small smile appeared at the corner of her mouth.

"Most of it. Maybe more than was supposed to. At least this time you don't have to sneak into my apartment to convince me."

She looked confused but didn't say anything. He'd been assigned to help Isis complete a few easy assignments. He loved her attention to detail. She was a cool and in-control-of-herself kind of woman. She planned every case with precise direction and never missed anything. He enjoyed learning from her, and she was willing to help him and teach him any way she could.

He was surprised that Solomon could not explain his dreams or how he could see into the future. His foreknowledge didn't happen all the time, and after the first time, the insights came in short bursts, like a bad headache or a daydream.

Solomon finally told him, "You've been granted a gift, son. Don't waste it. If it wasn't for your dream, your family would be dead right now."

K was supportive of his new job and never asked him to explain what he was doing or where he was when his work took him late into the nights on a few occasions. "I don't deserve you, babe."

"I know," K said, "but you've got me. Now run along and go be a hero."

He wondered how much she knew or what she thought he might be doing with the odd hours he worked. He doubted she bought the *working for the government* thing, and he didn't expect her to. It was a nice story to tell the neighbors at backyard barbeques. It meant a lot to him to know she loved, trusted and supported him.

They paid off the house—rather, Solomon paid it off that Christmas. He'd become part of the family and loved Sam as if she was his own granddaughter. Solomon came over for dinner often and sometimes played dress-up with Samantha. Bracelets and lipstick on the older man made quite a sight, but Sam loved Solomon's attention, and that was enough for him.

Today, Mark had to take the Taxi over to Vermont, where two brothers had been on a killing spree. They'd kidnapped eleven girls, usually from the local high-school hangout. It had taken the authorities ten months to find six of the girls. Their bodies were almost unrecognizable.

He cringed when he saw the file. The brothers had done horrible things to the girls, as if it was a sport to them.

WJA had sent in one of their undercover women. It was easy to make her look like a teenager. She'd been in the school only two weeks before she was taken. WJA had a tracking device on her, and Mark was going in to get her out.

He would be gone two days, between the rescue and the hit. He hoped to be back in time for the weekend. Zipping up his suit, he crawled into the Taxi and hit the start button. It was hard to believe, but he rather enjoyed using the device. It still made him a little sick afterward, but it sure saved time.

* * *

"MARK, WE NEED YOU. Come in immediately. We have something you need to see." Isis's urgent voice on his cell phone made him press the accelerator and promise to be there as fast as traffic would allow.

He closed the phone wondering what would make her sound so nervous. Nerves were not normal for Isis, but he was willing to do whatever needed to be done. Maybe the case involved an important person, maybe even a celebrity.

As usual, the streets were jammed with cars, bumper-to-bumper, and the cacophony of horns and swear words. It took thirty minutes to go five blocks. But it was New York, where the sound of cursing was an essential part of the city's daily symphony.

Mark smiled at Mr. Able, who was reading the morning paper. "You ready to celebrate the new year?"

"You bet. I got all the grandkids a bucket of candy and noisemakers." He chuckled and waved Mark in.

"That should make for happy parents."

"Ha! It's good for 'em."

Mark laughed. "Have fun!" He stepped through the door. It took a few minutes to get through all the checkpoints, but it had taken just forty-five minutes from the time Isis called him to the moment he sat down in his chair in the conference room.

Only three other people sat at the table—Big B, Isis, and a man named Johnny Jamison. He was a Class-D sniper who'd been active for over ten years. He had a mustache that looked like a caterpillar roosted under his nose, but he was in great shape for a fifty-something.

"Okay, we all here?" Johnny looked around the room with brown, flat eyes. "Solomon wanted me to get started with the briefing. He'll be down in a few minutes."

The room was silent as everyone looked at Johnny. Isis was taking notes on an electronic device that seemed to float in the air in front of her. Big B fidgeted with the toothpick in his mouth. Mark noticed everyone seemed to be avoiding his gaze. He frowned.

A picture of a tall man with a scruffy, blond beard and curly hair appeared on a screen that hovered in the middle of the large, wooden, conference table. "This is Tripp Maddock. He goes by the name of Geoff Martin and has been underground until just recently. These pictures were taken here in New York. He's been running with Detective Weston, Detroit PD. We don't know the nature of their relationship, but we have reason to believe he's involved with our FBI contact." Mark remembered talking with Isis about a case she was working on. They had taken out a prison filled with rapists and murderers. Detective Weston had been investigating it, so they'd had to get him out of the way until the case was under control.

But it didn't work. The kidnapping seemed to make him even more determined. In the meantime, their contact went rogue and hooked up with the leading crime boss out of Russia. They were trying to expose the WJA and would do anything to make that happen.

"Now, this trail gets twisted here. We all know Detective Weston. He was kidnapped about an hour ago. We have reason to believe Tripp Maddock had something to do with it. We know he has close dealings with a Russian general named Taras Karjanski, and we believe he has teamed up with our FBI contact."

A picture of a rough-looking man with a thick, black beard came up on the see-thru screen. "This is General Karjanski. He's our main target, what is called the *Don* of the Russian Mafia. He has Weston, and he may have others."

Mark studied the Russian's face. *Why would he go against the WJA and turn against his own country?*

His thoughts were interrupted by Johnny's stern voice. He was going over the details of their mission.

"We need two teams to go in to take out Karjanski and Maddock. Mark, you and Isis will take care of the hit on the general. Big B and I will take care of Mr. Maddock. Then we'll rescue Weston."

Jamison went over the blueprints and layouts of the building on the coast of Puerto Rico, where they believed the Russians were holding Weston. From the satellite images, the abandoned asylum looked like it was heavily guarded and would be hard to penetrate.

"We are only there to take out our two targets. Guards will be shot with non-lethal weapons. Our FBI informant has already been tagged and will be brought in alive for questioning. Any questions?"

They shook their heads.

Just as Johnny was wrapping up, Solomon walked in, a grim set to his mouth. He took the floor. "I have some new

information I think you should know before you go on this
mission." He took off his glasses.

"We just learned that General Karjanski has kidnapped
two other individuals. We learned this information from Agent
Seloent, whom we picked up thirty minutes ago."

Mark could feel his stomach tighten. Solomon was always
calm, never nervous. He took a breath and tried to focus as
Solomon went on.

"The two that were taken are very close to Mark—and to
me." He blinked and looked into Mark's eyes. "They have K
and Sam."

The world went white. For a moment, Mark thought he
was losing his mind and might never recover. Was this another
dream? He tried to speak but couldn't.

His mind flooded with a million thoughts of what could be
happening to his family. He tried to see the future, maybe force
a dream so he could see if they were okay. But he couldn't.

Isis put her hand on his shoulder. "I'm so sorry, Mark.
We'll get them back."

He looked at Solomon as his training took over and his
heart slowed to a normal beat. He had to be strong for his
family. He took a breath and nodded for Solomon to go on.

Solomon clenched his fists. "We believe they are being held
in the same building as Detective Weston. Our mission is now
one thing, and only one. Top priority is K and Samantha. We
are to ensure their safety at any cost.

"Second is Weston. We need him on our side." He
straightened. "We're on the clock now, people. This is a rescue
operation. If we come in contact with either of the two targets,
take them out, but don't go looking for them."

They were dismissed, and everyone headed to the main
Taxi room. Ten different locations were accessible from the
New York headquarters, as well as fifteen more throughout the
city at different safe houses.

Mark was scared, but he tried not to show it. He couldn't
understand why his family was taken. He wasn't connected to

the Russian or anyone else involved, as far as he knew. *Is it a random thing?* He didn't think so. It had to be a direct attack against him.

Isis smiled at him and tried to show her support as she suited up for the hour-long ride on the *Taxi of Death*, as she called it, saying if anything went wrong, "you'll be dead before you know what you hit."

Mark was soon suited up. The four looked at each other without saying anything. They all knew their part, and they knew what was at stake. With a nod, Mark climbed inside one of the tubes and soon was on his way to the most important mission of his life.

He had lost his family once. He was not about to lose them a second time.

* * *

BLOOD TRICKLED DOWN KIRK'S face from a large cut above his left eye. The beating was severe, but still he cursed and spit at his attackers. They wouldn't know how much he was hurting. They wouldn't break him.

All he could think about the last few days was the woman and little girl he had helped. *Are they okay? Did they make it out?* He hoped they had. The only thing that kept him alive was the possibility of escape and making sure they had survived.

He hadn't been looked at as a hero in a long time, and the look on the woman's face when he opened their cell door was worth every beating he'd endured since.

His captors had cut his feet with razorblades. Both were bloody and swollen, probably infected. One step would be enough to make a strong man pass out from the pain. The Russians mocked him and left the door open, just to see if he had it in him to try to escape. But he knew they were waiting for him just down the hall.

He stared at the open door and the light in the hall beyond. It looked so easy. Just walk out the door. But it wasn't so simple. His cell floor was littered with broken glass and metal shavings, as was the hallway. It was a cruel joke. The two masked men who scattered the glass and metal had laughed and had a grand old time, like torturing people was their only entertainment.

As Kirk sat in the middle of his cold cell stripped naked and bleeding from his hands and feet, he tried to work himself up to make another try for it.

Come on, man. You never give up. NEVER!

* * *

K SAT WITH THE AUTOMATIC weapon across her lap and a bad feeling in her gut. She went over in her mind what she was going to do when the guard awoke. She'd never killed anyone before and wasn't sure she could do it now.

Sam turned over and yawned.

K clamped her teeth together. She couldn't let her daughter die in this awful place.

Sam opened her eyes.

K put her finger over her lips and smiled. Sam knew she was supposed to be quiet. She was such a brave little girl. K was proud of her, loved her sweet little smile.

Rising to her feet, she picked Sam up and moved her to the back of the little shed. She wanted to hide her, just in case something went wrong.

She whispered in Sam's ear. "Stay here until Mommy calls for you, okay?" Sam nodded, leaned back against the wall, and hugged her knees.

"Good girl."

K stepped around one of the grinding, clunking pumps and looked at the gun in her hand. It had a silencer clipped to the side of the barrel. At least that's what she thought it was from watching CSI Miami with Mark every Thursday night.

Pulling it free, she threaded it onto the end of the barrel. It was easier then she thought it would be, which made her feel a little better. Sliding the action back, she loaded a round in the chamber with a click that she was sure should have awakened the guard.

Peering around the corner, she checked to see if he was still sleeping.

The spot where he had been was empty.

Looking wildly around, she stepped out from behind the second pump just as one turned back on with a loud whirring sound. The noise made her jump, but not as much as the hand that came around her mouth and pulled her to the ground.

The shock of the fall made her lose her grip on the gun. It went flying. Before she could turn over, she felt a kick to her side, which shot pain up her spine and knocked the breath from her lungs.

She flipped onto her back, kicked with both legs and made contact. Her attacker staggered back, hit his head on a metal pipe and fell to the ground with a thud and a grunt.

She rolled to her knees and scrabbled for the gun. It was three feet away but felt like a hundred miles. When she finally grabbed it, she spun around just in time to hear the growl and see the furious guard jump at her. She closed her eyes and pulled the trigger.

CHAPTER TWENTY-SIX

THE GUARD'S HOLLOW EYES stared at K as she pushed him off her body. Breathing hard, she leaned over his body and vomited. She'd never killed anyone or even dreamed it would ever be something she'd have to do.

Samantha came around the corner. "Mommy?" She looked at the dead man lying on the floor. K tried to cover her innocent child's eyes, but Sam pointed at the body. "Bad man."

K sighed and reached for her daughter. "Yeah, honey, he's a bad man. But he won't hurt us anymore."

Holding Sam close, she tried to think. It would be dark in a few hours. They could make a run for the gate or maybe try to get on one of the delivery trucks that came in through the gates in the evenings.

"I'm hungry."

"I know, hon. I'm hungry, too." She couldn't remember the last time they'd had anything to eat.

Avoiding the guard's unblinking stare, K searched his pockets and found a packet of trail mix plus a canteen of water. They shared the trail mix, morsel by morsel, until every crumb was gone. It wasn't much, but it was something.

They both jumped when the radio on the dead guard's belt squawked. The language was German or Russian. K couldn't tell. But the voice sounded urgent, and she had a feeling what that could mean.

They would be coming to find their missing guard.

* * *

MARK OPENED HIS EYES and tried to see the broken landscape out the window, but all he saw was K's face. They'd made it to Puerto Rico early that morning. After a long ride in a beat-up, old Jeep Cherokee, then a switch to a station wagon for the final trip through the interior of the island, they were almost to their checkpoint. They would arrive before dark.

The Taxi had put them on a part of the island farthest from where they wanted to be, but it was still faster than taking a plane and a lot less headache. Guns were frowned upon on airplanes, anyway.

Isis punched him on the arm and smiled. "How you holding up?"

"Okay, considering. Any news?"

"No, just that our FBI informant cracked and told us who else he had working for him."

"That's good news. Anyone I know?"

"Nope, just a CSI agent. He ended up dead along with his wife. That Geoff character is a hired hit man connected with the Russian Mafia as well as the FBI."

Mark remembered the picture of the man. He must have been good to have been able to fool Detective Weston. Judging from his file, Weston was a sharp guy and had solved more cases in the DPD than any other detective on the force. No one cared about his success rate though, due to his nonconformist personality.

"One thing I don't get," Mark said. "Why did they take my family? I'm not connected with them in any way. Do you think they know about my involvement in the WJA?"

"Not sure. That confuses me, too." Isis looked up from her tablet. "At this point, I don't think the reason matters. We just need to get Sam and K out of there. We'll sort through the whys later."

Mark nodded and watched as they passed run-down houses and fields filled with workers picking what he assumed were coffee beans. It looked like a tedious job, and from the looks on the natives' faces, he was right.

An hour later, they reached a small building made from old lumber and tin roofing material. A big, dark-skinned, Puerto Rican man smiled and waved as they drove up. He looked like he could be Big B's brother.

"Welcome to the island, my friends. You have a good ride, yes?"

They all nodded as they stretched, trying to work out their cramped muscles before they stepped inside.

The interior of the shack wasn't much better than the outside. The floor was dirt, and Mark could see through the holes in the walls. A large wooden crate sat on the floor in the center of the room. He walked over to it and read the label on the top. **Bananas**.

"Yes. It's our equipment, the good stuff!" Big B smiled and tore into the crate. The bananas were, in fact, M249s, Squad automatic weapons and one M2 50cal. sniper rifle. Big B tossed the sniper rifle to Mark, along with a scope and a few clips of ammo.

After the contents of the box were emptied, Big B loaded his backpack with Claymore mines, hand grenades, and a few biological bombs. Isis had a machine gun and a belt loaded with throwing darts dipped with a tranquilizer.

Jamison, wearing thermal glasses, threw each person a small earpiece that linked them all together. Jamison's call sign was *lookout*. He was in charge of clearing the way and being their eyes and ears.

Big B was *groundkeeper*, charged with ensuring they had whatever diversion needed and that their butts were covered in case of a problem.

Isis and Mark would go in hot. Mark had a long-range rifle. Isis had short-range charges and the knockout power. Mark inspected his weapon. His rifle folded in two parts. In the full lockout position, it was loaded with a plastic bullet filled with a chemical called Liquid Metal.

Similar to mixing concrete powder with water, Liquid Metal would hit the blood stream and mix with incredible speed. In a matter of seconds, the victim would lose all motor skills and vision. The blood would carry it through the body, which would harden head to toe in less than ten seconds, leaving the victim stiff and dead.

The best part was that the victim could not scream or cry for help, making it the perfect weapon for this type of mission.

Mark also carried a sidearm, a fifty-round air gun that could shoot semi-automatic or full auto. The tiny darts were filled with liquid explosives that would penetrate the skin and explode within half a second. The only sound was a puff of air, then a faint pop as the mini-bomb scrambled the victim's insides.

Johnny Jamison went over the plan one more time as they assembled their gear. As anxious as they all were, they had to wait one more hour, until it was completely dark. Mark tried to hide his fear. He wasn't afraid for himself, but for K and Sam. What if his team was too late? He couldn't bear to think he might fail them again.

* * *

KIRK COULD FEEL HIS head swim and the glass dig into his knees and hands as he crawled down the hall, trying to make it to an empty cell.

All he hoped was that the other cells weren't covered with glass, too. He made it to the last door, reached up, and turned the doorknob.

It was open.

He rolled inside and gritted his teeth as bits of metal and glass, already embedded into his back, dug in deeper. He felt around and discovered the new room was free of shards. He lay on his back, trying to get a second wind. He'd left a blood trail. It wouldn't take a genius to find him.

Let them come.

He was in the mood to tangle with a guard or two. Pain will either break or make a man, and it was making him madder by the minute.

After he worked the glass from his hands and knees, he found an old pillowcase on the mattress in the corner of the room. He tore it into pieces and wrapped his feet to stop the bleeding. Besides his feet, the busted ribs and miscellaneous cuts and bruises, he could tell he had a broken nose. He limped toward the door and looked out into the hall.

He needed a weapon. Something—anything. He scanned the floor. Most of the glass was broken into little pieces, but some of the metal chunks were just the right size for a makeshift knife.

He picked up two long, sharp, four-inch pieces and wrapped them on one end with the last bits of the pillowcase. He made his way through the door at the end of the hall and could hear voices coming from a door off to the left. It was also back the way he had come, over the glass-lined floor. Finding the same crate he had hidden behind earlier, Kirk shook his head. Déjà-vu all over again.

He spotted an air-duct cover in the ceiling that looked like a return, which meant it would be open to the dead space above. Though the pain was incredible, he crawled onto the crate, stood upright in all his naked glory and reached for the grill. He could barely get a handhold, but with some effort, he pulled himself into the open hole, scraping his bare back. He replaced the grill and peered down.

He heard footsteps. Two bearded men stopped to talk just a few feet from the vent. They were talking in Russian or some variation of it. One rolled his ski mask to the crown of his head, lit a cigar and moved on, puffing at the stogie as if it was his last meal.

The other sat on the crate, pulled a flask from his pocket, lifted his mask and unscrewed the top. Kirk saw the man's boots and coveted them, as well as the gun hanging from a strap on his shoulder. But the shoes had more appeal than the gun at this point.

He quietly removed the grill and placed it to one side and studied the guard. The big, hairy man outweighed him by a good twenty pounds, but if he surprised him, he might be able to overpower him. He leaned forward. *This is going to hurt.*

Jumping from his hiding place naked and bloody, he landed on top of the unsuspecting guard. The guard flopped to the ground without a sound. Kirk rolled to his knees and looked at the shard of glass protruding from of his victim's neck. It worked. The guy was dead. Apparently, he'd hit an artery.

Grabbing the huge man by the collar, he dragged his body into an open cell and closed the door. He quickly undressed him, slipped on the clothing and shoes, though they were two sizes too big. He hitched the belt tight, pulled the black ski mask over his head and stepped out of the cell. After checking the machine gun to make sure it was loaded, he trotted down the hall toward the exit.

* * *

A CROSSHAIR LINED UP with the head of an unknowing Russian guard making his rounds on the main site. Mark tracked him as he walked behind a small outbuilding, then dropped him with a single round.

The man hit the ground. Mark could see him stiffen as the fluids in his body turned as hard as steel. Mark scoped out his next target. He was patient—he had to be. The attack had to be done with the utmost care in order not to alert the others or further endanger his wife and daughter.

Isis lay next to him under the heavy camouflaged netting they shared. They blended into the brush and would be unseen, even if the enemy was right on top of them. She whispered in his earpiece that another guard was taking a leak in the bushes to the left. With a quick swing of his rifle, Mark took him out.

Big B made his way down to the main yard, through the double fence, and past the dogs. He placed charges under a Jeep and on the side of a fuel tank balanced on tall wooden stilts. Mark made sure he was covered. The computer screen inside the small hut was linked to a thermal imaging camera that could see through almost any material. It was like a big X-ray device, but live and very nice to have on an operation like this. Jamison announced that he spotted someone kill a guard and take his clothes.

"He's on the main floor, making his way in our direction. Don't shoot. I think it's Weston." Jamison laughed. "He's limping, but appears as determined as the file says he is."

"Any sign of K and Sam?" Mark tried to sound professional.

"Not yet, but I'm looking. Only one other prisoner that I can see—and he looks male."

Mark sighed and motioned for Isis to follow him. "Okay, we're going in."

* * *

K DECIDED TO MAKE a dash for a truck or some kind of vehicle. One of them had to leave sometime to go for a coffee run or supplies. K and Sam would try to hide inside a truck, and maybe, just maybe, escape.

Cracking the door open just enough to look out, she jerked back when she saw a guard standing a few feet away. Beyond him, she could see open grass, dirt, and a big truck.

She turned to Sam. "Okay, honey, you do like we talked about. We're going to play hide and seek. We're hiding from the bad, bad men. You follow Mommy and be very quiet, okay?"

Sam nodded as if she understood this was more than a simple game.

Gun in one hand, K grabbed Sam's hand with the other and pulled her along as they dashed for a bush behind the guard.

"Stop or I shoot. Stop!"

K froze as a guard, who must have been standing behind the small pump house, shone a flashlight on them. Before she could even think, a half dozen guards were pointing guns at them. She dropped her weapon and wrapped her arms around Sam.

But a guard grabbed her by the shoulders as another ripped Sam from her grasp.

"Mommy!" Sam screamed. "Don't let them take me."

K fought the men, clawing her way toward Sam, until a rifle butt was slammed into her head, followed by blackness.

CHAPTER TWENTY-SEVEN

THE COLD WATER JOLTED K awake. She looked around "Sam? Where are you, baby? Sam, come to Mommy! Where is my daughter? Sam!" She yelled and cried as she fought to get the attention of someone—anyone.

K struggled but found that she was strapped to a chair. Two guards looked at her and one spit out the side of his mouth.

"Shut up. You're lucky we keep you alive after you killed Gustavo." A short, middle-aged man with a scruffy black-and-silver speckled beard, he glared at K from beneath thick eyebrows, his dark eyes filled with hate. "You think you're so smart. You will die here. I will see to that." He slapped K, knocking her back in her chair.

A rust taste filled her mouth. Her front tooth felt loose, but all she could think about was Sam. She shook her head as he pulled her upright again. "You come with us to see the boss. You behave, or your child will pay. You hear?" The man's accent sounded childish to K, but she suppressed her smile. What she really wanted to do was mock him and use words on him that her mother would have scolded her about—and yet, her mother would have used even worse on the man herself.

They cut her duct-tape-bound wrists free and pulled her to her feet. Half dragging her to a cell directly across from the one she was in, they opened a door that led to a stairway. The basement was even more frightening than the rest of the building.

The lights overhead flickered, and the smell of sweat and blood filled the room. She would have never known the place had a basement. The doorway leading to it was in the back of one of the cells.

The stairs were carved from the earth itself, and in some places these had broken off. K stumbled and the two guards held her firm as to not drop her.

She could see the end of the staircase up ahead. It looked like it was all excavated by hand. Wooden beams stretched across the top and sides, making the room look like a mineshaft. The cave-like room was stacked to the beams with wooden boxes and crates full of explosives and guns—which K deduced by the printed lettering on the side of them. They led her to a rough-hewn door on the right and knocked.

She waited, and they waited. The guard to her left shifted his feet as if he was the one being marched to his death instead of her. *Who was this guy they were so afraid of?*

"Come in." The male voice sounded English or Scottish. She couldn't tell at first, but in the end she decided that it was English. The guards shoved her into the small room and shut the door.

Behind a desk made of stacked pallets sat. The laptop in front of him seemed out of place in the dirt-walled, dimly lit room, the glow of the screen illuminated his face, giving him an eerie look.

"Where is Sam? Where is my daughter?" K's legs were shaking.

"You have a problem, Mrs. Appleton. Your husband is a thorn in my side, and for that *you* must suffer." He glared at K, his dark eyes glowing. "Allow me to introduce myself. My name is Tripp Maddock. You may call me Geoff."

* * *

KIRK HELD HIS BREATH as a heavyset man came down the

hall toward him. He pulled out a cigarette and casually lit it. The cell door beside him opened and a short man with hairy eyebrows stepped out, shutting the door behind him.

Kirk eyed the door, thinking it must lead somewhere else, maybe to an exit.

The two looked at him as he sat on a counter that held two computers. A large window looked out into the main lobby and the guard station. Kirk grunted and puffed a cloud of smoke.

"You not hot in that thing?" the tall guard asked. "I only wear it if I have to."

The two didn't wait for a response and moved on, as if his opinion didn't matter in the least. Thank God the guard he'd killed was at the bottom of the food chain. He blended in better in that kind of uniform. Though the office door led into the lobby, every foyer exit was covered by a pair of guards. He had to find another way out.

The two guards he'd just encountered were standing in the main lobby, their backs to him. He stepped into the hall and walked toward the cell door he'd seen the short, scruffy guard come out of.

It was a carbon copy of all of the other doors that lined the hallway. But when he turned the handle, it opened, and he saw that this cell was different. He looked down the rough-cut stairway.

He checked his newly acquired gun then crept down the long, dimly lit stairway. When he reached the bottom, he scanned the room for guards then hid behind one of the crates. He heard voices from the other side of the door in the corner. A woman, maybe, and someone else—a man.

He crawled closer to the door and scrunched behind another stack of crates. It was a man, a man with a familiar English accent. *Geoff?*

His mind raced through the events of the past few weeks. The chance meeting in the desert, the ever-so-helpful gentleman, the private jet, the ever-ready credit card. He'd been played.

Jaw clamped to control his rage, he leaned over to lift the lid of a crate. Even in the dim lighting, he could see it was filled with detonators and C-4. He grabbed several blocks of C-4 and shoved some detonators in his pocket. He put one brick down on the floor next to where he sat and set the timer.

Twenty minutes—that should give him enough time to get the woman and child of here. *If not, then I'll be going out with a bang, as they say.*

* * *

ISIS AND MARK STEPPED over the guard dogs he'd shot and made their way around the back of the building. Three dogs lay dead after Mark shot them in the head. He was in no mood to play fetch.

The south end of the building featured a loading dock lined with roll-up doors. Grateful the grounds had obviously been abandoned long ago and natural undergrowth allowed to take its land back, Isis and Mark zigzagged from bush to bush toward the building.

Under an overhang next to some cargo doors, two guards sat at a makeshift table playing cards and drinking vodka straight out of the bottle. Mark held out his hand to halt Isis. She crouched behind a pile of pallets and extracted two blades from her boot. She lifted her arm to fling the first, then the second knife, before the first reached its target. The moment the first blade burrowed into the neck of a lanky man, blood gurgled from his mouth and he fell face-first into the stack of poker chips in front of him. The second guard's eyes widened, but before he could scream, the second blade caught him in his open mouth, slicing into the back of his neck.

They crept up to the two bodies, pulled them upright and shoved sticks in their jackets to keep them in a sitting position.

Isis retrieved her knives, wiped them clean on the shirt of one of the dead men and pulled her ball cap low over her forehead. Mark looked down at the man who held a full house. *And he thought it was his lucky day.* Grabbing a radio from the table, he shoved it in his pocket.

"I think we have a basement," Jamison said in their earpiece. "Weston just went into a room and disappeared. The blueprints don't show a basement, so that's my best guess."

"Where is it?"

"Southwest of you and down the hall. I'll send it on your com-stats."

Mark opened up his watch cover and looked at the map readout. A red dot on the blue background indicated where Jamison thought the basement was and a map of their current location.

"Okay. We're on our way in."

Mark took out a pair of sunglasses and slipped them on his head. Capable of imaging thermal, X-ray or night vision, the glasses also enabled the user to peer through wood and most metals. He looked over at Isis, who had her glasses on already.

The doorway looked clear, and in a swift, silent, fluid motion, they were inside. The place immediately went dark as Big B cut the main power. They could hear the pound of boots and the chatter of excited voices.

Mark and Isis hunched down and advanced through the building unnoticed in the dark. Though guards and gunmen ran past them, the two hugged the wall and made their way through the main level unhindered.

Holding cells with open wood-and-metal doors lined the walls. Reaching the only closed door, Mark looked inside but couldn't distinguish whether or not he was seeing a prisoner in the green-and-red glow that moved and shimmered like heat off a hot roadway.

He whispered. "Jamison, can you see in this cell?"

"No, too much in the way. You're on your own."

He signaled for Isis to cover him. She gave a thumbs-up and they rushed into the room.

A startled guard jumped up and grabbed his gun. Mark shot him with his air pistol, hearing a popping sound as the guard's heart turned into mush. The man fell to the ground, twitched and was still.

A child's scream echoed between the cell walls.

Mark rushed to the corner of the cell, where his daughter crouched like a beaten puppy. He took off his glasses and reached out his arms. "It's okay, baby. It's Daddy. I'm here. It's okay." She stared at him for a moment, then ran to him and fell against him, sobbing into his chest.

"I'm here, baby. Everything's okay." He fought to hold himself together as his little girl shook in his arms. He hugged her tight, and whispered in her ear. "We're going home, but first I have to find Mommy. This nice lady will take you to a safe place. Okay?"

Mark handed her to Isis, who took off down the hallway the same way they had come in. He heard her whisper into his earpiece, "We got Samantha, and I'm coming out."

"We'll take care of Sam." Big B's deep voice boomed in his ear. "Now go find your wife, Appleton, while I create a little diversion."

An explosion rocked the building. The radio in Mark's hand erupted with Russian curses.

He headed for the cell with the stairway but stopped when the shouts ceased and his vision was obliterated. After a moment of darkness, he saw a man holding a gun against K's head. He yelled for the man to put the gun down, then fired and hit the man in the hand, sending the gun flying. Instantly, the man pulled out a knife with his other hand and stuck it into the side of K's neck.

She fell to the floor. Mark screamed as he shot the attacker in the head, shattering his eye socket. He looked at K. She was lying on the floor in a pool of blood.

Holding his head in his hands, he tried to focus. These visions had come to him before, but now it came at him like a dream he couldn't control. He straightened and saw he was standing in the cell where Sam had been held. His blackout was over, but his head felt like it was in a vise. He stood up, put on his glasses, and turned the mode to thermal.

He had to find K. The vision would be his wife's future, if

he did not step in now to change it. Looking at his watch map, he could see that the door to the basement was down the next hallway, parallel to where he now stood.

"Sam's out and safe, Mark."

Mark whispered, "Thank God."

"You go on ahead," Isis said, her voice calm. "I'm going to secure the general."

A second explosion shook the building.

Mark rounded the corner and dashed toward the stairwell but was jumped by someone large and heavy as he passed an empty room. He hit the ground, a sharp pain slicing through his shoulder as his rifle slid down the hallway, rattling through some kind of debris.

He rolled over just in time to see a big boot coming at him. He grabbed it and twisted, at the same time kicking his assailant's other leg out from under him. The man dropped with a noisy crash onto the rubble-studded floor but jumped to his feet with unbelievable speed.

Mark jumped up to hit the man square in the jaw, which did not seem to faze him. With a swift second blow, he hit him in the throat with everything he had and felt the big man's windpipe crush. The giant man fell to his knees, gasping for breath.

Mark pulled his forty-five and fired point-blank at the big man's head. As he holstered the gun, he heard a woman scream.

* * *

"YOU SEE, K—MAY I call you K?" Geoff chuckled to himself. "I have a feeling you have no idea who your husband is or what he does."

K did not respond.

"He had to be the hero. Had to put his nose where it didn't belong. Now he must pay."

"You're crazy. My husband didn't do anything to you."

Geoff jumped to his feet. "He killed my brothers. My only three brothers are dead because of him!" With a quick swing of his hand, he smacked K across the room. "He killed my only family, and now I will kill his!"

The lights flickered and faded. She could hear yelling and gun shots from the floors above them and tried to crawl to the doorway, but Geoff grabbed her and dragged her toward him, his breath heavy on her neck. She hit at him with her hands, but it only made him laugh.

"You know," Geoff whispered, "Your dear little Samantha will scream and cry when I carve her up, but before she dies, I'll tell her Mommy is dead."

K screamed and kicked up with her knee as hard as she could. She could tell by the way he grunted that she'd hit her target.

His grip loosened. Pushing with all her strength, she freed herself from his grip and scrambled for the door. Everything was dark. She could only see shadows and a little light from the top of the stairs. She screamed and tried to squirm away when she felt a hand grab hers.

"It's me, the cop." He wrapped a strong arm around her shoulders and pulled her behind a crate. "Stay here, no matter what."

Before she could speak, he was gone. She could hear yelling and cursing and grunting as her rescuer struggled with her attacker. There was the sound of a fist hitting flesh, then a single gunshot reverberated out in the dark and the struggle stopped.

K held her breath. Her body shook, and she hoped and prayed the cop had fired the shot, not Geoff. *God, please help me. I don't want to die. Please!*

"Get up, you fat cow!" Geoff had found her hiding place. He loomed in the dark like a hate-filled devil.

A gunshot sounded a few yards up the stairs. She screamed and felt her hair being pulled almost out of her head as Geoff dragged her back into his office. He yanked her to her feet just as the lights came back on.

"Put the gun down, Tripp!"

Mark? It can't be. He came for me. He came for me!

Geoff pointed the gun at Mark and squeezed the trigger. But his hand flew back in a sudden jerking motion when Mark's bullet ravaged through his palm, removing two fingers. The gun flipped through the air and landed on the floor. The roar that filled the underground room pulsated through her chest as she watched Geoff grasp his injured hand, a horrified look on his face.

A second shot rang out, hitting Geoff in the shoulder. As he stumbled backward, K dropped to her knees just as a third bullet pierced her attacker between the eyes. His head caved in like a bashed watermelon, and exploded into a mess of hair and bone. He landed on the cop's body, which was lying on the floor, facedown in a pool of blood.

K sobbed as Mark rushed to her side. He knelt beside her, rocking her in his arms, kissing her on the back of her neck, whispering in her ear, "I'm here. Everything is okay, sweetheart. I'm here."

* * *

MARK'S EARPIECE SOUNDED AS Jamison asked if everything was okay. "Yes, K is secure. We're on our way out."

"Any news on Detective Weston?"

"He's dead," Mark said.

"Copy that. Get out of there and report back to the drop-off point. We've got your back."

"On my way."

"Sam! We've got to—" K jerked from Mark's grip and tried to get up.

"Sam's safe." He helped her up and held her close, kissing her lips, her cheeks, her neck.

She laughed through her tears. "What took you so long?"

"Traffic."

Gripping her hand, he led her through the smoke-filled building and out the back door. Just as they cleared the hill above the parking lot, an explosion behind them made both of them jump. They turned to see the entire building erupting in a fiery mass of concrete and metal.

When they arrived at the van, Isis informed them that General Karjanski had escaped in a helicopter hidden in the woods south of the building. But no one seemed to care.

Teary-eyed, they all watched Mark and his family hug each other. Sam climbed in Big B's lap. "Did you help save me?"

"You bet I did, sweetie, but your dad did most of the work."

She reached around his huge neck and hugged him hard. She slid down his shin to sit on his big boot. "Do you know how to play horsey?"

Big B laughed and wiped tears from his cheek. "I sure do."

Chapter Twenty-Eight

KIRK OPENED HIS EYES and felt the dead weight of a body on top of him. Using all the strength he could muster, he rolled over and shoved the body aside. A pain stabbed at his chest. He grasped his ribs and felt something warm and sticky ooze between his fingers. Blood. Just an inch higher, and the bullet would have gone through his heart.

He was lightheaded but coherent enough to know he had to get out of there. The bomb would be going off at any moment.

He looked around. The woman was gone. He hoped she was okay. But Geoff, the double-crosser, whose headless body he'd shoved away, was dead, which was fine with him. Getting to his feet, he staggered up the stairs, down the hall and into the main lobby. The guards and a few men in business suits were all scrambling for cover. He could see flames coming from the outside of the building.

Finding a side door, he rushed outside and ran into the trees just as the building burst into flames. He smiled and dropped behind a boulder. He'd always enjoyed blowing stuff up.

* * *

LIFE WAS DIFFERENT FOR the Appleton family now. K was taking a self-defense class and learning how to shoot a gun under Mark's careful eye. Mark spent every minute he could spare with his family.

Samantha went on as if nothing had ever happened. That made K happy knowing her child wouldn't be scarred for life and wouldn't need counseling because of nightmares.

Mark sat in the conference room at the WJA headquarters, being briefed by Johnny Jamison.

Tripp Maddock, or Geoff, had three brothers who worked for him and the general. The plan was to blow up three supermarkets and two schools and blame the bombings on WJA. Mark had thrown a wrench into their plans when he killed Geoff's brothers in the cabin in the woods the previous year.

The general had escaped, and no one knew where he was. The consensus was that he was likely in Russia or the Czech Republic, but they didn't know for sure. The agent who had double-crossed them was in prison for selling secrets to Russia, which was provided by an anonymous tip to the director of the FBI.

"You with us, Mark, or are you dreaming again?" Jamison smiled as he pointed to the picture on the screen.

"I'm here."

"Good. This man is connected with General Karjanski and is involved with smuggling nuclear weapons into Iran. His name is Hokamend Mahmud-e-Raq. He is also part of the terrorist organization involved in the bus bombings last year in Oakland, plus the one in Los Angeles.

"We have a contact and a safe house waiting for you. You are to leave in twelve hours. This mission, mind you, could last a year or so. We need you to first get all information possible from his personal computer and locate his nuclear weapons warehouse. Then take him out."

Mark nodded. He'd been studying Hokamend for the past few weeks. The terrorist's twisted web of destruction was about to unravel. If the mission went as he dreamed it would, the mission would end with Hokamend dead on the floor of his palace in Tehran.

* * *

KIRK READ HIS OBITUARY and laughed out loud. He couldn't believe all the lies his friends wrote about him. There was even a blip from his ex-wife. *He was a kind and caring man.*

"Bah, what does she know?" He took another sip of his peach margarita and set it on the table beside his chair. He dropped the back of the chair down, closed his eyes and relaxed, soaking up the sun's healing rays. He loved Bali, which was always warm and smelled like the ocean. He loved the feel of the soft sand under his feet and the warm breeze that filled his mind with happy thoughts.

It felt good to be free of his past. Here, there was no one to bother him other than the local women and the occasional parrot that flew into his hut every now and then. He smiled as he thought about the million dollars he'd found in the rubble of what was left of the old asylum. He'd almost missed it—but when a dead man is handcuffed to a suitcase, it usually means something.

He couldn't believe how cheap Bali was. The fully furnished villa he bought only cost two-hundred thousand dollars, and it came with hired servants, maids and gardeners.

His drink was replaced with a fresh one by a petite, brown, young woman. She smiled at him and wandered off to do whatever she did when she wasn't waiting on him. He smiled. Life was good in Bali. Real good.

One day soon, he would pick up his gun again. He still had work to do. General Karjanski lived just two villas down the road.

Kirk smirked and reached for his drink. He wasn't finished yet. Not by a long shot.

The End

Check out more titles by Aaron Patterson at:
www.StoneHouseInk.net

About the Author

Aaron Patterson is the author of the best-selling WJA series, as well as two Digital Shorts: 19 and The Craigslist Killer. He was home-schooled and grew up in the west. Aaron loved to read as a small child and would often be found behind a book, reading one to three a day on average. This love drove him to want to write, but he never thought he had the talent. His wife Karissa prodded him to try it, and with this encouragement, he wrote Sweet Dreams, the first book in the WJA series, in 2008. Airel is his first teen series, and plans for more to come are already in the works. He lives in Boise, Idaho with his family, Soleil, Kale and Klayton.

Available Now

Dream On
Book Two in the WJA Series

CHAPTER ONE

I WATCHED IN VAIN as my life slipped away and there was nothing I could do about it. Time is a heartless father, and in its never-ending *ticks and tocks*, time smiles at me as if to say, "I have you, I control your life, and you will do as I bid—or else!" I can feel my own heartbeat, and that, too, is ruled by time, beating in perfect rhythm as if my own heart conspires against me.

You can never take your future and bend it to your own will. If you try, then time, or maybe even your own heart, will throw a banana peel on the ground and you'll tumble and end up in the same place I am. I was a careful man and tried to keep my eyes on the ground in order not to step on something or into something that would take me. I was ready for anything. However, nothing could have prepared me for this…this place, and this feeling of finality and judgment!

Mind-numbing darkness crept all around me with a stench that hit my senses like a freight train. At first, I thought I'd been buried alive in someone else's grave, and the smell was the decomposing body I shared a box with. Then, after a few days, or weeks, I can't say which for sure, I figured out that the stench was me. I was the terrible taste in the stale air that I tried to breathe! I was trapped in a wooden box that gave me about a

306 | AARON PATTERSON

foot below my feet and six inches above my head. I felt around and touched the lid, only to find that there was a mere foot of space in front of my nose.

I am dying! The thought made me want to scream and struggle, kicking and smacking with everything in me to free myself and drink in the sweet morning air that used to swim through my lungs. I did, in fact, do just that for so long that I passed out with exhaustion and woke up in the same dark place, but this time my head ached with a pounding that not just one aspirin would cure. I would have believed I was already dead; however, the pain shooting through my body told me otherwise. I understand that you don't know me and that I'll never see you or know your name, but I need to tell someone what happened, and how I was to end up dead, or almost dead!

My name is Mark Appleton. I know, not too flashy or "in your face" hero kind of a name. I'm no different than you, the stock broker working his sixty plus hours a week, or the guy standing on a highway holding a stop sign in a construction zone. I am your everyday, ordinary, run of the mill American guy, and I'm in a casket—my casket. I was buried alive and from what I can tell, I'll not be escaping any time soon. So, why would someone do that to me, you might ask?

Well, I have a job that involves a little different approach than your average mail carrier. You might say my job is to deliver messages to those in this world who think they can commit any evil they dream up without repercussion. I encounter people every day who would love to see me dead... hung by my neck and swinging in the breeze.

That's where I come in, I am their repercussion! I'm an assassin, who is what some might call a vigilante or a mercenary of sorts. I know, I know, but lying here in a cramped box, talking to myself, I can't help but wonder how I got the job or how I ended up in a pine box underneath a ton of dirt.

The voice recorder in my watch is the only way you will ever know my story, so here goes...

Well, I have a job that involves a little different approach than your average mail carrier; you might say my job is to deliver messages to those in this world who think they can commit any evil they dream up without repercussion. I come into contact with people who would love to see me dead, hanged by the neck and swinging in the breeze.

That is where I come in. *I am their repercussion!*

I'm an assassin who is what some might call a vigilante or a mercenary of sorts. I know, I know, but laying here in a cramped box talking to myself, I cannot help wondering how I ended up doing what I do and how I ended up in a pine box underneath a ton of dirt.

The voice recorder in my watch is the only way you'll ever know my story, so here goes...

CPSIA information can be obtained
at www.ICGtesting.com
Printed in the USA
LVOW12s1717060716

495333LV00002B/197/P

9 780982 607817